In the dark of the unlighted street, he quickly pulled Isabel onto his lap. He drew the cloak around her and with it his arms. In the next moment, he kissed her.

Isabel's "Yip!" of surprise became a soft moan as Brett's mouth moved hungrily over hers. She had kissed men before, but never had she felt this inferno that roared through her, burning away all thought, all sense of danger. Her arms, of their own accord, wrapped around the earl's neck as she returned his kiss with equal hunger, luxuriating in the fire he had ignited. "Yes," she said to herself over and over again. This was what she had wanted for so long. . . .

"Ms. Martin is a delicious discovery whose exquisitely precise dialogue sparkles like the finest of jewels."
—*Romantic Times Magazine*

By Michelle Martin
Published by Fawcett Books:

THE HAMPSHIRE HOYDEN
THE QUEEN OF HEARTS
THE MAD MISS MATHLEY
THE ADVENTURERS

Books published by The Ballantine Publishing Group are available at quantity discounts on bulk purchases for premium, educational, fund-raising, and special sales use. For details, please call 1-800-733-3000.

THE ADVENTURERS

Michelle Martin

FAWCETT CREST • NEW YORK

A Fawcett Crest Book
Published by Ballantine Books
Copyright © 1996 by Michelle Martin

http://www.randomhouse.com

Library of Congress Catalog Card Number: 96-96465

ISBN 0-449-22340-X

Manufactured in the United States of America

First Edition: September 1996

10 9 8 7 6 5 4 3 2 1

*

Prologue

April 26, 1804   Midafternoon

Ravenscourt, the country seat of
the Earl of Northbridge, near Forton, Lancashire

"How IS HE, Doctor?" demanded the Earl of Northbridge.

"A simple case of exhaustion, my lord," replied the young, ruddy-faced physician as he closed the study door behind him. "With proper rest and nourishment, he should be fully recovered within a se'ennight."

"Did he say anything to you?" inquired Sir Henry Bevins, turning in his chair before the earl's desk.

"No, Sir Henry," the doctor replied, "nothing intelligible. I caught a few words that sounded like Jamie and another akin to Howard or Horace or perhaps even horse. That was all."

"Is there nothing more we can do for the fellow?" asked Lord Northbridge.

"I've given full instructions to your housekeeper, my lord. I will visit the poor man daily. I anticipate no complications."

"When may we question him?" the earl demanded.

"Not for a good twenty-four hours, perhaps even forty-eight. He's thoroughly done in."

"Blast!" said the earl, his face grim.

"We must remain in the dark, it seems," said Sir Henry mildly.

"It is very unlike Monty to have created such a tangle," said

1

the earl, "and remarkably foolish of Dick to place speed over food and sleep. Well, at least he will recover. Thank you for coming so quickly, Dr. Montrose."

"It is, as always, my lord, a pleasure," said the doctor. With a respectful bow, he decamped, closing the study door behind him.

"Well," said Sir Henry Bevins, turning back to the earl, "this is a fine kettle of fish. Is the letter genuine, do you think?"

The Earl of Northbridge lifted the soiled document from his desk. "It might have been forged, of course. But I know Monty's hand, and I would swear this came from him. More importantly, I know Dick Rowan. He accompanied Monty from England thirty years ago and hasn't been from his side since. He would not have left his master save in the most dire circumstances."

"Then Montague Shipley *is* dead, just as his brother and son claim."

"If that *is* Monty's son lolling around Thornwynd."

Sir Henry adjusted his pince-nez. "But Montague Shipley's letter specifically refers to his son returning to England with a protector. Would that protector not be the boy's uncle, Horace Shipley?"

The earl rose from his chair and began to pace the dark green Chinese carpet. "I would have said yes a day ago. But Dick Rowan's sudden appearance and collapse today, this letter, and Monty's will have thoroughly muddied the waters. Monty's letter says the boy will not reach England for another week or so. Horace and his supposed nephew have been here nearly a fortnight!"

"Two pretenders to the baronetcy," murmured Sir Henry.

"Precisely. Which is the real James Shipley?"

"The documents of the boy at Thornwynd seem all in order, and he knew the password."

The earl waved away such an argument. "Documents can be forged, and Horace could have taught him the password. It has been in the Shipley family for generations."

2

"The boy certainly *looks* like a Shipley."

"Yes. That's worrisome." The earl thrust his hands deep into the pockets of his riding breeches, for he had been touring his estate when Dick Rowan had suddenly appeared. "It makes sense that Horace would claim young Jamie and bring him to England, not through any benevolence on his part, for he hasn't any, but from the hope that he could gain control of Thornwynd through Jamie."

"Quite probable from what I know of Mr. Shipley," said Sir Henry, taking a large pinch of snuff.

"But here we have Monty's letter," said the earl, striding to his desk and lifting up the single sheet of paper. "It also makes sense that Monty wouldn't put his son's life in Horace's hands, for there was no love lost between the brothers. It is very likely that Monty would entrust his son's care to someone else. If only he had named Jamie's protector!"

"Well, the poor fellow was dying, after all. Says so himself in the letter. Couldn't expect him to think of everything at such a time."

"Yes," said Lord Northbridge, staring at the letter as if by sheer force of will he could make it tell him what he needed to know. He sighed and let it fall to the desk before taking his chair once again. "If that *is* a letter from Monty. A knotty problem, Bevins."

"Yes, my lord. What do you propose to do?"

"The only thing I can do: my duty. Monty's will names me James Shipley's guardian. Forgery or no, it is my responsibility as a leading member of the ton to insure the proper succession at Thornwynd, and that means insuring the boy's safety. One Jamie is already free from danger at Thornwynd. Therefore, I shall fulfill Monty's supposed last request and meet this second James Shipley in Northamptonshire. I'll find out the truth of the matter, if not on the road back to Lancashire, then certainly when we bring the two boys together."

"If this letter of Monty's is a forgery, you could find yourself

3

in some danger on the road," Sir Henry observed. "Only a villain would attempt such a charade."

"Oh, I'll be on my guard," said Lord Northbridge dismissively. "But my presence alone should prevent any trouble."

Sir Henry Bevins began to chuckle. "It would give me no end of pleasure to have this second Jamie the heir and Monty's will a true document, for then all of Horace Shipley's hopes would be dashed. He undoubtedly expects to be named the boy's guardian. With you appointed in his stead, he won't be able to plunder Thornwynd."

"The moment James Shipley, number one or number two, is named the next baronet, Horace Shipley will find himself out on his ear," the earl agreed with grim satisfaction.

"Shall we tell Horace about this second Jamie?"

Lord Northbridge leaned back in his chair and sighed. What should have been a simple matter was becoming damnably complicated. "We'll have to. He's already making plans to permanently install his charge at Thornwynd. He will have to be stopped. The only way to do so legitimately is to announce a second claimant to the baronetcy."

"How he'll roar," said Sir Henry with a happy smile.

"Yes," said Lord Northbridge, without the smile. He was seldom amused. The earl was a serious gentleman who took his position, his estate, and himself seriously. His father had spent most of their time together impressing upon him the responsibilities, rather then the frivolous pleasures, of his position as the only son and heir to an important title and a massive property. Thus, when Lord Northbridge succeeded his father as quite a young man, he had not veered toward open-handed debauchery but wholly in its opposite direction.

He dressed simply but well, for he knew himself a model for other young men in the district and did not wish to lead any of them down the ruinous road to dandyism. He was a skilled and noted whip, pugilist, and swordsman, an all-around athlete to his acquaintance, but this he considered a mere prerequisite for any man in his position.

He rigorously administered his estate, was noted as an improving landlord, and paid close attention to his tenants and servants and business concerns. Everyone in the district gave him a good name. He was respected by all but not loved. They might not boast his university education, but his tenants and staff knew enough to understand the difference between a gentleman acting from the dictates of his duty and one who acted from the dictates of his heart.

His sister Fanny—who had suffered repeatedly from his chilling set-downs during her girlhood and adolescence—gave it as her opinion that the earl had no heart, and their mother, when she could bring herself to consider anyone beyond herself, vaguely agreed. Her son had categorically refused year after year to act as host in their town home in Grosvenor Square during the London Season, and the Dowager Northbridge thought this very mean. Despite his advanced years, the earl was still considered a brilliant catch in the ton, and his presence would have added considerable luster to her balls, routs, Viennese breakfasts, and card parties.

Had anyone had the temerity to inform Lord Northbridge that the world in general thought him a cold fish, he would not have been perturbed. He prided himself on his cool, rational approach to his family, his business, and his neighbors, for he firmly believed that only in this way could he properly do his duty by them all, and Duty was his god.

Fanny, upon her marriage three years earlier, had bluntly asked her brother why duty alone had not driven him to the altar long ago. He had civilly replied that he had yet to meet anyone suitable to become the next Countess of Northbridge. He informed his sister that his wife must possess—in addition to great beauty, noble birth, and a decent fortune—a well-informed mind, a good knowledge of the modern languages, skill on at least one instrument, superb taste, an excellent knowledge of the poets, both ancient and modern, and a certain regal bearing that set her apart from the common herd of the ton.

Fanny, with considerable disgust, informed him that in that case he would die a bachelor. Clearly it was up to her to supply the next heir to the earldom. Lord Northbridge replied that she must do what she thought best, and then calmly led her down the aisle to her pale but eager bridegroom.

Unlike the rest of the world, the earl did not consider himself capricious. He was, in his own reserved way, fond of his sister, he liked her husband, and he tolerated his mother. He was simply used to having his own way, which, in his opinion, was always the best way. His ability to quickly and coolly sum up a situation was his chief attribute, he thought, and it served him well now.

The unconscionable mess at Thornwynd had been placed at his door, and there was no one better than Lord Northbridge to settle the matter. Horace Shipley was a blackguard; that was incontrovertible. But whether he hoped to gain control of Thornwynd through "protection" of the true heir's interests or by out-and-out fraud remained in question.

"Study him closely in my absence, Bevins," the earl commanded. "His reaction to this news and his deportment during the delay may tell you if he is outraged at an impostor trying to unseat his nephew, or if he is frightened that the true James Shipley will reveal his fraud to the world. A large fortune and an important estate are at stake. We must judge carefully."

Sir Henry Bevins, though a justice of the peace and twenty years the earl's senior, was noted for his amiability and quite used to the earl's commanding ways. "You realize, of course, that if you don't get this second James Shipley up to Thornwynd by the seventeenth of May, it won't matter if he's the real heir or not?" he said. "He'll have forfeited all claims to the baronetcy by the terms of the Thornwynd legacy."

"The legacy is not far from my thoughts. A devious family, the Shipleys, to put such a time constraint on the heir. And how typical of them to give us two heirs to choose from."

"When do you leave for Northamptonshire?"

"Today," said Lord Northbridge, sitting upright and begin-

6

ning to jot down a list of the things he would need on his journey. The earl was always peremptory in business matters, a characteristic to which his associates had long resigned themselves. "The weather has made the roads nearly impassable. I want to give myself plenty of time to reach the rendezvous the letter names. I'll leave you to question Dick Rowan, once he regains consciousness, and to keep Horace Shipley in line until I return."

"I wonder which of us has the more difficult task," Sir Henry said with a smile.

"Oh, you do, to be sure," Lord Northbridge replied as he continued to write. "Whatever adventures I encounter on the road will be a welcome respite from Horace Shipley's noxious company. How sensible of Sir Barnaby to disinherit the blackguard so long ago. I am at least spared the threat of having such a man as my near neighbor."

*
Chapter 1

May 3, 1804   Late afternoon

Rockingham Forest, between Braybrook and
Little Bowden, Northamptonshire

"CAN IT BE fixed, do you think?"

"Not in our lifetime. Does it seem to you, Tony, that we
have been singularly short on luck of late?"

"Now, Jack, you're mistaken. We have had an abundance of
luck . . . all of it bad."

Jack's smile was distracted as gray eyes surveyed first the
wrecked gig and then the wilderness around them. The road
was little more than two ruts surrounded by the thick woods of
Rockingham Forest: an excellent place to encounter mischief.

"Perdition to Hanson's Livery," she said. "Well, we've been
left at least with a horse that is sound. We can ride double.
Thank heavens I shall not have to wrestle with petticoats."

"There are advantages to affecting masculinity," Tony
observed.

"Yes," said the faux Jack. "Locomotion for one. There is an
inn just five miles down the road. We should be able to rent or
purchase saddle horses there."

"But your ankle—"

"I have been coddled long enough," Jack said in a voice that
would brook no opposition. "My ankle will do very well.

Besides, saddle horses are faster and cheaper than purchasing another gig."

"Very well, *big brother*," said Tony. "I'll release the horse from its traces and we'll be off."

A hand on his arm kept Tony from putting action to words.

"What is it?" he asked quietly.

"There is someone on the road behind us. One horse coming quickly. On your guard."

They stood together calmly, with pistols at the ready, as a long-limbed rider on a black Arabian gelding came toward them at a canter. Seeing two guns aimed at his broad chest, he pulled to a stop ten yards from their gig.

"Is this a robbery?" he inquired with a frown.

"Merely caution in perilous times," Jack replied, lowering the gun held with quiet assurance.

"Ah yes," said the rider as he patted his gelding's strong neck. "One cannot be too cautious. Highwaymen, footpads, Radicals. You've had some trouble, I see. Perhaps I can help." He dismounted. "Must you continue to point that gun at my heart?"

Jack glanced at the offending pistol. "Put up, Tony."

"But—"

"He means us no harm. Put up, I say."

The boy reluctantly drew the pistol to his shoulder. "How can you be sure we are safe in the tall gentleman's company?"

"My vast years of experience have honed my intuition to a fine edge. Be at ease."

The boy's dark brown eyes were puzzled, but a slight shake of Jack's head told him he would have to wait for an explanation. Jamie had learned long ago to maintain whatever character or disguise he had adopted. Right now he and Isabel were the Cavendish brothers; he would act accordingly.

They turned to observe the interloper as he strode to their gig with the grace of a born athlete. He was a most attractive gentleman. His riding clothes, though dusty, were clearly of the first stare and molded themselves gracefully to broad shoulders and long, well-shaped legs. His hair was flaxen and tied back by a black ribbon; his blue eyes knowingly surveyed the wreckage. The quality of his horse, the cut of his clothes, and his somewhat regal beauty and bearing made a most impressive package.

"Faith, 'tis a nonesuch," murmured Isabel.

"Do you admire the type?" Jamie queried.

"Upon occasion," Isabel retorted, a touch of pink in her cheeks.

"Well, it was not much to begin with," said the tall gentleman as he left the gig, "and now, I'm afraid, it is much less. It cannot be repaired."

"That was our opinion," said Isabel.

"There is an inn," said the gentleman, "just a few miles down this road in the village of Little Bowden. You can procure a worthier carriage and team there. I understand the food is tolerable, so you may expect a pleasant night. I would be happy to accompany you there. My name is Avery. Brett Avery."

"Avery? An elf king?" said Isabel, gray eyes alight with mischief.

"Impossible," Jamie stated. "His towering height prohibits any relation to elfdom."

"But don't you think the mantle of golden hair upon his head a suitable crown for a king?"

"If you have quite finished dissecting my name," said Mr. Avery with some severity, "I should like to know yours."

"Oh, now, where are our manners?" Isabel exclaimed. Apparently the nonesuch was not used to being teased. A pity. "I am John Cavendish," she lied fluidly, "and this is my little brother, Anthony."

"Little?" inquired Mr. Avery with the lift of one brow.

"He may be larger than me, sir, but I do surpass him in years. I have the brains of the family, you see. Tony has the brawn."

"Well I like that," said Jamie with some indignation. "I've

done extremely well with my Latin of late. Our tutor has said so."

"Yes," said Isabel, "but how is your German?"

"Miserable," agreed Jamie with a grin.

"For shame, Mr. Cavendish," chastised Mr. Avery. "The study of German is a prerequisite for any man of quality. How is it," he said, brushing some dust from his superbly cut coat, "that two such well-educated young gentlemen come to be on so abominable a road?"

"Ah," said Isabel, "it is our penchant for adventure, sir, which has brought us to our current plight. You see, our father died a few years ago, and our mother has insisted on keeping us close to home ever since."

"Mother is an extremely estimable woman," said Jamie, happy to embroider the tale, "but she has no sense."

"Now, now," said Isabel, not to be outdone, "she has some sense, just not masculine sense. She has no understanding, sir, of a young man's need to kick up his heels on occasion. As I am to attain my majority in two months' time—"

"I felicitate you, sir," said Mr. Avery.

Isabel bowed. "I have grasped this as my last opportunity to enjoy any fun in life, for I shall probably be saddled with a wife within a year of my succession. I could not bear the thought of marrying without some adventure beforehand. So Tony and I have run off to sample the more disreputable delights of the world before returning to our stately manor . . . and peace . . . and quiet." This last was said with a grimace.

"Indeed," said Jamie, "it is a pity you have come upon us, Mr. Avery, for we had hoped to meet no one of good character while adventuring."

Mr. Avery's blue eyes widened in surprise. "I beg your pardon. I shall try to lower my character for as long as we travel together. The Crown and Bull is not so very far, after all."

"And how comes so respectable and well set-up a gentleman to be on so abominable a road?" Isabel inquired in all seeming innocence.

Mr. Avery regarded her in greater surprise, as if unused to having any of his actions questioned. "I had some business in Braybrook," he replied, "and took this shorter route to Little Bowden to avoid being caught on the road at night, though this forest makes things dark enough. My horse has been shying at goblins this last hour."

"Perhaps a wreath of garlic around his neck?" Isabel suggested.

"No, no," said Jamie, "that's for werewolves."

"No," said Mr. Avery, "for vampires. A firm hand is all that is required for goblins."

Isabel had no doubt that Mr. Avery's hand was very firm.

In the midst of this instructive conversation, she suddenly stiffened and touched Jamie's arm. Without a word, they checked their weapons. There was a knife in Isabel's boot. A pocket pistol in Jamie's coat. Swords, though currently unfashionable, were at their sides. They drew their pistols once again.

"So, this is to be a robbery after all?" Mr. Avery inquired.

"Hush," said Isabel with no respect for the gentleman's superior years and sex. "We are in some danger, sir. Pray stand aside and let us attend to it."

Mr. Avery was not used to being shushed nor to being ordered about by a stripling. Curiosity, however, got the better of him. He studied these overly confident lads a moment. Then he led his horse off the road behind the broken-down gig.

Three profusely sweating horses galloped into view, their equally perspiring riders leaning over their necks, urging them on with spur and whip. Seeing two guns drawn and aimed at them, they, as had Mr. Avery, jerked their horses to a halt.

"Throw down your weapons," Isabel commanded.

"You're mine, boy!" said the first man of little intellect as he charged his horse at her.

Isabel waited until the brigand was but four feet away and then fired, the bullet catching the man in the shoulder and

12

knocking him off his horse, which bypassed Isabel and continued to gallop down the road.

"Damn your eyes!" said the second of the three as he pulled his gun. Jamie did not hesitate. A single shot dropped the man from his saddle.

Isabel calmly pulled out a Spanish sword as the rotund third rider drew his gun with a grin. He was missing two front teeth.

"You've overshot the mark this time, me lads," he said.

"Not entirely," said Mr. Avery in a pleasant voice. He stood safely shielded by the gig. His pocket pistol, which had not appeared before, was aimed at the third man's heart. "Kindly disarm."

Scowling and swearing under his breath, the gap-toothed man dropped his gun into the dirt.

"I am appalled," said Mr. Avery with some feeling, "at the poor quality of highwaymen this country is breeding. A babe in arms could have made more of a success of this venture than you. Charging armed men! Not even looking to see if an ambush had been laid. I am ashamed to call you Englishmen. Kindly collect your friends, vagrant, and decamp."

The expletives in response to this command were extremely colorful and uncomplimentary to Mr. Avery's parentage. "Three men can't bloody well ride one horse," continued the rotund man.

"Very true," said Mr. Avery without a blush. "As you are unharmed, I suggest you walk and allow your two fallen brethren to ride back from whence you came. I find I don't enjoy sharing the road with you."

Glowering and perspiring, the third man helped his wounded compatriots onto his horse and, muttering several more uncomplimentary epithets, led them back down the road.

"*Au revoir, mes amis,*" said Isabel softly, watching them go.

Mr. Avery pocketed his pistol and walked up to Isabel and Jamie. "I am all admiration," he said. "That was extremely able teamwork and use of arms."

13

"Why, thank you, Mr. Avery," said Jamie as he reloaded his pistol. "It was good of you to step in when you did, although we could have handled the fat one without your aid." He drew his pocket pistol from his coat pocket, checked it, and returned it to his pocket.

"Of that I have no doubt," said Mr. Avery, raising an elegant eyebrow at the breadth of this pair's armory. "How comes it that two coddled lads can so easily rout a greater force of arms?"

"Why, sir, 'tis no mystery," said Isabel smoothly as she returned sword to scabbard and gun to belt. "Our father was a practical man and taught us the ways of the world."

"Unbeknownst," said Jamie, "to our mother, whose nerves are too delicate to withstand such knowledge of her babes."

"Father gave us a fair understanding," continued Isabel, "of arms—pistols, shotguns, rifles—swordplay, and fisticuffs. As we have been on the road for nearly a month, we have already encountered one or two bands of brigands intent on relieving us of our purses."

"We're not that plump in the pocket," said Jamie, "but highwaymen will be highwaymen."

"Thinking us ripe for the plucking because of our beardless chins—"

"Speak for yourself, Jack," said Jamie.

Isabel returned the grin. "Thinking us ripe for the plucking, sir, they were careless in their assaults, as you have seen, and were therefore easily routed. We left this last trio yesterday morning strung up by their heels from a stout oak tree just outside Tidbury in Bedfordshire. I don't understand how they came to escape so soon. Perhaps my knots were at fault."

"Oh, I can't think that likely," Mr. Avery said sardonically. "Mayhaps they were rescued by some innocent passerby."

"It is certainly a more reasonable supposition," Isabel gravely agreed. "In any event, yesterday's retaliatory measure seems to have upset them, for they came at us just now with some heat. I trust we will see no more of them."

"I think they have learned to keep their distance," Mr. Avery said. "Come, will you accompany me to the Crown and Bull and allow me to purchase you a dinner to celebrate this recent victory?"

"Why, sir, you speak to the point," said Jamie. "I am famished. Lead on. Lead on!"

Their horse was removed from its traces and then mounted first by Isabel, then by Jamie. With Mr. Avery once more upon his Arabian, they rode at a sedate pace the five miles to Little Bowden, a village with but one church, one pub, and one inn, the Crown and Bull, whose huge painted signboard of a heavy-breathing bull wearing a golden crown spanned the street and quite belied the rather diminutive stature of the inn, a two-story affair of Stuart lineage and several smoking chimneys.

Size, however, did not dictate service. Two ostlers came running to greet them and led away their horses while Mr. Avery, Isabel, and Jamie entered the inn.

"You have a slight limp, John Cavendish," Mr. Avery observed. "Are you injured?"

"An accident of my own making a se'ennight ago," Isabel airily replied. "I no longer notice my wretched ankle. It is late in the day, Tony. What say you, shall we stay the night?"

Jamie, seeing the look in Isabel's eye, choked back his startled protest and replied instead, "Yes, I think we shall. My hunger requires at least two hours at dinner and by then it will be dark and the sheets will have had time to air."

"A wise decision," said Mr. Avery.

Isabel cast an amused glance at Jamie as Mr. Avery now took full charge of the situation. He ordered their dinner, specified the wine, and demanded clean rooms for the night to be well aired and tricked out with the inn's best linens.

"A most domineering nonesuch," murmured Jamie. "Do you still affect admiration?"

15

"If it procures me a decent bed, I do," Isabel retorted.

"You were always so damnably practical," Jamie muttered.

The tiny innkeeper, noting the quality of Mr. Avery's clothes, bearing, and horse, was all obsequiousness in attempting to serve his guests but paled when informed they wanted three rooms for the night.

"Three?" he croaked. "I am prostrate, sir. I have but two that I can offer. Two excellent rooms, sir. Clean, well kept, but alas, only two."

"Have no fear, landlord," said Isabel to the innkeeper. "My brother and I shall batch together. Mr. Avery may have the second room to himself."

"Oh, sir, I *am* grateful for your understanding," gasped the innkeeper. "Pray step this way to our private parlor, and I will have your meal served at once."

While Mr. Avery went to check on his horse, Isabel and Jamie sat down at a clean table to await their dinner. The parlor, timbers darkened by the passing centuries, was comfortable enough. A fire blazed in a huge fireplace, effectively removing the night chill from the air.

"This is madness!" Jamie said to Isabel once the innkeeper had hurried from the room to secure their dinners. "We should be stuffing food in our pockets and riding off now!"

"I know it," Isabel replied in a low voice. "But there is Mr. Avery to consider. It will not do to arouse his suspicions. He has a knowing pair of eyes, that one."

"But our pursuers—"

"Are not accustomed to us stopping at an inn. Be at ease, Jamie. We will bid Mr. Avery adieu in the morning and continue on our journey. For now," Isabel said as Mr. Avery entered the parlor, "let us enjoy the pleasures at hand."

Their meal, though not fashionable, was plentiful and well cooked. The three spent a leisurely hour supping, enjoying a decent burgundy and conversation.

"Whither are you bound, Mr. Avery?" Isabel inquired after a sip of the burgundy.

16

"North, with no inclination to get there quickly."

"Try the syllabub, Jack, it's wonderful!" Jamie exclaimed.

"Thank you, no. I am full."

"Shall I eat it, then?"

"Yes, of course."

"You are a generous brother, Mr. Cavendish," Mr. Avery observed.

"My brother is a growing boy, sir, and needs his sustenance."

"But do you not grow as well?" Mr. Avery asked.

"Alas, sir," said Isabel, pushing her syllabub across the table to Jamie, "I follow my mother's side of the family in coloring and appalling lack of height. Tony is our father's son. He shall tower over me within a few months, you mark my words."

"Your father was a large gentleman, then?"

"Oh, sir, a behemoth," said Isabel. "Tall, broad in the shoulder, with a stomach of iron. Witness Tony."

Mr. Avery glanced at Jamie, who had advanced well into the second syllabub. "I take your point. Tell me, in the midst of all this adventure, how can your estimable mother survive the loss of her two adored—and hungry—sons?"

"Ah, sir, I fear she survives the loss badly," Isabel replied. "But we write her once a week and assure her of our continued good health and happiness. There comes a time in every young man's life when he must think of himself. Don't you agree, Mr. Avery?"

"It was my impression that young men do nothing *but* think of themselves," the gentleman coolly replied.

"Perhaps. But we were raised with better manners and hopefully more sense."

"So it would appear," said Mr. Avery.

Isabel leaned back in her heavy oak chair and surreptitiously considered Mr. Avery. There was a certain pleasure in the gentleman's company. He was intelligent, sensible, skilled in the delicate art of bruiting about power, and undeniably

17

attractive in a cool, English manner. More important, he was a second, albeit temporary, bravo who, should another attack come in the night, would undoubtedly defend Jamie first and ask questions later. 'Twas a pity he would have to be abandoned on the morrow, but it was not right to further endanger the proper gentleman through private troubles.

"You're a very accommodating gentleman," Isabel observed. "Taking up two unknown youths, procuring us decent beds, buying us dinner, agreeing with everything we say. I've never known a more harmonious companion."

Mr. Avery permitted a slight smile. "You are most kind."

"You are a man of some position and responsibility in the country?" Isabel asked, already guessing the answer.

"Yes," said Mr. Avery. "In addition to a rather large estate, which takes up most of my attention, I have many obligations to my family, to my tenants, to the parish poor, and to my neighbors."

"Sounds damnably dull," Jamie opined.

"It is an honor," said Mr. Avery coldly, "to be of service to others."

"Your sentiments do you credit, sir," Isabel said hurriedly, giving Jamie a swift kick in the shin under the table. "Many gentlemen in this day and age think only of their own pleasure, not of their duty."

"An excellent recover, sir," murmured Mr. Avery, an appreciative glint in his blue eyes.

Isabel affected not to hear. "In addition to your many familial and social duties, are you also married?"

"I? No, no. I have yet to meet a suitable wife."

"But are you not advanced in years to be unmarried?" Isabel inquired.

Mr. Avery stiffened. "If you wish to continue in my excellent company, I would advise you to watch your tongue, boy. I am five-and-thirty and still well able to marry and father heirs!"

18

"Indeed, sir, I did not mean to impugn your virility," said Isabel, her gray eyes twinkling mischievously. "But with all the obligations that you've enumerated and your keen sense of duty, how is it someone has not yet dragged you kicking and screaming to the altar?"

Mollified and amused in spite of himself, Mr. Avery had some difficulty in suppressing a smile. "Why, I am taller than most, and they have found it difficult to move me."

"More wine anyone?" said Jamie.

Isabel shook her head.

"And you, Jack Cavendish, are you not pursued by all the young females in your set?" Mr. Avery inquired. "You're a handsome youth, I protest, with a good leg and charming manners. Are you not hotly pursued by matchmaking mamas?"

"Indeed, sir," Isabel replied, fighting an incipient blush, "why else do you think I have run off?"

"My brother," offered Jamie with a wicked grin, "is accosted wherever he goes by dewy-eyed females fluttering their fans and simpering at him."

"It is enough," said Isabel with a frown at Jamie, "to give one a distaste for all female kind."

"There are, I assure you, a few nonsimpering females in the world," said Mr. Avery. "Be of stout heart."

"I wish I had your height," Isabel said wistfully, "for I fear it will be a simple matter to bind and carry me to the altar, kick and scream though I might. Can you imagine, sir, being married before you are five-and-twenty?"

"A lowering thought indeed," Mr. Avery murmured.

"That is nothing," said Jamie. "Think of *my* plight. Mother is already throwing Lucy Moriarty at my head, and I'm four years from my majority! Lucy is an admirable young woman, I assure you, Mr. Avery, but she has spots, and one eye is blue and the other eye yellow, and I cannot for the life of me decide which to look at when I am talking to her. Should I be forced to marry the wench, I shall go cross-eyed!"

19

"A fate to be avoided at all costs," Mr. Avery agreed.

Isabel smiled over her burgundy. The nonesuch had a sense of humor buried beneath all that propriety after all. It was a happy discovery.

The hour was advanced when the three, escorted by a sallow chambermaid, slowly climbed the narrow stairs to the first landing, which boasted three guest rooms: one of which was occupied by an itinerant wine merchant, another which Mr. Avery claimed, and the third which was entered by Isabel and Jamie.

"Well, Tony, we shall sleep tolerably well tonight," Isabel said, surveying the two beds in the room, one a trundle bed, it must be confessed, but still a bed.

"It will be a pleasure not to sleep upon the bare ground," Jamie agreed. "What say you, big brother? Shall we toss a coin for the trundle?"

"Nay. Your longer bones require the larger bed. I'll sleep on the trundle and gladly. Help me out of this coat, will you?"

Jamie obliged.

"Ah! I long for clean clothes," said Isabel, stretching with relief.

"And some fetching evening gown, no doubt," said Jamie, and he won a grimace in reply.

"It is not that I miss dresses so much but, oh my, Tony, for a bath and someone to attend me and clean clothes! Now that, to me, would be heaven."

"You were always singularly lacking in ambition, *Jack*."

With a lazy salute Jamie left the room so Isabel could change in private.

With many sighs of relief she removed boots, trousers, shirt, and the corset that had bound her breasts for nearly a week without respite. It was all well and good to have the freedom of traveling as a man, the ease of movement of breeches, the comfort of going anywhere unfollowed by speculative glances, but oh how she hated that corset!

It had taken her two years to perfect the design. It was built to pull in rather than push out her breasts and to make her clothes fall deceptively over slim feminine hips. It had served its purpose well in the intervening years, for Isabel had often had to play the boy—but never for such a continuous stretch of time. Sleep in it had been, at best, uncomfortable. Release for one night was bliss.

Using the basin, she quickly washed what dirt she could from her face and body and vigorously brushed her black hair. To be able to wash her hair was her next goal in life. To be a boy was one thing, but to be a filthy boy quite another.

Her well-scrubbed reflection peered at her from the tiny mirror as she plaited her hair. What would the very proper, very handsome Mr. Avery say if he discovered her to be a woman? This was a lowering thought. Mr. Avery seemed a man of very decided opinions. He could not approve her charade. Few gentlemen would.

She sighed, pulled a nightshirt from her valise, and tugged it over her head. Masquerading through perilous adventures— what a life! Certainly it had had its amusements and pleasures in the past, but there were none now with the fear gnawing at her breast. That that slovenly trio should attack them again! Isabel shivered. She could not draw a safe breath in this England.

She slipped a pistol under her pillow and wondered, not for the first time, if she would ever be free of danger. Not for a moment in the last two months had she doubted her abilities nor regretted the heavy burden placed on her shoulders. But oh, she was weary! She longed for the peace that continually escaped her and for the safe harbor she had never known.

Isabel suddenly grimaced. "Giving way to self-pity, for shame! Be grateful for what you have, my girl," she sternly ordered herself. She glanced around at the room, at the high feather bed that would be Jamie's, at the large fire in the grate burning so reassuringly. For one night, perhaps, she might claim that safe harbor. Brett Avery was next door, and for all his propriety, she suspected he was skilled in the art of self-defense. She would not lament the adventurous life she led nor the danger she faced now. She had a bed, a fire, and Brett Avery close at hand. She would not want for more.

Chapter 2

May 4, 1804   Early morning

Hanning's Brook, Northamptonshire

BRETT AVERY STOOD at the entrance to the inn's private parlor and surveyed the charming scene before him. A table was laid with a plentiful breakfast, and seated at that table talking quietly together were Jack and Tony Cavendish. Jack was a handsome youth with gray eyes that looked their best when alight with mischief, which was regrettably often. It was a pity for the boy that he was not taller, but he had well-shaped legs, intelligence, an attractive voice, and he wore his cleaned riding clothes with a certain authority that surpassed his twenty years and his five and a half feet of height. Mr. Avery could well believe that every female in his county had set her cap for him.

As for Tony, he might be four years from his majority, but he bid well to reach six feet within the year. He was not a handsome boy, but his face, with its long thin nose, was striking. When his brown eyes were alight with deviltry, as they were wont to be, Mr. Avery doubted that few females could gaze on him unaffected.

"Ah, youth!" he exclaimed. "You must have been up at dawn."

The Cavendishes turned to him with welcoming smiles.

"Come join us, sir!" Jamie cried. "We've held breakfast for you."

23

"That is most generous of you, lad," said Mr. Avery as he took his chair. "I know what it must have cost you to wait with so much food before you."

"Oh come, Mr. Avery," said Jamie with a grin. "You quite misunderstand me. I do not think only of food; it is just that I think of food with great pleasure."

Mr. Avery smiled as he poured out his coffee. "I admire the distinction."

The three set to their breakfasts with gusto as Mr. Avery regaled them with some deliciously scandalous London *on dits*, a description of Mr. Kean's newest triumph on the stage, and a complaint against some of the more ridiculous knee ribbons to appear on some of the more adventurous sprigs of fashion strolling down Bond Street.

The hour passed quickly and with pleasure on all sides. Isabel knew a sinking feeling in her heart when she saw Mr. Avery sit back in his chair to pronounce himself full and satisfied with the repast. They must part soon, and with all the necessity for the separation staring her in the face, Isabel acknowledged the unhappiness in her heart. She caught herself. What folly! She had regretted no man's absence before, and she wasn't about to begin now.

"As you purchased dinner, sir, you will allow me to provide breakfast," she said coolly, drawing out her purse.

"As you will," said Mr. Avery.

"Tony and I wish to thank you for your company and your many kindnesses on our behalf, but we feel that the time has come to part. Whilst you were at your morning toilette, I was able to procure two able horses."

"They are nothing to your Arabian, of course," said Jamie. "But they are strong and will carry us as far as we need."

"And so," Isabel said, standing up and extending her slim hand to Mr. Avery, "we must say good-bye and wish you health and happiness on the rest of your journey."

The tall gentleman looked up at her and smiled. "I think not."

Isabel and Jamie became very still. Jamie's hand clasped the

24

pistol in his coat pocket as Isabel—heart pounding in her breast—mentally went over the weapons she had secreted about her person and debated whether the parlor door or window would promote the best escape.

"I have come to fetch you to Lancashire," Mr. Avery continued, "at the personal request of Montague Shipley."

Mr. Avery had created all the sensation he could have desired. Isabel and Jamie goggled at him.

"You are mistaken, sir," said Isabel, recovering first. "We know no Montague Shipley and cannot conceive why anyone would ask you to accompany us anywhere."

"You are very cool," Mr. Avery said approvingly, "but do give over the playacting. I have known Montague Shipley these last twenty years and more, just as *Tony* has known him all of his life, for how should a son not know his father? You are very like Monty, you know, young James. Particularly about the nose. I had rejoiced at Monty's succession to Thornwynd, I have mourned his death, and have come to insure his son's succession to his rightful inheritance. But perhaps this will explain and defend me to your better understanding."

Here Mr. Avery withdrew from his inside coat pocket a letter, which he, glancing at Jamie, handed to Isabel. A quick glance told her all: it was Monty's hand.

"Read it aloud," said Avery.

With a nod from Jamie, Isabel began to read the letter, very much aware of Mr. Avery's close scrutiny.

" 'My dear Brett,

" 'I am dying. I am sending my son to England with a protector whom I trust with his life. I have given them full instructions to take them to Ravenscourt where, I hope, they may rest in some ease and safety until Jamie is declared the true Baron of Thornwynd.

" 'To better protect my son from any treachery or delay he may encounter in England, I ask that you contrive to meet

25

with them and escort them on the road north. I anticipate that Braybrook or Little Bowden in Northamptonshire will serve you best, not before the first of May, for they will encounter many difficulties in removing from the Continent. Any debt you owed me will be amply repaid by these efforts on my behalf.

" 'If this does not bespeak my enormous trust in you and the friendship I have long cherished, then nothing can do so.

" 'Your friend in life and death,

" 'Montague Shipley, Baron of Thornwynd.' "

Isabel's voice faltered only on the last. Jamie had already turned away to stare out the small window.

"How came you by this, sir?" Isabel demanded in a low voice, her gray eyes fixed grimly on Mr. Avery.

"You will know the name, I believe, of Dick Rowan, Monty's servant for many years? He brought me this letter, as well as a will."

Isabel glanced at Jamie. From his deathbed, Monty had sent Dick Rowan to England not an hour before they, too, had fled Vienna.

"Dick might have fallen in your way, sir," she calmly observed. "You might have killed him and stolen the letter."

"Possible, I grant you, but not at all true. Perhaps a word in your ear?"

Jamie started and turned from the window. "Do you know the password, sir?"

"There will soon be a fair wind over Thornwynd," Mr. Avery pronounced.

Isabel gasped and hurriedly sat down in her chair. "You have proved yourself a friend, sir, and are well met." She calmly met his speculative blue gaze and wondered what could be behind it. She handed him back the letter. "We will trust you . . . as far as we are able."

Mr. Avery hesitated. "Monty taught you well. You are rather young, I think, to be Jamie's protector."

26

"I am older in years and experience than my appearance reveals."

"And your true name?"

"Jack Cavendish will do as well as any other."

"Very well, Jack," said Mr. Avery, a note of disapproval in his voice as he returned the letter to his coat pocket. "May I inquire your relationship to the young baronet?"

"We are a form of cousins, sir. I was unofficially adopted by the Shipleys many years ago and have been Jamie's constant companion ever since."

Again that measuring gaze. "I am puzzled," Mr. Avery said, "for you seem familiar to me. Have we not met before?"

Isabel's heart clenched. How could he recognize her? "No, sir," she replied. "I assure you I would have remembered the event."

"Yes, I dare say I should have as well. It must remain a mystery, then," Mr. Avery said with a sigh. Apparently, he did not enjoy mysteries. "The morning is advanced. I have ordered my chaise to meet me here, and I suggest we decamp. The Thornwynd legacy has yet to be fulfilled."

There was a moment of silence. Mr. Avery regarded his erstwhile traveling companions in some puzzlement.

"I don't like it," Jamie said.

"Neither do I," said Isabel. "It was not right of Monty to involve you, sir, in the great danger surrounding us. I beg you remain here with your carriage and let us go on alone."

"No," said Avery, "I will not shirk my duty to a past debt."

"Abandon duty to reason, sir," Isabel urged. "You have no understanding of the trouble you are bringing on yourself and no real right to interfere. Monty made me Jamie's protector. He also appointed a guardian for Jamie, the Earl of Northbridge, who will surely keep him safe once we reach Lancashire. Your company, entertaining though it is, is yet unnecessary."

"Counsel well worth heeding, Mr. Avery," said Jamie.

"Leave me to Jack's able care and the tender mercies of the fat and crotchety Earl of Northbridge."

"Crotchety?" said Mr. Avery with a lift of his elegant eyebrows.

"Jamie is wont to embroider the facts of the case," Isabel said with a frown at her charge. "Monty once described the earl as a most punctilious gentleman chained to his estate without the adventurous spirit to want or even know that he should escape it."

"Ah."

"It was most unfair of Monty to saddle me with a gout-ridden antiquity," Jamie complained. "You'd think he would have done better by me."

"Let us do better by you, Mr. Avery," said Isabel. "Do not accompany us on our journey. You cannot understand the grave danger in which you stand."

"Then you may explain it in greater detail to me when we are on the road."

Again Isabel and Jamie exchanged a glance.

"A most determined gentleman," said Jamie.

"Would Monty befriend any other?" said Isabel.

"I would point out," Avery said, "that whoever your enemies may be, they will not be expecting you to travel in a comfortable chaise, and they will not expect you to be a trio."

"That is true," Isabel conceded. "But you have been seen assisting us. You will be remembered, and sooner or later we *will* be discovered and the danger will be as great as it was before we met you."

Mr. Avery consulted his watch. "I trust I may be of some use should it come to a fight. You cannot rid yourselves of my company, gentlemen. Resign yourselves to that fact."

"We will undoubtedly encounter further oak trees strong enough to hold even Mr. Avery," said Jamie to Isabel. "We can string him up by his heels at our leisure."

She smiled. The plan was not wholly ridiculous, though she thought it would take some effort to catch the nonesuch unawares. "Very well, Mr. Avery, we will accompany you . . . for a while."

Mr. Avery bowed. "You honor me with your trust. I will go attend to my chaise and coachman while you gather your things together. I will meet you outside."

Mr. Avery strode to the door and then turned back with a grin. "Lucy Moriarty indeed!" He was gone in the next moment, leaving Isabel and Jamie to stare at each other in some consternation.

"Are we safe in his company?" Jamie asked.

"For now," Isabel replied. Her fingers drummed on the table. "I think."

"You do not trust Mr. Avery?"

Isabel's laugh was grim. "I trust no man, and I dare trust no one until you have fulfilled the Thornwynd legacy."

"You will not exchange your breeches for petticoats?"

"Not just yet. For now, it is important that Mr. Avery learn to accept my role in this adventure of ours. There may be some sense in Monty soliciting his aid. Mr. Avery seems a most capable gentleman."

"You always fancied the nonesuch."

Isabel frowned at the boy. "Admired, Jamie, if you please."

Jamie went to the window and watched the preparations in the yard. "Why did Father not tell us he had arranged for Mr. Avery to meet us?"

"Monty was always very fond of a secret," Isabel said slowly. "Besides, it was safer for Mr. Avery to search for us and prove himself to us, rather than for us to search out Mr. Avery and perhaps fall into a trap of Horace Shipley's making. But why did Mr. Avery not reveal himself to us last night? Why did he wait until now? There is more here than we are being told; I am certain of it."

Jamie turned to her. "Are we in danger, then?"

"There is certainly danger from what he knows that we do not," said Isabel, her brow furrowed. "But what could it be?"

"At least Dick got through unscathed. Our own journey is not hopeless."

"So it would seem." Isabel sighed. All was not right here, but she could not put her finger on what. "Come. We'd better join our new traveling companion."

They left the inn and advanced into the bright early-morning sunshine. The tall gentleman had not lied. The forest-green chaise was of recent make and well sprung.

"Why, sir, we are to travel in luxury," said Isabel with open admiration.

"Comfort, merely comfort," said Mr. Avery dismissingly. "The Cavendishes will accompany me, Dawkins," said he to his grizzled coachman, who stood at the heads of a high-spirited team of grays.

"Yes, sir," said Dawkins with no trace of enthusiasm.

Jamie inspected the horses while Isabel secured their valises behind the carriage. With a dour look, Dawkins laboriously climbed onto his perch.

"To Lichfield, Dawkins," said Mr. Avery.

"No, sir," Isabel countered, "to Nottingham."

Mr. Avery turned with a most forbidding look. "Mr. Cavendish, or whatever your name is, you are in my charge now and will follow my direction."

"On the contrary," Isabel retorted, not all cowed by this masculine display. "Monty specifically enlisted your aid as *escort*, not leader or guide. To me he gave the charge of Jamie's safety until he is installed at Thornwynd and claimed by the Earl of Northbridge. Therefore, we go at my direction."

Blue eyes glinted at this challenge to his authority. "You have fulfilled your charge, boy, for *I* am the Earl of Northbridge."

Isabel and Jamie stared at him a moment and then regarded each other.

"I thought he was Brett Avery," said Jamie.

"Or at least a secret elf king," Isabel said lightly, despite the sinking of her heart. An earl, forsooth. Her luck could not be worse.

"You are not the only ones to indulge in playacting," said the earl, a trifle miffed at their calm reception of this momentous news. "My Christian name is Brett. Avery is an old family name."

"Yes, of course it is," Isabel said soothingly.

Jamie burst out laughing. "And I thought you'd be a crusty old chair-bound codger! Well met, sir! Well met," he said, shaking the earl's hand.

"Thank you," said the earl coolly, smoothing a coat sleeve. "As I am your guardian and you have reached me safely, you will now allow me to dictate your course."

"No, sir," Isabel reiterated. "Monty placed Jamie in my charge until he is safely named heir to Thornwynd. Until that time, you will go at *my* direction."

"I will do no such thing," said Lord Northbridge testily.

"Then you will travel alone."

"My dear child," said the earl with the greatest condescension, "I know this country as you or even Monty could not. I will get you to Thornwynd safe enough."

"You will escort us at my direction, sir, or you won't go at all," Isabel retorted.

Lord Northbridge jerked open the chaise door. "Into the carriage, boy, and no more of this nonsense."

Isabel bowed and stepped back from the chaise. "Jamie, fetch our valises. It has been a pleasure knowing you, my lord," she said, offering her hand. "I trust we may meet again at Thornwynd."

The earl was clearly taken aback but still game. "I could have you gagged and tied and thrown into the chaise," he observed.

"You could try," Isabel retorted.

The earl's glare was routed by an appreciative smile. "A most loyal and determined puppy, indeed. I begin to think

31

Monty chose his son's protector well. Very well, I concede, stubborn Jack . . . this one time. Whither are we bound?"

Isabel let out her breath. She would not like to do battle with the tall gentleman on a daily basis. 'Twas most agitating. "For now, we must advance toward Bardon Hill in Leicestershire and from thence to Nottingham."

"You have your directions, Dawkins," the earl called to his coachman, and received a grunt in reply.

With a bow to his lordship, who held the door open for her, Isabel climbed into the chaise and sat beside Jamie. Their host ordered Dawkins to drive on as he followed Isabel into the carriage.

"How the mighty are fallen," Jamie murmured, his brown eyes alight with suppressed laughter.

The Earl of Northbridge cast him a quelling glance. "Remember that you are my ward and that it would be wise to curry my favor," he said, sitting opposite them and crossing his long legs. "Come, gentlemen. Tell me your history. How has it come about that Monty should die and you tread perilously close to the time constraints of the Thornwynd legacy? It does not seem at all like Montague Shipley to arrange such a precarious situation for his son . . . and friend."

"But did not Dick Rowan tell you?" said Jamie.

"Dick, I'm afraid, was in no condition to tell anyone anything when he reached Ravenscourt."

"Good God, sir, was he injured?" Isabel cried.

"No, no, do not alarm yourself. He was merely suffering from exhaustion and quite unable to tell me anything of Monty. The doctor assured me he would be fully recovered by now, so have no fear. But you must tell me why you have been tramping England's back roads disguised as the Cavendish brothers."

"You may thank my uncle for that," Jamie said bitterly.

"Horace Shipley means to stop Jamie from claiming his inheritance," Isabel stated.

"Have you proof of this?" the earl demanded.

"We had little opportunity to secure affidavits from those who have attacked us," Jamie snapped.

Lord Northbridge studied him a moment, his expression masked. "You've had a hard time of it, it seems. Tell me your tale from the beginning, if you please. I am quite in the dark."

Jamie glanced at Isabel. He was not feeling communicative.

"We received a letter from Monty's solicitor on the evening of February twenty-fourth last," Isabel reluctantly began. She, too, had no desire to relieve that awful night. It haunted her dreams and pressed upon her heart during the day. "The letter was to the point, informing Monty of his inheritance and detailing the time constraints of the Thornwynd legacy. Monty or his successor had to appear at Thornwynd by the seventeenth of May or lose his inheritance. The difficulty lay in that we were in Vienna at the time."

"Vienna?!" said the earl. "And you reached Northampton-shire in only two months? There's a war on!"

"We know," Isabel said dryly. "It caused us a devilish amount of trouble. We had already lost two months in receiving the notification of Monty's succession, and then there were Horace Shipley's agents to combat."

Lord Northbridge's blue eyes narrowed. "I begin to think Monty's death was not from natural causes."

Jamie stared at him in surprise. "But did you not know, sir? Father was murdered on my uncle's orders."

The earl was silent, his face cold and forbidding. "I know Horace Shipley is capable of many foul deeds—but murder?" He stared out the window at the clouds dappling a bright blue sky. "Tell me what happened."

February 24, 1804   Evening

Vienna, Austria

"That's a very fetching gown, Isabel," said Montague Shipley approvingly as he rose from the table. He was a tall, robust gentleman who seemed to fill the dining room. "Is it new?"

"Yes," Isabel replied as she and then Mr. Shipley took their chairs. "Green is the Citizen de Saville's favorite color. You did say you wanted me to distract him tonight, did you not?"

"Ah, my attentive Isabel," Mr. Shipley said fondly, raising her slim hand to his lips, his brown eyes displaying that roguish twinkle she had come to know all too well. "We shall have the citizen pouring all of Bonaparte's secrets into your delicate ear before the night is out."

"A charming prospect," said Isabel with a grimace, retrieving her hand. "I have never liked playing at spies, Monty,"

Mr. Shipley appeared affronted. "Spies? Piffle! A Shipley would never be so vulgar. I merely delight in acting now and again on my country's behalf."

"It is my opinion that if we are going to lure de Saville into a good enough humor to speak freely into my delicate ear, we will have to spend a good deal to let him win at the tables tonight. Where is the profit in that, Monty?"

"Ah, my child," said Mr. Shipley with the greatest condescension, "still after so many years you fail to perceive my genius. We will have de Saville's secrets and a full purse before the night is out, never you fear."

"Well," said Isabel, still a bit disgruntled by the part she was about to enact, "ten percent of *anything* will be better than I had hoped for this evening."

"You should have insisted on claiming twenty percent of your winnings in my establishments."

"Twenty?! It was all I could do to bring you up to ten!"

"That is because at one-and-twenty you were not yet experienced enough at the bargaining table to gauge my intentions. You might try to renegotiate our agreement at some point in the near future."

"You are a rogue," Isabel pronounced.

"Thank you, my dear. You will have a bountiful old age, Isabel. I shall see to it," Mr. Shipley assured her.

Isabel grinned at the old rascal. "As long as I *make* it to an old age, I'll be content, Monty."

"Good evening, Father, Isabel," said the scion of the house as he strolled into the dining room.

"You have been primping," Isabel commented, looking the boy up and down.

Indeed he had. A younger version of his father, James Shipley was wearing a chocolate-brown evening coat with a collar that nearly covered his ears, and white pantaloons with pale yellow knee ribbons, the newest kick from Napoleon's court.

"For once I do not have to be a footman, a croupier, or a waiter," Jamie stated as he took his seat, "and I intend to enjoy such novelty to the fullest."

"All I ask is that you not fall into that appalling Viennese accent you affected at last week's ball and all will be well," said Mr. Shipley a trifle sternly.

"When have I ever made a misstep in any role I've undertaken?" Jamie demanded, piqued. "I am a consummate actor. You have said so yourself innumerable times, and you know, Father, that you are never wrong."

"That is very true," said Mr. Shipley, considering the matter.

Footmen in perfectly understated livery brought in the first course of their dinner. With them came a slight man, with a tuft of gray hair, and a letter in his hand.

"This just came for you, sir," he said in a broad Lancashire accent.

"How many times have I told you, Dick, how dangerous it is to bring correspondence into a dining room?" Mr. Shipley said sternly to his servant.

"It's just the three of you, sir," Dick stolidly retorted, "and the letter bears the mark of your father's solicitor."

Three pairs of eyes stared at Dick Rowan.

"Does it, now?" Mr. Shipley murmured. He took the envelope. "I rescind my chastisement, Dick. Let us see what Mr. Stone, Esquire, has to say for himself."

He broke the seal and quickly scanned the letter comprising two pages, closely written. Knowing he had an audience, and always glad of one, he took his time with his task before finally setting the letter on the table before him and looking up at Jamie, Isabel, and Dick.

"My father has died," he announced simply.

"But that's impossible!" Jamie declared. "You've always said he was too contrary to die in your lifetime."

Far from appalled at this indecorous outburst over such grave news, Mr. Shipley Senior merely shook his gray head at his own lack of foresight. "Sir Barnaby's stroke three years ago weakened him more than I suspected. And in more ways than one. He wholly failed to disinherit me as he did Horace. I am now the Baron of Thornwynd."

"Good God," said Isabel, thunderstruck.

"Precisely," said the new baron with the greatest satisfaction.

"My condolences on your father's death, sir," said Dick. "He was a crusty and ill-tempered old weasel, but at least he was consistent in his bad character."

"Yes, something he always criticized *me* for," said Mr. Shipley with a sigh. "Odd to think that Father can no longer hound me with his damned letters. Well, I dare say he'll do his level best to haunt me now. If ever someone was meant to be a ghost rattling his chains about all night long, it was Sir Barnaby. It would be just like him to be so irritating."

"But this is astounding!" Jamie cried. "With you the new Baron of Thornwynd, *I* am suddenly advanced to the status of an *heir*! The fairest damsels in England will throw themselves at my feet!"

"You are seventeen," Isabel reminded him, "with more than enough time to languish in bachelorhood until the appropriate damsel hurtles herself at you."

"Enough of this chat," said Mr. Shipley. "We must make plans to return to England at once."

"Good God, sir, why?" Jamie demanded.

"You are forgetting the Thornwynd legacy, my boy," Mr.

36

Shipley replied, leaning back in his chair and raising his wine glass to his lips. A sigh of deep contentment followed. "Any heir to the baronetcy who does not present himself at Thornwynd within five months of the former baron's death forfeits all rights to the inheritance, and the next direct male heir—that would be you, and after you my nephew Nigel Clark—succeeds to Thornwynd. I've no fancy to see you becoming a baron just yet, my son. So I shall claim the baronetcy for myself. Your turn will come in time."

"A very long time, I trust sir," said Jamie, raising his wineglass in toast.

The baron acknowledged this homage with a fond smile. "Well, this will alter our plans. We will dine, attend my French and Viennese guests at the Golden Chariot, fleece de Saville of his secrets, and return here no later than two in the morning. We'll have the servants pack our things betimes so that we can be off by dawn."

"So soon?" said Isabel with a start. "Why the haste?"

"It relates to the date of my father's death," said the baron, showing her the solicitor's letter. "He died on the seventeenth of December; this letter is dated the nineteenth of December. That gives us less than three months to reach Thornwynd before the legacy removes me from succession, and there is a war on, after all."

"Not to mention a blockade," Jamie added.

"A decided impediment," his father agreed. "We'll need all our wits to outmaneuver Bonaparte, the Austrian army, and the English army and navy."

"Well," said Isabel after a fortifying sip of wine that did nothing to mask the pain cascading through her, "I wish you Godspeed with all my heart."

The baron and his heir stared at her in the greatest astonishment.

"What are you babbling about?" the baron inquired somewhat testily. "Why wish *us* Godspeed when you will be with us?"

"But I will not be with you," Isabel calmly retorted.

"What foolishness is this?" the baron demanded.

"No foolishness," Isabel replied, staring into her wine, ordering her fingers on the stem of the glass not to tremble. "There is the little matter of an outstanding warrant for my arrest in England, or had you forgotten?"

Truth be told, the baron *had* forgotten this minor difficulty in the excitement of the moment. But now that this stumbling block was recalled to his consciousness, he brushed it aside as he would a mildly irritating fly.

"As baron, I will have both wealth and power," he declared. "The warrant will be of no moment."

"It is of considerable moment to me, sir," Isabel wryly retorted. "You may have all the faith in the world in Thornwynd's influence. I cannot be so sanguine."

"What is all of this talk of warrants and not coming to England with us?" Jamie said impatiently. "You *must* come with us, Isabel. We cannot get on without you."

"You fend for yourself very well already, child. You will not regret my absence."

"How can you, Isabel? How *can* you say such a thing?!" Jamie demanded, his young face flushed with outrage. "I'd rather England sank into the sea than live a day without your company!"

"I'm sorry, Jamie," Isabel said gently, covering his clenched hand with hers. "I was trying to be brusque and brave and doing a lamentable job of it. I cannot bear the thought of parting from you and Monty. You are my family. But I am not safe in England. I cannot go."

"Have no fear, Jamie," said Montague Shipley. "Our separation from Isabel will be of short duration. Once I am installed at Thornwynd, I will arrange to have the warrant quashed, and then Isabel may return to England with impunity."

The next two courses of dinner were spent discussing their plans for departure on the morrow and where Isabel would stay until Monty could safely summon her to England.

It was in waiting for the fourth course of their dinner—a

haunch of venison—that the trouble began. No footmen had entered the dining room in a good twenty minutes. The baron had rung the silver bell at his plate twice already. He had just raised it a third time and meant to shake it with the vigor his outrage demanded, when an army of men, all wearing masks, burst through the door where the footmen were expected.

They were armed to the teeth: a decidedly bloodcurdling crew.

"A unique attack, perhaps," Montague Shipley conceded amiably to these interlopers, "but the very height of rudeness. Even the basest of thieves knows not to interrupt their victims at dinner."

"It's not your gold we want, Shipley," growled a burly man reeking of beer, "it's your life. And the boy's!"

"You see, sir," said Jamie, turning from the carriage window, "my uncle had had much more time than we to think of what must be done and to hire enough men to insure that it was done properly."

"Our servants had either been tied and gagged or beaten senseless," Isabel continued. Oh, it was hard to play the stalwart boy when the grieving woman longed for a surcease from this pain! "Our attackers thought to catch us unawares. They succeeded. They had hoped to find us without weapons. Here they failed. Gilt can hide a surprising heft to a dining room chair and produce a welcome degree of unconsciousness with whomsoever it connects. Knives were at hand. We were able to escape the dining room and make our way to where true weapons might be found: the main hall, the study, the library. We separated; it was our only chance."

"How many did you fight?" asked the earl.

"I counted ten, didn't you, Jamie?"

Lord Northbridge stared at them.

"Yes, ten," Jamie replied grimly.

"With guns, with swords, we were able to kill or wound many of our attackers," Isabel continued. "But Monty was the

39

main target, and while Jamie and I were otherwise engaged, the bulk of the force was turned upon him. He fought off three. The fourth . . . struck home with a sword."

Jamie pulled his hat over his eyes as Isabel continued in a stilted voice.

"Jamie and I came to him as soon as we could, but the wound was mortal. We knew it. So did Monty. We had two servants left to us, the man who carried the will and letter to you, sir, and our cook. With their help we got Monty to a couch and made him as comfortable as possible. He was . . . agitated. He believed Jamie to still be in deadly peril and charged me with safeguarding him until his succession. He had not to ask. I had already vowed to protect Jamie with my life."

"Clearly you were in danger. But how could you be sure it was Horace Shipley's men who attacked you?" the earl demanded.

"We had trussed those that we had wounded," Jamie replied with grim satisfaction. "I was able to persuade them to name their master."

"Horace is as tightfisted as reported. His bravos were vastly underpaid for their labors," Isabel said in a low voice.

"Where are those men now?" the earl demanded.

"I don't know," Isabel said, forcibly pulling herself from her black reverie. "I assume the Viennese authorities took them in hand. If they were handled appropriately, it is doubtful they are still alive."

"Blast!" said the earl. "How am I to prove . . . Well, let it go for now. Continue your tale, Master Jack."

Isabel took a steadying breath. "While Jamie and I packed and prepared for our departure, Monty wrote the letter to you and then, strength failing him, dictated his will to Dick Rowan and the directions that might get us to Ravenscourt. He died a half hour later. We could not stay to bury him. Our chef—who had been with us eleven years—agreed to take charge of Monty's body until we could send for him to be buried in England. We left that very night.

"Fortunately, we knew Vienna quite well, having resided there for some weeks. Our attackers, though Viennese, did not know us nearly so well, and we were able to escape the city undetected. But the war created many difficulties and delays, as Monty anticipated. We were followed. Twice we were attacked. Twice we inflicted far more harm than we incurred.

"We reached Hamburg about a fortnight ago and searched three days before we found a ship with a master we could bribe into running the blockade to England. We were at sea nine days."

"Nine miserable days," Jamie put in. "I was never meant to be a sailor."

"Sick?" the earl inquired.

"As a dog," Jamie replied. "Too sick to defend myself when one of the ship's mates attacked me."

"Jamie is usually quite capable of taking care of himself," said Isabel, "but on this occasion I was forced to intervene and wrenched my blasted ankle in the process."

"The accident of your own making?" the earl inquired with the sardonic lift of one brow.

"Quite my own fault, sir, I assure you," Isabel coolly replied. "I should have noticed the stool. Monty would have been appalled at my carelessness."

The earl's blue gaze dwelled on her face a moment. "And what of the attacker?"

"The mate confessed to having taken fifty gilders from one of my uncle's agents. He was keelhauled for his pains," Jamie said with a satisfied smile. "The captain objected to any threat to paying customers."

"We landed at the Nave," Isabel continued, the tale coming easier now, "and have been on the road these last three days. At first we thought ourselves safe. Horace Shipley's sphere of influence was the Continent, not England. No one followed us from the boat. For the first day of travel nothing untoward occurred. And then, two days ago, the trio whom you so obligingly helped us rout first came upon us and, thinking us but two

41

callow youths, met with a far stronger resistance than they had anticipated. That they made a second attempt indicates both Mr. Shipley's determination and his open purse. Who knows how many more men he has hired to stop us? Time is on his side. We've but a fortnight to reach Thornwynd and satisfy the requirements of the legacy."

"I never knew Horace to have an open purse," murmured the Earl of Northbridge. "But then, he never had so much at stake."

"I wish to emphasize to you, my lord," Isabel said earnestly, "that this is not a lark where a man of responsibility and duty may kick up his heels. 'Tis a life-and-death undertaking; it could be your death. Will you not reconsider accompanying us?"

"However able you may be," the earl replied quietly, "and every moment with you has proven your many abilities, you have shouldered a burden of overweening weight for your years. It is my duty to honor Monty's deathbed request and to give my protection to Jamie. There isn't an argument you can make that will change that."

Isabel's sigh conceded defeat. She had done *her* duty in trying to dissuade the earl, and truth to tell, she was glad he had refused her. It had been a relief to tell the story to another. She had not known the pleasure one could derive from a warm, compassionate blue gaze. She had no desire to give it up.

"I confess," Lord Northbridge continued, "that I gravely underestimated Mr. Shipley's ruthlessness. I hope my error does not bring you further trouble."

"What puzzles me," said Isabel, "is why Horace is going to all this trouble. Is it merely spite or jealousy? Sir Barnaby disinherited him long ago. If Monty and Jamie are dead, Thornwynd passes to Jamie's cousin, Nigel Clark. What scheme does Horace have up his sleeve? How can he benefit from Jamie's death?"

"You don't know?" said the earl.

"No," Isabel replied. She became very still. "Do you?"

"A suspicion or two," the earl conceded. "I'll tell you them later."

"Very well, sir," said Jamie gruffly as he pushed back his hat and sat up. "We have answered your questions. It is now time for you to answer ours. How did you come to know my father, and what debt did you owe him to bring you out on such a dangerous course?"

The earl was a little taken aback. He was accustomed to being accepted on the strength of his title and fortune, not challenged for all he was worth by a mere boy. Still, *if* they had endured all that they claimed, it seemed a fair request. "I originally met your father in the company of my father," he began slowly. "They had gone to school together. My father was fond of traveling on the Continent, and it was in Brussels that I first met Mr. Shipley at a dinner which my father gave."

"How many years ago, sir?" Isabel inquired.

"I was then but fourteen, so it would be twenty-one years, well before Jamie's birth and your unofficial adoption." He raised an inquiring brow to Isabel, but she only smiled and shook her head. It was her life's practice never to explain herself. The earl sighed as one ill-used and continued. "Monty and my father corresponded thereafter and whenever in a city together, such as Paris or Rome or Cádiz, they would often meet, and I was privileged to sit on the outskirts of their conversation and thereby gain a much broader understanding of the world."

Isabel could not suppress a chuckle. She had a very good idea of the education Lord Northbridge had received in Monty's company. The earl shared her smile. She found herself warmed by his blue gaze and hurriedly looked away.

"A few years later I entered upon my grand tour," he continued. "The Shipleys were then in Florence. Jamie had just been born, and I had the pleasure of visiting often with Mrs. Shipley and admiring your red, wrinkled little face, young James."

"You must have observed a different child, sir," Jamie said. "I was a handsome infant."

43

The earl's mouth quirked up. "As I was eighteen and rather full of myself and my own self-importance—"

"Oh no, sir," Isabel murmured wickedly, "not *you*?!"

Lord Northbridge cast her a most forbidding frown. "I was careless in my treatment of many," he continued frostily, "including a gentleman whom I happened to best one night at the baccarat table in the gaming house which Monty then owned. Not only did I best the gentleman, I had the great incivility to tease him about his loss to a young cockerel like myself. The gentleman took it badly, and when I left the house, he accosted me on the street and forced me into a duel then and there. As he was ten years my senior, Italian, and well schooled in the art of swordplay, I was ill-equipped for this attack and was about to perish when Monty, suspecting trouble, came upon us. He defended me to such effect that the gentleman died the next morning, and I and your family, Jamie, were forced to flee Florence for the more comfortable climes of Lyons. There Monty undertook my education in swordplay and good manners, lessons which I hope I have not since forgot."

"Once instructed by my father," said Jamie, "you have his teachings for life."

Lord Northbridge gravely nodded. "Very true. After my tour was completed, we maintained a fairly steady correspondence. He even came to England some three years ago, after his father had suffered a stroke, and spent a few days in my company before returning to . . . I believe you were in Spain at the time. And thus I hope my history of association with your father is successfully concluded."

"Admirably," Jamie said.

"You have accounted for yourself very well, sir," Isabel agreed.

"As I think on it," the earl continued, turning to her, "Monty never mentioned a lifelong companion to Jamie."

"At my request," said Isabel with great unconcern. "He knew there were some in England curious as to my whereabouts, and I wished not to be discovered. I believe he made it a practice not to mention me to anyone."

"You committed some crime whilst in the nursery?"

"No, sir, the schoolroom."

The earl gave her a hard look. "You will not explain yourself, then?"

"I see no need," Isabel said with a shrug. She had always prided herself on how well she could hide her fear. She suspected she had only to say her true name and this earl must know everything. She could not let that happen. Jamie's life was in her hands. Her own life depended upon secrecy. "Monty has vouchsafed my ability in protecting Jamie, as he has vouchsafed for you. May we not trust each other through his good auspices?"

"As you will," the earl said, inclining his head. But there was a curiosity and a determination in his blue eyes that Isabel did not like.

*

Chapter 3

May 7, 1804   Early afternoon

Near Bardon Hill, Leicestershire

ISABEL GLANCED OUT the chaise window at the soggy but towering Bardon Hill rising gray-green through the mist. She sighed. They had been traveling four days, three of them hampered by incessant rain, which often reduced their travel to a crawl, uphill, on an ill-kept road. They were only halfway through Charnwood Forest.

They should have been in Yorkshire by now. Still, there were nine days left to the Thornwynd legacy, plenty of time to reach Lancashire and Thornwynd. She would not worry ... well, at least not much.

"I declare two aces," said Lord Northbridge.

She surreptitiously studied the earl opposite her as he considered his cards. She had grown more and more fond of studying the nonesuch as the days had passed. She particularly liked sitting with him over dinner, lamplight shining in his golden hair, the shadows softening his face until she could forget, for a moment, that she dared not trust him.

He wore today a coat of blue superfine cloth that emphasized the breadth of his shoulders. His yellow breeches molded themselves to his long, muscular legs. His flaxen hair glinted in what there was of the afternoon light. In short, he was an extremely handsome man, clearly a gentleman of fashion, but without ostentation. And he played a wicked game of piquet.

"Not good enough, I fear, Brett, against my three queens."

The earl stared at her cards. "Where did you get that third queen?"

"You were so obliging as to deal it to me, sir. It was singularly rash of you," Isabel replied, pocketing the money from the small table that lay between them.

"That brings us equal once again," said the earl as he began to shuffle the cards. "However do you contrive it, Master Jack?"

"I like to think we are all well matched, sir."

"And for years I had believed piquet to be my forte," murmured the earl.

"Oh, it is," Isabel assured him. "You've a most devious mind for the game, sir. But I had Monty as my tutor, and that must count for much."

"Too much," said the earl with a smile.

He had a most charming smile, which he had revealed more and more these last few days. Isabel noted, not for the first time, that his smile lightened his lordship's face, removing every hint of autocracy. She wished that she might find some way to make him laugh, for she was curious to hear that sound. But he could not quite give up that last bit of reserve.

"How are you at whist?" Brett inquired.

"Oh, I much prefer it to piquet," Isabel blithely assured him.

Brett considered her a moment. "Do you have a sister?"

"No," said Isabel, caught by surprise.

"Pity." He began to shuffle the cards as thunder rumbled far in the distance.

Though the weather was unpleasant, the company was not. Lord Northbridge, Jamie, and Isabel were soon fast friends, Jamie quickly reducing them to a first-name basis. The earl was now Brett to them and they Jamie and Jack to him. They played at cards and dice, but conversation was their mainstay, primarily between Jamie and Brett, for Isabel, noting the

47

continued hooded survey she received from the earl's blue eyes, was careful to reveal as little of herself as possible.

Thus, Brett and Jamie discussed the many places each had visited on the Continent, the war with Napoleon, and the difficulties that had entailed for the Shipleys and "Jack" as they traveled from place to place ahead of the French or Austrian or English armies, occasionally being subsumed by them. Monty, as always, had turned every difficulty to a profit.

With Isabel, Brett discussed literature, for that she would converse on. They discovered a similar taste in the poets but wildly diverging tastes in the playwrights, for Isabel cheerfully confessed a liking for the comedies and romances, while Brett preferred the tragedies and the dramas.

These debates were the moments Isabel liked best. Though he believed her to be a youth far more deficient in education and experience than he, the earl yet debated her as an equal. Often she would have been swayed to his course had she not wished to continue the fun of their verbal battle. She felt as if Brett were a lifelong friend, so easily did she laugh in his company.

Their one real source of discord was Isabel's determination that she should guide them to Lancashire and not the earl. It was a daily, often bitter, fight, for the earl deeply resented being ordered about by a calfling, as he called Isabel. He was forever holding up his vast years of experience, superior education, and formidable knowledge of the countryside . . . to no avail. Isabel had placed her life in Monty's hands years ago and had known some security because of it. She would not be swayed from his course now. Thus, at the end of each battle— the earl threatening to tie and gag Isabel at the least, and vivisect her at the worst—they continued on Monty's course. Wisely, Isabel forbore challenging Brett on any other matter of import.

Thus, at Brett's insistence, they had stopped at an inn each night of their travels together, and Isabel had happily indulged herself in a bath each night.

Jamie, seated beside Isabel and munching on an apple, watched Brett deftly deal the cards. "I don't suppose Jack mentioned to you that he once took fifty thousand gilders from Baron Erslitz in one night of play at Father's gaming house in Brussels? The game was piquet, wasn't it, Jack?"

Brett calmly settled back on his seat and studied his cards. "I thought I was playing with a shark."

"On the contrary," said Isabel, frowning at Jamie, "I am only a wolf occasionally disguised as a pigeon. The baron had plucked too many feathers from one of Monty's best friends. Monty asked me to attend to the matter and I did."

"Monty asked a good deal of you over the years," Brett commented, glancing at her over his cards. "I declare a point of five."

"He asked no more than I was willing to do, sir. I concede you your point of five."

"May a quarte also succeed?"

"Anything is possible in this world, Brett. What heads it?"

"Why, a stalwart nine, of course."

"Alas, sir, I hold a quarte to the jack."

"A pity. Will two tens suffice?"

"Oh, indubitably . . . had I not two kings."

"Why did Monty never take me in hand?" sighed the earl.

Isabel cast him a kindly smile. "My lead, I believe, and I count six."

"Very neat," Jamie informed Isabel as she gathered up the cards.

"And very even," said Brett. "Do you not wish to lighten my pockets as you did for the Baron Erslitz on that memorable night?"

"I keep trying, Brett, but you won't oblige me. You are not as easily led into deep waters as the baron. Nor do you lose your head, as he did. In the end, he was so incensed that he wagered all on a very bad hand of cards. It was almost an embarrassment to take his money."

"But not an embarrassment to work in a gaming house?"

49

Isabel looked up at Brett in surprise. "How should it embarrass me to be employed in the best gaming house in Europe?" she inquired.

"Monty was always very particular about the company he kept," Jamie explained. "Only the rich and titled graced our houses."

"It was perhaps not the best environment to raise a young boy," Brett said somewhat grimly. "I should say two young boys, for I gather you were not kept in the background."

"I was a footman or a waiter," Jamie said with a grin, "depending on the city. I overheard many choice pieces of conversation which profited us no end."

"A unique upbringing, to say the least," murmured Brett, his blue gaze dwelling on Isabel's face for a moment.

She shrugged. "I am grateful for it, sir. It taught me the ways of the world and showed me how to stand on my own two feet. I have been a gamester, a baker, a musician, heir to a dukedom, actor in a troop of strolling players, footman, soldier, and acrobat, amongst others."

"Courage, dexterity, and intellect. They fit you well for your current role, my boy."

"Sir, you honor me," Isabel replied, fighting back an incipient blush.

For all her caution, she found the earl's open and growing regard for the youth she played most gratifying, and troubling, for she had begun to react to his praise not as the boy she played but as the woman he made her feel. Never in her long career with Monty had she encountered this difficulty before. She was at a loss to explain it now.

She ought to tell Brett the truth and so diffuse this complication. But she thought that if she revealed herself as a woman to Brett she would lose the easy camaraderie she now enjoyed. She liked seeing the respect in his blue eyes when she won a game of cards or disputed his literary edicts. She liked that he fought with her as an equal.

It was impossible that he would consider her an equal when he knew her to be a woman.

A gentleman of rank and fortune and one, moreover, as proper as Brett could not but deplore the deception she now enacted. He must have decided views on the behavior, attitudes, and beliefs with which a well-bred woman should be endowed. Isabel suspected that she fell far short in each category. Having known him but five days, Isabel yet valued the earl's good opinion and was reluctant to part with it. It was not that she had formed a *tendre* for the gentleman; Isabel congratulated herself on having far too much sense for that. But these five days in his company had brought her to esteem his many worthy qualities, and she had enough pride to wish to keep even a small share of that esteem in return.

So, she took his money at the conclusion of the next hand.

"You are an even more devious card player," the earl complained, "than Jamie's cousin, Nigel Clark."

Isabel looked up from the cards she was shuffling. The change in the earl was unsettling. "I hope you do not bear me the enmity which you appear to bear Mr. Clark?"

"No, no, boy, not at all," Brett assured her as he straightened a signet ring on his little finger.

"Is there bad blood between you and my cousin?" Jamie inquired.

Brett considered him a moment. "More of a mutual agreement to loathe each other," he replied.

Isabel felt very cold in that moment. She fervently thanked Heaven that the earl did not regard her as an enemy.

"I smell gossip. Tell us all!" Jamie eagerly implored.

"I'll do no such thing," Brett retorted. "No gentleman would reveal—"

"High card?" Isabel interposed. "Loser answers any question proffered by the other?"

The earl studied her a moment. They both knew how much he wanted to question her on her past. He reached out and cut

51

the cards, showing her a jack. Isabel blithely palmed an ace and that was that.

"Oh, very well," Brett said grimly. "Clark married an acquaintance of mine, a girl I had known and admired from infancy. He was . . . a bad husband. She escaped him by dying in childbirth. There is no more to tell."

Jamie regarded the earl for a moment. "I do not think I will like my cousin Nigel."

"You will, alas, have to meet with him often," Brett replied. "He managed Thornwynd the last three years of your grandfather's life and continues to do so now as executor of Sir Barnaby's will."

"But when I succeed to Thornwynd, my cousin becomes a mere nothing," Jamie riposted.

"On the contrary," Brett countered. "Clark's experience of Thornwynd will stand you in good stead. Never spurn valuable experience out of hand, cawker."

"You will deal civilly with an enemy, sir?" Isabel inquired.

"As long as I find it useful to my purpose," he replied, his blue eyes hard.

Isabel shivered inwardly. Was his civility with Jamie and her a mere pose to serve some unknown purpose? Often she caught him studying Jamie, a slight frown crinkling his eyes. And never was she free from his scrutiny. Isabel shivered again. Nothing untoward had yet occurred, but she could not help but wonder: How safe *were* they in his company?

"Will my cousin attend me when I fulfill the legacy, guardian?" Jamie inquired.

"Indeed. The legacy requires him to do so as the next male heir."

"Who else will attend?" Isabel asked, hoping to dispel this unexpected and unfathomable tension curling within her.

"Sir Henry Bevins, the local magistrate, will attend, of course," Brett answered, "as well as Lord Farbel, Thornwynd's nearest neighbor; Reverend Dillingham, the parish cleric; and Squire Babcock."

The cards slipped through Isabel's hands. She knew she was pale. She felt as if all the blood had drained from her body. "Babcock, sir?" she managed as she hurriedly collected her cards. "Monty said there was a Squire *Davenport*, not Babcock."

"Davenport sold to Babcock two years ago," Brett replied. "Do you know the Babcocks?"

Aye, Isabel thought grimly. *I've killed one of them.* "I have heard of them, sir, more in relation to Yorkshire than to Lancashire. I believe they are a . . . hard family."

"I would not be surprised. I know only Jonas Babcock, and he is not at all to my liking: hard on his servants, hard on his tenants."

"Jonas?" Isabel said, desperately staring at her cards.

"Squire Babcock, Jack!" Jamie said impatiently. "Haven't you been paying attention?"

"This hand has distracted me," Isabel replied, her voice steady. Oh God, *Jonas* Babcock, brother to the man she had killed! He would not fail to recognize her, dressed as a woman or a man. She had met him several times while in her step-father's household. Not only would Jonas have a say in Jamie's succession, he would have a say in her death, for the closer they came to Lancashire, the closer *she* came to a gallows tree!

Monty must not have known. He couldn't have! He would not have named her Jamie's protector and bid her come to England to face certain arrest and hanging if he had known. He would have given that charge to Dick Rowan and ordered her to remain on the Continent.

But she *was* Jamie's protector and it mattered not that Jamie was now in the Earl of Northbridge's company. She could not trust the earl to safeguard Jamie as she would, for how should an esteemed member of the *haut* ton know anything of villainy? Besides, how could she trust this earl who had secrets of his own?

She was very neatly trapped. She had now not the vague fear of discovery but its certainty. Her loyalty to, and love of, both

Jamie and Monty would not allow her to now abandon Jamie and flee for her life. She must get him to Thornwynd, see him formally installed as baronet, and then somehow escape the country before Jonas Babcock had her clapped in jail.

How this was to be accomplished, Isabel could not fathom. She had a few days yet to make her plans if she could free herself of this terror that was like a block of ice around her brain. She felt as if she were thirteen again and cowering in Hiram Babcock's house. It was hard to remember the woman she had become in the intervening years, the woman who owed all that she was to Monty.

Isabel forced herself to take a deep breath. Panic would help neither her nor Jamie. Somehow she must and would keep her promise to Monty, whatever the cost. In the meantime, she would say nothing of this to Jamie. He knew of a *warrant*, not of murder. She would not worry him with her own troubles when he had so many of his own. There might yet be some escape at the end of this journey. If only she could think!

"Another hand, sir?" she inquired as Brett pocketed her money.

"Not now, I thank you," Brett replied, settling back in his seat. "Your play is too deep, Master Jack. I must needs recover my wits."

"I would not purchase such a declaration for all the gold in Christendom," Isabel retorted as she gratefully put the cards away.

Blue eyes drilled into her. "You doubt your abilities, Jack?"

"On the contrary," Isabel lightly replied, fighting the unease such scrutiny always provoked. "I have every confidence in my abilities and in your ability to successfully play at piquet for twenty-four hours without respite. I'll not be gammoned by such a paltry ruse. Recover your wits indeed!"

"I am found out," said the earl tragically.

"A very knowing fellow is Jack," Jamie said.

Isabel permitted herself a smile and turned her attention to

54

the rain. *Jonas Babcock, Jonas Babcock, Jonas Babcock* drummed on the window.

This fourth day on the road together was as gray and as wet as the third day had been. It fit her mood precisely. How she longed to indulge herself in a good case of nerves, but she still had a role to play, a promise to fulfill. "To work, my girl," she muttered to herself. She pulled a walnut from her coat pocket, cracked it between her slender fingers, and trusted that Brett noted this masculine accomplishment.

"Faith," she said, feigning a huge yawn, "if I had known our travel through England would be accomplished with so much comfort and so little trouble, I should have worn my nightcap and slept the entire way."

"Do you grow lax in your vigilance, young protector?" Brett inquired.

"So well sprung a carriage would certainly promote laxity, but no, I have observed carefully no one following us and have some hope, but not much, that we may continue the journey without further danger. You might leave your carriage in our care and return to London to enjoy the pleasures there rather than the boredom of a rain-soaked road."

"Have you noted," said Brett to Jamie, "that not a day goes by that Jack does not try to remove me from your company?"

"Very unhandsome of him," pronounced Jamie. "It shows a decided want of gratitude for your many kind offices on our behalf. You bought us a wonderful dinner last night, sir, and the breakfast this morning was most filling."

"But Jack did just as well by us at lunch," the earl noted. "We shall come out even in the lightening of our purses. I feel certain that Jack will see to it."

"Monty encroached on your time and safety, Brett, in charging you as our escort," Isabel retorted. "I see no reason to encroach on your pocketbook as well."

"I believe I could stand the charge," said the earl with a smile.

"Are you very rich, guardian?" Jamie inquired.

Brett considered him a moment, his gaze hooded. "Vastly rich, ward," he corrected.

"How comforting," said Jamie. "I have great hopes for my allowance."

"I am now convinced," said the earl grimly, "that it is a good thing Sir Barnaby never met you, James."

"Why is that, sir?" Jamie inquired, not at all abashed.

"Your tongue would have got you disinherited by the age of ten!"

"Well," said Jamie with a grin, "it does run in the family."

"I pity Sir Barnaby more and more," Brett said feelingly. "What other man was cursed with such sons as Horace and Montague? The first a blackguard and the second a hothead with more independence than sense. Sir Barnaby disinherited and exiled Horace to the Continent, as any honorable man would do, then turned to his second son for filial love and comfort, and what did he find?"

"A boy with a violent dislike of any guiding hand?" Isabel mildly supplied.

The earl grinned at her. "An ungrateful, undutiful wretch," he pronounced, "who must needs fly off the handle at the least provocation and exile *himself* to the Continent, leaving Sir Barnaby but one daughter to console him, and there was little consolation in having Maria about."

"Was she a harpy?" Isabel inquired with interest.

"She succumbed to vapors."

"Oh, good God," said Isabel with disgust.

"Precisely."

"I would begin to pity my grandfather," said Jamie, "if I didn't know he was a cantankerous old slowtop too bent on having his own way to tolerate anyone else's opinions or desires."

"Somewhat like the Earl of Northbridge," Isabel observed with a sweet smile.

"I will have to thrash you one of these days," the earl pleasantly informed her.

She grinned at him and cracked another walnut.

The chaise-and-four suddenly lurched to a stop. Instantly Isabel and Jamie drew their pistols as Brett lifted the ceiling trap.

"What is it, Dawkins? What has happened?" he demanded.

"I think one of the lead horses has thrown a shoe, sir," Dawkins replied.

"The mud sucked it off, more like," the earl said. "I'll come and help you."

"Some caution, Brett, if you please," Isabel said, forcing her heartbeat back to a calmer pace.

He cast her a quick smile and then stepped from the chaise. He returned a minute later well covered with rain.

"One of the lead horses has cast a shoe and bids fair for going lame soon. We follow your route, Jack. We must exchange this team as soon as possible. Whither shall we turn?"

Isabel had memorized Monty's instructions long ago. "Just after Bardon Hill there is a country lane that will take us to Lennox. But it's another nine or ten miles, I fear. Will the horse do until then?"

"I think so. He's a strong animal. With this rain, we should probably reach Lennox in an hour or two."

The earl climbed back into the chaise, and Dawkins drove them through the mud to a larger town than they had thus far encountered. Lennox boasted two or three notable families and a number of fashionable shops. The dark green chaise passed these establishments and churned up to a sprawling posting house. Its passengers quickly alighted, sinking ankle deep into the mud. The rain, for now, had faded to a fine mist.

"A pleasant town, this," Jamie said. "I think I'll stretch my legs while you attend to business."

"You will be cautious, Jamie," said Isabel.

He grinned at her. "As always," he said before crossing the muddy street.

"I'll attend to the horses, Brett," Isabel said. "Your legs are longer than Jamie's and undoubtedly in need of some judicious stretching as well."

"As you will," said the earl with a weary sigh. He turned in the direction of a bookstall.

Isabel breathed in the rain-washed air with some relief. For a brief time, she could escape both her thoughts of Jonas Babcock and the increasingly close confines of the chaise-and-four.

It took several minutes to agree to the horses for the next stage of their journey. Once satisfied, and trusting Dawkins to get them into their traces, Isabel recollected the shops they had passed. A new shirt or two would not come amiss. She made her way through the mud, which sucked tenaciously at her top boots, and spent a quarter hour considering the display of goods in several shop windows. Lennox, though nearly two hundred miles from London, was yet graced with proprietors of some taste.

She purchased three new shirts, a wonderful riding coat, and a fetching pair of pantaloons before returning to the street. Jamie was nowhere in sight. A sudden unease led her around a corner . . . to find Jamie standing with his back to her. He faced a fat man. The man held a gun on Jamie.

Isabel's heartbeat pounded in her ears. Here was their old gap-toothed pursuer from the day they had met Brett!

Quickly she ducked back around the corner. Her breath came in sharp puffs. Leaving her new clothes on the wooden sidewalk, she ran to the far side of the mercantile building. To shoot the blackguard would draw too much unwanted attention. The rotund man might have friends in this town.

Desperately she searched amidst the mud and finally found a good-sized rock. She eased around the building. The brigand's back was to her; Jamie was facing her. He saw her, as she intended, but experienced as he was, his young face revealed nothing.

"You're going to bring me a pretty penny, me lad," the gap-toothed man was saying. "Almost enough to repay me for all the trouble you've—"

He got no further, for Isabel hurled her rock with decent accuracy. It struck the side of the lout's head. He dropped to his knees with a groan. She then brought the butt of her pistol down upon his head with all the strength she could muster. He fell like a stone onto the street.

With one strenuous heave, Isabel turned him onto his back, so he would not suffocate in the mud. She checked his pulse and found it steady and strong. He would not die. Nor would he awaken for at least an hour.

"What took you so long?" Jamie said jovially as he sauntered up to her.

Isabel whirled around on him. "I thought you promised to be careful!"

Jamie flushed. "I was . . . distracted."

"Pray do not let it happen again," Isabel snapped.

"I'm sorry, Isabel," Jamie said quietly. "I'll be careful in the future. How the devil did he find us here?"

Isabel began to breathe more freely. That danger should come upon them so suddenly! "Either he followed us," she replied, "which I cannot think likely, for I have watched the road carefully, or knowing our destination and the roads available to us, he guessed that we must pass through Lennox at some point. There are other, rougher roads leading to this town. A single determined man on a good horse could have accomplished much, despite the mud."

"Are there others with him?" Jamie said as they turned back toward the posting house.

"I think not," Isabel said, collecting her packages from the sidewalk, hands shaking slightly. Her head on new clothes when she should have been thinking of danger! How Monty would have lambasted her. "Having been bested twice by us, he knew us to be difficult to capture. If there were others, he would have had them with him just now. He has undoubtedly communicated with your uncle, either by letter or messenger.

The weather probably delayed any reinforcements he might have expected."

"A plausible scenario and a dangerous one. Would he have mentioned Brett to my uncle, do you think?"

"It's possible. He certainly would have described us and our course to insure our capture if he should fail."

"A change in disguise seems paramount."

"Yes," said Isabel hollowly. How was she to explain herself to Brett? It seemed impossible. "I must take on the meeker garb of a woman; you will disguise yourself accordingly. Take these packages back to the chaise and mind you stay with Dawkins until I return. I must venture into Grey's Ladies Emporium. I shan't be long."

"What shall I tell Brett?"

Isabel felt cold inside and almost mistook it for misery. "Say nothing for now. Secure a private parlor at the posting house and effect your own disguise. I will join you shortly."

Brett, two new books under his arm, returned to the posting house to find several carriages in the yard and Dawkins on his perch, a strong team of bays in the chaise's traces.

"Where is the brat and Master Jack, Dawkins?" Brett demanded.

"Master Jamie said he wanted to wash some of the dirt and mud off before continuing on the road, sir. I expect him any moment. Master Jack has yet to return."

Brett glanced sharply up at his coachman. "Do you fear trouble?"

"Nay, sir," Dawkins assured him. " 'Tis a canny young gentleman. He'll no doubt make his appearance in good time."

"You're right, of course. Well, with this delay, I might as well enjoy a glass of ale."

He entered the posting house and worked his way through a rather heavy crowd to the taproom. Within ten minutes the rain had started once again and the earl had finished an excellent glass of ale.

He would then have sauntered from the house to the yard, but there was some congestion at the front door. A cleric and his ample family were all trying to walk through the doorway at once. After they had finally disentangled themselves and made their rambunctious exit, a portly squire rudely shoved his way past Brett. Then, when he finally saw daylight at the door, Brett was waylaid by an elderly gentleman who bid him mind his manners and allow a lady to pass.

Brett obligingly stepped aside and observed the couple with some interest. The old gentleman barely reached the first button of Brett's waistcoat, hunched over as he was with age and rheumatism. He had a profusion of white hair on his head and an even greater profusion of white whiskers on his face. Tiny and ancient he might be, but the fire of a tyrant still stirred in his veins.

"Stand back, I say!" he cried in a querulous voice, taking a swipe at Brett's leg with his walking stick.

The Earl of Northbridge nimbly avoided the blow and then glanced at the young woman for whom he had nearly been maimed. She was tall and slender with an abundance of black curls framing a face that promised beauty, what little he could see of it, for she seemed more than a little shy as she stared determinedly at the floor. The modish green traveling dress revealed a most pleasing feminine form.

A rare admiration was conjured in his breast. He had not even a clear view of her face; he could attest only to the soft blush in her cheek. And yet, the earl thought in amazement, he could actually imagine the rest of her! Her lips would be full, her eyes sparkling with wit and intelligence as she regarded him openly, without the petty masks of coyness and flirtation. Her voice would be . . . intoxicating.

For a moment Brett did not know himself. Unused to this disturbing stab of emotion, he could only stare as the elderly gentleman, scowling forbiddingly at the earl, escorted the young woman out of the posting house.

Feeling unhappy and on edge at the same time and not at

all sure what to do about it, Brett advanced at last into the yard. The interesting couple was nowhere in sight. "Blast!" he muttered.

Dawkins sat grimly waiting on the carriage box.

"Have they returned?" Brett demanded.

"Oh aye," Dawkins muttered, "*they've* returned."

Accustomed to his coachman's perpetual gloom, Brett merely nodded at him and allowed an ostler to open the door of the chaise-and-four for him.

It was now that the earl's nerves sustained a severe shock, for seated within were not the two youths he had expected but instead the elderly gentleman with whiskers and the ravishing young woman in the modish green traveling dress.

"Close your mouth, Brett, and get in," said this vision. "We will explain all on the road."

*

Chapter 4

May 7, 1804   Midafternoon

Lennox, Leicestershire

BRETT CLOSED HIS mouth, climbed into the chaise-and-four, and was jostled into his seat as Dawkins cracked his whip and set the horses moving.

"Jack?" Brett inquired.

The composed smile was familiar. "Charlotte, for now."

Several different, and heretofore rare, emotions assaulted the Earl of Northbridge in the same moment: exultation that the lovely young woman at the posting house had not slipped through his fingers; astonishment that any woman could be so beautiful; understanding about how his imagination had conjured her so perfectly; mortification that he should have been on such intimate terms with Jack, speaking and acting improperly with what had instead been a woman; an even deeper mortification because somewhere deep within him a voice was rejoicing at Jack's true self; anger that he had not trusted the increasingly nagging voice of his intuition, which had insisted that Jack was not what he had seemed; humiliation that he should have been deceived and used by this woman; fury that he had not been trusted with the truth; and confusion at the excitement leaping in his heart.

This internal conflict could have but one outcome.

"A woman?!" the earl exploded. *"You are a woman?!"*

"Yes," she replied, composure intact.

"By God, this is unconscionable! It was bad enough being ordered about by a stripling with more mischief than manners, but to be ordered about by a rag-mannered, indelicate, unnatural *woman*—!"

"A *gentleman*," she said coldly, "does not insult a female, however unnatural, to her face."

Brett was taken aback, but only for a moment. "I have never been more *outraged* in my life!" he seethed. "That any woman should parade about in *breeches*, cavorting like a *man*, thumbing her nose at society and propriety and . . . and . . . "

"Duty?" she mildly inquired.

"Yes, by God, your *duty* to uphold the strictest bounds of decorum!"

"I am afraid, sir, that Horace Shipley's *unnatural* desire to see Jamie dead supersedes my feminine duty to uphold the strictest bounds of decorum."

"Do you honestly expect me to believe that Monty would entrust his son's life to a woman? A *woman*?!"

"Far easier to believe that than that Monty would saddle his son with the guardianship of a sanctimonious, self-righteous prig!" she snapped, the color high in her cheeks.

Brett gasped. For a moment he could not find his voice. No one—and certainly no *female*—had ever dared to address him thus!

"Aren't I rather young to be witness to so bloodthirsty a scene?" Jamie inquired.

Brett turned to stare at the elderly bewhiskered gentleman seated beside him. "You still claim to be Montague Shipley's son?" he demanded.

"To my last breath."

"And why should I believe so consummate an actor? Or should I say actors?" Brett amended, directing a frosty glance at "Charlotte."

"Why should you not believe us?" she calmly retorted. "You have Monty's letter and will and his likeness before you.

64

Knowing the danger in which Jamie stands, our masquerade is wholly reasonable."

"To one of *your* background, perhaps," Brett sneered.

He suddenly found the speaking end of a pistol shoved under his chin.

"Insult my protector once more, sir," Jamie growled from the other end of the pistol, "and I shall not be responsible for my actions!"

"Jamie, that is quite enough!" his protector broke in sharply.

The boy glanced at her in surprise. "But—"

"Put up, Jamie! The earl's reaction to my disguise is perfectly reasonable. No gentleman of Brett's upbringing can be expected to understand the kind of life we have led. Now stop acting like a silly calfling defending his lady's honor. Monty would be appalled by such a display."

To the earl's surprise, the boy flushed up to the roots of his wig and returned his pistol to his pocket.

"As for you, sir," Charlotte continued before Brett could utter a word, "you will try to remember your manners while in my company or I shall remove Jamie from your chaise and get him to Thornwynd myself!"

It was now the earl who flushed. Whatever *her* background might be, *he* was a gentleman and he had acted badly. For one who could not accuse himself of ever having acted badly in his life, this was a leveler.

"I apologize, madam," he said stiffly, "for any insult. I am not used to such blatant deception." He found the steadiness of her gray gaze almost unnerving. "What am I to call you? Charlotte Cavendish?"

"No, no, Charlotte *Hampstead*. And Jamie is my aged and crotchety grandfather, Charles Hampstead. *You* are William Fanley, my fiancé."

"Your what?!"

"You must have some excuse for riding with us, sir."

"I will not engage in playacting on *your* behalf, *Miss Hampstead*!"

"It is not on my behalf but on Jamie's. We ran into a bit of trouble in Lennox, which is why we have changed our disguises."

"You ran—" began the earl, openly appalled.

"It seems that Horace's men now have instructions to search for three men traveling in a luxurious chaise. We cannot yet exchange the chaise, so we must exchange the Cavendishes for this newest masquerade. Horace's men look for a boy, not an elderly grandfather traveling with his newly betrothed granddaughter. We should be safe for another day or two."

Brett could not but stare at her. She treated danger as if it were an everyday occurrence! But was there danger? He had seen no evidence of it in Lennox. Certainly these two were adept liars. The Cavendish brothers and the Hampsteads were ample proof of that.

Oh, why had the world suddenly become more complicated?!

Charlotte reached into a small valise by her feet and pulled out a red wig and mustache. "For your disguise," she said, handing these items to Brett, who regarded her with the utmost horror. "My grandfather and I reside in Worcestershire, and you are very kindly escorting us there after a brief but delightful sojourn in London, where we met and were betrothed."

"You do not honestly expect me to wear this ridiculous—"

"But I do," she said calmly.

"I will not lower myself to such a shameless charade!" the earl declared. "Every feeling revolts at the idea."

"As you will," she said coolly, and opened the carriage door. Rain spattered in. "The village of Isleton is but a thirty-mile walk."

"You cannot throw me out of my own carriage!" Brett sputtered.

"Yes," she said with a sweet smile, "I can."

What appalled the Earl of Northbridge was that he believed her! A woman who would disguise herself as a man was capable of anything. "Very well," he growled, beginning to affix the wig to his head.

Charlotte serenely closed the carriage door.

Silence ruled for several minutes. Awash in a sea of outrage, embarrassment, and honest perplexity—how could any woman behave in this manner?—the earl was at a loss for anything to say.

"Jamie, have some consideration for the earl's feelings," Charlotte sternly advised her charge, "and stop grinning like an idiot."

"How did Monty come to name *you* Jamie's protector," Brett muttered as Charlotte withdrew a small bottle of spirit gum from her reticule and handed it to him so he could affix the horrendous mustache to his stiff upper lip.

"Why, I was unofficially adopted by the Shipleys some thirteen years ago. Having trained me himself, Monty trusted my abilities and my loyalty completely."

The earl could think of nothing to say to this, and so said nothing.

They traveled for several hours more, primarily in silence. The easy camaraderie Brett had come to enjoy with this pair had been shattered. Staring into one of his recently purchased books, he felt the loss keenly. He had never known with any of his acquaintance the connection and ease he had shared with "Jack" and Jamie. It was a surprisingly bitter blow to lose it now.

They came at last to the tiny village of Isleton, which boasted two inns. Brett insisted that they stop at the larger of the two. But even this precaution was not enough to insure their comfort, for the innkeeper complained that the rain had brought many travelers to his door and he had but two rooms to offer, one of them quite small.

"Mr. Hampstead and I," Brett said grimly, "shall share a room, and Miss Hampstead shall have the other."

"The smaller, of course," said Charlotte. "I'll not have *dear* Mr. Fanley cramped on our journey."

"As you will," said Brett with a scowl.

While their rooms were readied, the three dined on unpalatable

67

food in the crowded dining room, the other travelers trapped by rain and mud loudly complaining of their misfortunes. Brett—his upper lip itching from the unaccustomed presence of the red mustache—listened with growing outrage as his *fiancée* described the last ball she had attended with Mr. Fanley in London and the great pleasure she had taken in dancing with him, for despite his height, he was an extremely graceful and able performer. She voiced the hope that Worcestershire would supply them with innumerable betrothal balls so that she might know such pleasure again.

The elderly Mr. Hampstead assured her that he would hold as many balls as she liked, so glad was he to finally get her off his hands.

Charlotte then engaged her grandfather in conversation as to whether or not they could convince her dear mama to accept her sweet Mr. Fanley into the bosom of their family when he had no title and but three thousand a year.

The Earl of Northbridge was about to put a stop to this insulting spectacle when the innkeeper announced that their rooms were ready. They quickly fled the dining room and its indigestible offerings. Charlotte was shown to a tiny garret room possessed of a narrow bed, a battered dresser, a cracked mirror, and no window. Before Brett could utter a word of complaint about such shabby accommodations, she pronounced it more than she could have hoped for and bade gentle goodnights to her fiancé and grandfather, almost as if she really were a gentlewoman and blushing bride-to-be.

Brett accompanied Jamie into their far more commodious room. It boasted a large bed, a dresser, a cracked mirror, a fire, and a window.

"Only one bed?" said Brett to their host.

"Why sir, I thought you would not mind sharing a bed with the old gentleman, seeing as you're soon to be related," the innkeeper replied.

"I have never in my life shared—" Brett began.

"This will do well, host," Jamie said in a querulous, phlegmy voice. "You may leave."

The innkeeper, with a rough bow, departed.

Jamie straightened and looked up at Brett. "Shall we toss a coin to decide right and left sides of the bed?"

"Have your pick, aged sir," Brett snapped, pulling off his red mustache with palpable relief.

"Oh dear. You are still peeved."

Brett gasped. "I gave you my protection, and what did I receive in return? Lies!"

"The less you knew, the less you could accidentally reveal."

"By God, this is the outside of enough!"

"Monty would have praised my protector for the skill with which she hid her true self from you."

"Then *Monty* was no gentleman!"

"You will not disparage my father in my company, sir!"

Brett considered the boy. His sudden anger seemed real enough. But then, so had the friendship of Jack Cavendish. "I beg your pardon," he said stiffly.

Jamie stared at him a moment and then removed hat, wig, coat, and boots. In stocking feet, he walked over to the rickety stool in front of the cracked mirror and proceeded with great dexterity to remove the bushy white eyebrows, mustache, and beard from his face, Brett watching him with reluctant interest all the while.

"You have done this before, I gather?"

"But of course," Jamie said coolly. "I have played everything from a grandsire with one foot in the grave to a blushing vestal virgin."

"You what?!"

"I was younger, sir," Jamie said haughtily, "and shorter."

Brett wondered if the world would ever return to its sane, uneventful course. "And has *Charlotte* often played the boy?"

"She's been boy as much as girl," said Jamie. "And when she's been a girl . . . oh my! Those were exciting times. Father had her play at being his wife, my mother, my sister, my aunt, his mistress, *Napoleon's* mistress—the list goes on and on. She could not help but make an impression wherever she went. As for boys, she's been my brother, my valet, Father's valet, an Italian count, a French colonel, and any number of other roles, even a stable boy at one point. She's quite good with horses, and we were rather desperate for accommodations in the Netherlands."

"Amazing," the earl said, and he meant it. That any woman should lead such a life! A woman, moreover, possessed of such beauty and understanding—the earl hurriedly stopped his wayward thoughts. This was not a path he intended to travel. "Well," he said, shrugging out of his coat, "despite the gross impropriety of such a masquerade, I suppose I am forced to now do what I can to play the lover to so fair a damsel."

Jamie stood up, his brown eyes grim, his young face cold. "You will do nothing improper toward Isabel," he intoned. "Her many masculine abilities and charades in no way detract from her status as a gentlewoman."

"Lower your hackles, puppy, she is perfectly safe with me," Brett said in some amusement. As if he would dally with such a creature! "So, her real name is Isabel, eh?"

Jamie flushed. "My wretched temper! She'll have my head for this."

"Nonsense. Her duty is to protect your head, not claim it. Or so she says. How came she to be under Monty's protection? And if you tell me that she was unofficially adopted thirteen years ago, *I* will throttle you!"

"I know very little of Isabel's history," said Jamie with a reluctant smile. "She came to us when I was but four or five. Her past has always been a mystery. Monty, I think, knew of it. He somehow met her while visiting in England and invited her to join our family. I know nothing else."

The earl sighed heavily. "Do you at least know how old she is?"

Jamie chuckled. "She is seven-and-twenty, sir."

"Impossible."

"Isabel has the amazing ability to appear as old or as young as she chooses or the charade requires."

"Why has she not married?" Brett demanded suspiciously.

"Truth to tell," Jamie said, sitting back at the dressing table to remove the last vestiges of his disguise, "I never thought about her marrying. She never seemed that interested in the subject."

"How very extraordinary," Brett retorted, wholly unconvinced. It was his experience that a single female was always on the hunt for a husband. But then, his experience had never prepared him for this preposterous pair.

It was bad enough that a woman had paraded about as a man, but far, far worse was the knowledge that Brett had begun to consider that young man a friend, to admire his mind and his many skills, to enjoy their debates—in effect, to take pleasure in his company. Well, his eyes were open at last. "Jack" was no friend, "he" was an adventuress and—in spite of her beauty—the Earl of Northbridge felt nothing but disgust for the woman. Nothing.

The following morning, when he had paid for their wretched beds and disgusting breakfasts, the three settled themselves into a shabby post chaise, and Dawkins drove out of Isleton. The sun was shining, the water receding from the roads. With luck and good weather, they would be at Ravenscourt in three days.

They had been fifteen silent minutes on the road when Jamie began to remove his whiskers.

"What now, child?" Isabel said.

"I am sick to death of being boxed in with you two," Jamie said amiably. "Particularly when you can't look at each other without growling. I am plotting my escape. Now that the sun is out, I shall act the groom. As an aged grandfather cannot undertake so strenuous a task, I revert to my youthful exuberance. Dawkins needs my assistance; I am sure of it."

"I would not tell him that to his face, puppy," said Brett.

"Well, Jamie, if you are to be a groom, I, too, must change

71

my station," Isabel said with a sigh. "I cannot travel as a single gentlewoman in the company of a single gentleman of Mr. Fanley's undoubted charm. We look nothing alike. Therefore, I must either transform myself into a Cyprian or a wife. Which shall it be?"

"My wife," Brett said with great firmness.

"The wedding date has been advanced," said Jamie with a grin.

"So it would seem. But are you sure, Brett?" Isabel inquired, mischief dancing in her gray eyes. "I make an entertaining Cyprian."

"I've no doubt," Brett sneered. "But I've a reputation to maintain. Only think of the blushes my mother and sister would endure if it should ever come out that a fair Cyprian had traveled in a Northbridge coach."

"Very well," Isabel said brittlely, "I shall play the almost dutiful wife. I have played it before. I assure you I will make you an estimable mate."

"I depend upon it," Brett snapped.

He ordered Dawkins to stop the carriage. Jamie jumped gleefully to the ground. Isabel handed him a new coat from his valise. He pulled on a cap and, after a moment's conversation with Dawkins, was quickly up behind the chaise, grinning from ear to ear.

"Forward! Forward!" he cried gaily.

With a crack of his whip, Dawkins obliged him.

Brett found himself alone in company with Isabel as a woman for the first time in their acquaintance. A host of conflicting emotions swept through him, rendering him mute, as Isabel reached into the small valise she had brought into the carriage with her and, after a moment's search, produced a wedding ring, which she slid onto her finger.

"There. That makes it official, Harcourt."

"Harcourt?" Brett gasped.

"Your new name. Harcourt Fitzwilliam Gollings. I am Matilda."

"Madam, I will not continue in these degrading charades!"

"Oh, *do* stop calling me madam. You make me sound like a fifty-year-old dowager, with a lace cap on my head and a lap-dog napping on my knee."

Brett's lips quirked up, for this image clashed so vividly with the beautiful creature in pale blue opposite him, a pert Italian cap on her black locks. "Very well," he pronounced, "I will call you *Isabel* instead. It is certainly preferable to Matilda."

He had the felicity of seeing Isabel flush slightly. "I'll have Jamie's head for this."

Brett's smile broadened with grim satisfaction. He liked having the upper hand with this hellion at least once in their acquaintance. "So the boy said. It was an accidental revelation, I assure you, Isabel. He felt himself goaded."

"*That* I can well believe."

"*I* do not believe that any female of your background has any right to sneer at *me!*"

"How dare you!" Isabel gasped. She raised her gloved hand as if she actually meant to strike him.

"Have you abandoned all attempts at civil conversation?" Brett coldly demanded.

Isabel glared at him, something the earl was not used to. What most perturbed the earl, however, was that an admiration—wholly unbidden!—had arisen in his breast for the way this provocateur's gray eyes sparkled with anger and the proud way she held herself she addressed him.

"I can recall civility whenever *you* choose to do so as well, *my lord*," she retorted.

The earl flushed. He was also not accustomed to being taken to task for his behavior, which had always, prior to this lamentable adventure, been exemplary. "As we are forced to travel together for the next few days, I will endeavor to treat you with the civility due any female," he said coldly.

"Oh, sir, you are too good to me!" Isabel turned her head to stare out the window.

73

A silence fell between them.

"Do you always carry a wedding ring with you?" Brett asked at last, feeling it incumbent upon him, as the superior of the two, to begin the conversation anew.

Isabel turned—reluctantly, it seemed—from the window. For a moment Brett thought there were tears in her eyes but then deemed it a trick of the light, for she spoke calmly enough. "You never know when such an item will be needed. I have had to pretend to be a wife or a widow at a moment's notice. Monty taught me to be prepared for any contingency."

An unaccountable anger rose in the earl's breast. "Monty should be horsewhipped!"

"Too late," Isabel replied. "He's dead."

"What I meant," said the earl between clenched teeth, "is that no gentleman of Monty's upbringing should have led a girl—whatever her birth—into any situation requiring her to masquerade as a boy or a wife!"

"True enough," Isabel agreed. "But then, Monty was no ordinary gentleman, and in the end the masquerades he devised did me a world of good."

"Oh yes, they taught you duplicity!"

"On the contrary, they taught me to value honesty, courage, and honor. Of equal import, they taught me to stand on my own two feet, to depend on no one and nothing save my own wits. You would not credit it, my lord, but before meeting Monty, I was a timid, pasty-faced creature with no more pluck than backbone. I owe Monty a good deal."

Brett could not credit this response. To actually value an adventurer's life?! It was counter to his finest feelings, his deepest beliefs. Better to let the conversation die than to encourage such blatant depravity. He hurriedly sought sanctuary in his book. They rode in silence for the next three hours.

It was not yet noon when Dawkins drove them into the village of Oakham. It was a pretty place. Flower boxes and gardens abounded. The small inn where they stopped was ivy-covered and picturesque. Remembering that he was a gentleman, whatever the company he now kept, Brett handed Isabel down from the carriage as if she were the lady she pretended, and then had to stoop to pass through the low doorway to the inn.

As Jamie remained in his role of groom, he attended the carriage and team with Dawkins, enjoying his luncheon in the sunlight while Brett grimly seated himself across a table from Isabel in the small coffee room. As there were several others also partaking of an early luncheon in the room with them, Brett bitterly acknowledged to himself that he could no longer continue in silence with the female opposite him. Propriety demanded conversation and—as she seemed to know nothing of propriety—it was incumbent upon him to speak first. But how did one converse with a hardened adventuress?

Fortunately their waiter appeared and Isabel, playing the demure and dutiful wife, deferred to *Mr. Gollings* in the selection of their meal. Feeling petulant, Brett would have enjoyed ordering every dish she disliked, but thus far in their travels she had yet to voice any dislike for any of the food offered her. Thus rescued from petulance, Brett ordered their meal, selected a wine, and then turned reluctantly back to his erstwhile "wife."

"I trust, *madam*, that you are not too fatigued by our journey?"

"Oh la, Mr. Gollings," said Isabel, whipping out her fan, "you know I am as hardy as an oak. I am so eager to return home, I could drive five hundred miles in one day if necessary. I am longing to see our dear children again."

Brett had never gaped in his life. He did so now.

"Nurse is an excellent creature, of course," Isabel blithely continued, "but I do feel that children do best with a mother's care."

"The wine is rather good, don't you think?" Brett said sternly.

She smiled sweetly at him, as any devoted wife would do.

"You always know best when it comes to food and wine, Mr. Gollings."

Their meal was now served. Brett tasted none of it, for Isabel prattled on and on about their dear childrens' accomplishments: Tommy's studies, Sally's needlework, and little Robbie's wonderful mastery of the English language at only three years.

He wanted to be outraged at the vast range of this charlatan's imagination. He was, in fact, convinced that he should be outraged. Instead he found himself increasingly interested in this fictional family of his. At several points in Isabel's monologue, he actually thought of breaking in with his own suddenly created memories of their childrens' activities!

He damned himself for this heretofore unknown weakness and then doubly damned himself when he realized how wholly Isabel had lured him into the charade, for in her company he had forgotten Jack Cavendish entirely! Indeed, looking at her now, the pert cap upon her shining black hair, her gray eyes alight with merriment as she smiled at the admiring glances from all the other men in the room, Brett found it impossible to believe that only yesterday morning he had been convinced that she was an intelligent, whimsical boy whose company he had wholeheartedly enjoyed.

Had he fallen under some sort of spell? Where was the cool, rational mind for which he had long prided himself? Had Isabel's skill as an actress actually overcome his long-cherished scruples?

No! It could not be. Yet he found himself watching her every movement, her every expression as he paid for their meal and they walked from the inn. She made not the slightest misstep in this newest role. She was beauty and light, and every male—from innkeeper to groom—seemed wholly entranced by her.

He—the Earl of Northbridge—was not entranced, of course. He could never forget himself entirely. Yet he was, in spite of himself, intrigued. He had never met anyone like

Isabel, someone who moved so easily from role to role, station to station as if born to each and enjoying each. She was becoming a puzzle to the earl, and the earl was a man who could not rest until any puzzle presented to him was solved.

*

Chapter 5

May 8, 1804   Early afternoon

Oakham, Leicestershire

WITH JAMIE ONCE again upon his groom's perch and Dawkins on his box, the ribbons in his hands, Brett helped Isabel into the carriage, took the forward seat opposite her, and studied her a moment, quite openly, as Dawkins set the team off at a trot.

She irritated him anew by openly regarding him in return. "Yes, Mr. Gollings?"

He flushed. He doubted if he would ever be comfortable in this female's company. "You have an extremely ... active imagination."

"Thank you."

"Loathe though I am to admit it," Brett said with a grimace, "you were right: You *do* make an estimable wife."

"Sir! I am overcome."

Brett glared at her. Could she not even accept a compliment? "You acted as if you were actually ... enjoying yourself."

"I have always preferred the female roles to the male. They require less work and attention to every word and deed."

In spite of himself, Brett was interested by this declaration. "Have you enjoyed your vagabond life?" he asked.

"On occasion."

He blinked. "What aspects have you not enjoyed?"

Isabel glanced out the carriage window a moment as she twisted the wedding ring around and around her finger. Then she looked directly at the earl. He doubted if she even knew what a coy glance was. "I confess to growing weary of forever being thrown into danger. And I miss not having the stability of a single home. You see, Monty could never be brought to stay in one place for more than a few months at a time."

Brett regarded her a moment. "It sounds a lonely and unpleasant life for a girl."

Isabel's smile was grim. "Believe me, sir, it had its advantages over what I had known. Besides," she added, her smile brightening, "I was not lonely, for I had Monty and Jamie with me. We were—are—a family, and a better family than any other I have known. Whatever unpleasantness I met in our travels was more than compensated for by the pleasure of their companionship, their unequivocal love, and the enjoyment I took at sitting at Monty's knee and listening to his life lessons. 'Tis a pity he never took *you* in hand, my lord, for he might have prevented you from forever looking for the duty in a task, rather than the pleasure. You must have shouldered your onerous responsibilities at an early age to be so badly corrupted."

The earl's eyebrows shot up. "I am the farthest thing from corrupted!"

"Bosh," Isabel retorted. "Any man who deliberately holds happiness and laughter at bay is thoroughly corrupted. Your devotion to duty has denied you all the fun of life."

The Earl of Northbridge was wholly confused. "Life is not *fun*."

"Perhaps your life isn't, but mine has been. Monty's was, too. I never met a man who derived so much enjoyment from life. He was a revelation to me. It is a pity you didn't spend more time in his company. It might have proved beneficial, or at least taught you the difference between the *choice* of responsibility and the *burden* of duty."

The earl, now wholly awash in confusion, could think of

nothing to say, for he could not quite make out what the devil she was talking about.

"You said you have a sister, sir?" Isabel said after a moment's pause.

"A younger sister, yes," Brett said with considerable relief. With his family he was at least on firm ground. "Fanny. She is married to Sir Robert Clotfelter."

A laugh escaped Isabel. She quickly clapped her hand to her mouth.

Brett could not hold back a smile. Damn the woman! It seemed amusement was infectious in this vagrant's company. "Yes, that was my reaction as well when first introduced to him," he said.

"Oh, I pity you, sir, and her even more. How could she have the courage to marry such a name?"

"Well, the name was attached to a genial young man who adored her, and that seemed to do the trick."

"Very sensible of her. But for the great Earl of Northbridge to allow his only sister to marry a mere baronet? Unthinkable!"

"Normally, yes, but then the Clotfelters own half of Cumbria and a most impressive shipping fleet. They will be a power to reckon with in the coming decades."

"A suitable match, therefore."

"Most suitable," the earl replied. He could not understand her smile.

"And your mother? What of her? Does she reside with you?"

"For part of the year," Brett replied. "Another part of the year is spent with Fanny and Clotfelter, and the last third in London, for she is a woman who enjoys the social whirl of the ton and is never happier than when planning and executing a ball or a card party."

"The Dowager Countess sounds as if she knows how to enjoy herself. Why ever did she not take you in hand and teach you to enjoy life?" Isabel inquired.

"I enjoy life!"

"Piffle. You enjoy doing your duty, and they are not the

same. Did you never realize that you might have fulfilled your duties to your tenants and your family and still have raised an occasional rumpus with a college friend or night on the town?"

"Oh, that is entirely out of the question," Brett assured her. "I am known throughout the ton for my common sense, steadiness of character, and disapproval of light entertainment."

Isabel wrinkled her nose. "Ugh! How awful!"

"If I were to kick up a rumpus, as you suggest," Brett said severely, "I would shock a good many in my acquaintance and bring a great deal of condemnation down upon my head."

"But if you were happy, Brett, what would that matter?"

He stared at Isabel in the utmost surprise. "You must be an anarchist."

Isabel laughed and the earl found that he liked her laughter very much. It was light and musical and wholly entrancing. He blinked. He was not supposed to like anything about this . . . this *creature*!

"Poor Brett," she said in all sincerity, "you *have* led a narrow, rigid life, haven't you? Happiness is a human right, didn't you know? That master of phrasing Alexander Pope declared in his "An Essay on Man" 'O happiness! our being's end and aim!' Why, Rousseau in *The Social Contract* stated that 'The thirst after happiness is never extinguished in the heart of man.' He did not qualify that statement by saying 'except when one has position and duties.' He was unequivocal in his statement."

"I might have known *you* would quote a French revolutionary."

"Very well, then, what of that noble patrician who stated that we are endowed by our creator 'with certain unalienable rights; that among these are life, liberty, and the pursuit of happiness'?"

"Worse and worse," Brett replied, shaking his head. "Now you quote an *American* revolutionary. Have you returned to England to foment rebellion, then?"

"No, no, only to 'End in one purpose, and be all well borne

81

without defeat.' *King Henry the Fifth*, act one. I mean to see Jamie installed at Thornwynd, sir, and no more."

Brett could not mask his surprise. "You possess more than a vagabond's education, it seems."

"Monty taught me to love books and learning. Jamie's tutors instructed me as well. Why do you stare at me so?" she asked with a smile. "Even a tenant farmer in this country may quote Shakespeare."

Brett was utterly still. It was as if a veil had lifted or the sun had emerged from behind a cloud. "I begin to think," he said slowly, "that your character was not wholly wrought at Monty's hand. Your education, manners, presentation, all suggest that you have not always been an adventuress."

"True," said Isabel, reluctantly. "My life was not always danced to the tune of Montague Shipley's piping. I have known in my time the respectability of a private life."

"Surely you must miss such a life?!"

"Not the respectability," Isabel replied, and Brett found himself gaping at her, "for it caused a good deal more harm than good. But a private life," she said slowly, "the quiet and ease of sitting in a chair and reading all afternoon without worrying if the authorities mean to swoop down on the house; having the same bed, the same clothes, the same pattern of the day; knowing whom to trust and whom to avoid, rather than continually worrying and guessing at it; these are gifts that I have missed on occasion. But in the end my love for Jamie and for Monty more than made up for such fripperies."

"Having a home and security," Brett said grimly, "are not fripperies."

Isabel's gray eyes met his in open surprise. He knew that feeling. He had been suffering from it this last half hour and more. Her gaze dropped. She studied her wedding band. "Very true," she said.

"You never thought of marrying to obtain that happiness and security?"

Isabel gave a shout of laughter. "Never," she said wryly. She glanced out the window and suddenly became quite still. There was the oddest expression on her face as she gazed at the country landscape. Brett doubted that she was even aware of the silence between them.

He could no longer deny his first impression of her as a woman. She was lovely! She had made a handsome youth, but she was a beautiful woman, and he was man enough to feel the full effect. What would he have thought of her if he had first met her at some country house party or been introduced to her at Almack's? He didn't know. He couldn't imagine her in those settings.

He shouldn't even be trying to do so. The earl chastised himself with some vigor. He had a duty to find the truth in the midst of this unconscionable morass of duplicity, and that, at least, had not changed with her disguise.

"Why do you look so?" he asked. "What are you thinking?"

With a start Isabel turned from her own thoughts to Brett. "I have just realized," she said in amazement, "that I have missed England!"

This raised a host of questions in the earl's mind, but he ordered them to compose themselves. There was time and the informant was wary. "You have been away from England for some time?" he mildly inquired.

"Nearly thirteen years," she said. "I never thought to return. Certainly I never thought to enjoy being here. And yet," she said with a quirk of a smile, "I find that I do." She glanced out the window again. "It's so *green*. I had forgotten."

"England has much to recommend it," Brett said casually, crossing one leg over the other. "Healthful and plentiful countryside, vibrant town life, similar company, a pleasing degree of education and advancement."

"Yes, isn't it odd?" said Isabel. "I never knew it till now."

Brett cast her a curious glance. How could she not know what she was born to? "You left no one in England whom you missed?"

"Not a soul," Isabel said firmly.

"Surely there were some who would have missed you?"

A sardonic smile touched her lips. "None that wish me well."

Brett felt a sudden chill. "But you couldn't have been more than fourteen when you joined Monty on the Continent. Yes," he said in answer to her startled glance, "I know your true age. You put no threat on Jamie to preserve *that* secret, you see."

"I had hoped," said Isabel with a sniff, "that Jamie had learned to be more gallant."

"That brat gallant at seventeen? Pshaw! My point being," Brett relentlessly continued, "that you were only a child when you left England. Surely your family—"

"I have no family save Jamie," Isabel icily broke in. There was an equally icy lull in the conversation. "How glad I am the sun is out," she suddenly said, looking out the window. "Jamie was beginning to chafe at the bit. He has spent more of his life out of doors than in it, you see." She paused. "He has not yet had the opportunity to grieve for Monty."

This declaration startled Brett. Would an impostor—however clever—have made such a comment? "And you, Isabel?" he said. "Have you wept?"

"Not yet," Isabel said, avoiding his gaze. "I have been preoccupied."

She would not permit him to interrogate her further. After one or two more attempts at conversation, Brett retreated once again into his book.

They drove on until nearly dusk, finally entering the village of Bilby. Dawkins pulled them to a stop before a large coaching inn, its yard crammed with carriages and curricles and multitudinous other vehicles of travelers also seeking to break their journey for the night.

They entered the inn and Brett, stepping up to the thin and quarrelsome innkeeper, announced that he and his wife and her grandfather required rooms for the night. The innkeeper began to complain of the many customers he had to supply and would have gone on at some length had Brett not pressed a guinea into his startled, knobby fingers. A room was instantly procured for the Gollingses while Jamie, once again in wig and whiskers, agreed to share a room with a portly solicitor. They followed their host upstairs.

The room into which the innkeeper bowed Brett and Isabel was large, commodious, and airy and boasted but one bed.

"This will do admirably," Brett informed the innkeeper as he waved him out of the room. "Pray see to my grandfather-in-law."

He shut the door and turned to regard Isabel, an amused smile on his lips. It might be unpardonable, but he knew a perverse pleasure at finding the adventuress trapped in her own shocking charade. "I will leave you to refresh yourself, *Mrs. Gollings*. Pray come down to dinner when you are ready."

He decamped before Isabel could throw the water pitcher at his head.

She looked around the room with a rather grim expression. She had not been thinking of the difficulties of being "married" to Brett. In the past, when she had played wife to Monty, they had had an understanding as to bedroom arrangements. The Earl of Northbridge presented an entirely different problem. He had made it abundantly clear what he thought of a vagabond female at home in both breeches and petticoats. Well, she had had to fend off more than one gentleman during her adventures with Monty.

Isabel paused. It was a lowering thought to place Brett in their league. Still, she must be practical. She was an adventuress; he was an earl. There were expectations on both sides.

With a sad little sigh, she washed herself, brushed her hair, and changed from her traveling dress into a gown of white sprig muslin, a red ribbon trimming the bodice. She then walked downstairs and entered the dining room, a serene expression masking her face.

Brett rose from the table, blue eyes alight with admiration as he complimented her on her gown and the cunning way she had styled her hair. He played the adoring husband to perfection.

Isabel longed to jab an elbow into his diaphragm, but he—perhaps prescient—kept himself just out of reach.

"Your grandfather is in fine fettle this evening, *Mrs. Gollings*," Brett said expansively as he poured her a glass of wine. "He has ordered nearly everything in the kitchen."

"I hope you do not begrudge him a bit of meat now and then?" Isabel tartly retorted. "The Lawrences were always renowned for our excellent appetites. When Grandmother Lawrence was alive, she was the most noted hostess in all of Shropshire. No one set a more bountiful table. I remember one ball . . ."

Isabel spent the whole of the meal fondly recalling with her "grandfather" the wide variety of food provided at the Lawrence Christmas Ball of 1798. Alas, the current meal could not be prolonged forever. Even Jamie had his limits.

Brett paid their bill and and led Isabel up two flights of steep stairs to their bedchamber.

"A charming room," said Brett, closing the door and leaning against it, tall and self-assured, "is it not, my dear?"

"Oh, indeed, Mr. Gollings," Isabel replied, regarding him warily. Her heartbeat began to quicken. If only this were some other man, she would not be so badly frightened.

" 'Tis a far more commodious bed than we have enjoyed thus far."

"We are fortunate indeed." There was always, Isabel thought desperately, the possibility of escape through the window.

Brett began to advance on her. "You shall have the bed, *Mrs. Gollings*, and I shall take the couch."

To keep the relief from her voice and her expression required all of Isabel's skill. "Nonsense, Mr. Gollings! You are much too big for so small a space. You would be cramped and uncomfortable all night long. You shall take the bed. I will be perfectly happy with the couch."

He stood almost toe to toe with her, smiling down knowingly. "No, my dear. As a gentleman, I cannot permit."

"Mr. Gollings—" said Isabel with some severity.

"Mrs. Gollings, the matter is settled," Brett interrupted with that tyrannical touch she had come to know and loathe so well. "I will go see to Dawkins and give you a chance to change and retire. I shall return in the half hour."

Brett strode from the room.

Isabel stuck her tongue out at him, or what had been him, and then looked about the room. "No, Mr. Gollings," she said, "the matter is far from settled."

Thirty minutes later when Brett returned to the room, he found the curtains pulled and a good fire casting a warm glow over everything, including Isabel ensconced on the couch, several blankets tucked neatly around her.

She had not exchanged her stubbornness with her breeches it seemed. Pity. Without a word he strode to the couch, picked her up, and carried her to the bed, though she struggled and demanded to be set down.

"Certainly, madam," he said, dropping her on the bed. "That is enough of that nonsense," he said.

"I trust I may sleep where I choose!" Isabel cried, glaring up at him from the mangled blankets.

"Certainly," Brett calmly replied. "As long as you make the choice which agrees with my own."

"Oh, you are vile!"

Blue eyes twinkled down at her. "But at least I know my duty."

Brett then strode to the couch, removed boots and coat, settled himself on the makeshift bed, pulled a blanket over himself, and promptly went to sleep.

Isabel sat on her bed feeling murderously angry to be bested in such a manner. Muttering uncomplimentary epithets at the slumbering lord, Isabel finally lay down.

It was, of course, wholly impossible for her to ignore the fact that the very handsome and occasionally charming Earl of Northbridge was sleeping opposite her. It wasn't fair that while he slept so peacefully *she* should be plagued by doubts and

87

fears and a secret rejoicing that, despite all her worries, he *was* a man of honor who would take no liberties with her despite her past and her disguises. "Oh bother," Isabel muttered. Here she was, supposedly outraged at the autocratic oaf sleeping uncomfortably on the couch, and at the same time thinking how wonderful he was.

With a sigh, she pulled the covers up to her chin. It took almost another hour for her to fall asleep.

Her dreams were jumbled and unfocused for several hours, and then, though her heart protested, they carried her back to her stepfather's house, to her girlhood. She had been out riding, as she rode every day, to escape her home for as long as possible. But this time she had stayed out too long, coming in after dark. Hiram Babcock stood there, waiting for her in the entry hall, drunk and already raging. He seemed to loom over her, face red, throat corded with fury.

Her stammered apologies, her quick excuses, her pleas for forgiveness were of no avail. Her stepfather grabbed the riding crop from her hand and lashed at her. She cried out, "No, I beg you do not!" But again it was of no avail.

With a stunning blow of the back of his hand, he sent her crashing to the floor, and then, standing over her, he raised the crop and lashed at her back as if she were some mortal enemy he meant to destroy. Her screams, her cries for mercy brought her no respite from the searing pain. No one came to her rescue. There was only the pain and the terror and the riding crop biting mercilessly into her flesh like a vicious metronome.

"No!"

She felt him grasp her arms. She struggled desperately to free herself. She heard his voice.

"Isabel. Isabel!"

She screamed and tried to pull herself free, but his hands were large and strong and held her still.

"Isabel, wake up! You are having a nightmare. *Isabel!*"

With a gasp she forced her eyes open and stared up into Brett's taut face and realized that it was he, and not Hiram

Babcock, holding her, sitting on the bed beside her, trying to wake her.

She had betrayed herself.

With a gulp of air, she tried to make her voice calm. "It's all right, Brett, I'm awake now,"she said.

And still he held her.

Oh, how she longed to throw herself against his broad chest and weep away all the old terrors, his strong arms holding her fast.

"You cried out," he said roughly. "I was afraid for you."

"You will think me a great ninny," she replied as she casually moved herself free of his hands. "It's an old dream, best forgotten."

" 'Tis an old nightmare that still haunts you," he retorted, one hand cupping her cheek, his thumb tilting her chin so that she must look him in the eye as his other hand smoothed back a few strands of hair.

She could not suppress a shiver at this touch, so warm, so gentle. Every sense seemed heightened. It was as if she felt more than saw his broad chest partly exposed by loosened shirt buttons, his breath harsh, his tension mirroring her own. The room seemed huge around them as she sat in this bed with Brett beside her, her hair disheveled, her nightdress a thin shield offering no protection. "I am sorry to have disturbed you," she managed. "Pray do not think any more of it."

"Isabel—"

"I am quite all right. Go back to the couch which you have chosen in your tyrannically masculine way and get what sleep remains in the night."

His fingers brushed against her cheek. She shivered at the soft caress. For one wild moment, she thought he meant to pull her into his arms. It was shocking how much she wanted that. Then the bright light in his blue eyes faded.

"Very well," he said. "Good night."

He went back to the couch.

Slowly Isabel sank back down onto the bed and pulled the

covers to her chin. Only then did she allow the trembling to overtake her, the memories to bludgeon her, that one horrific pistol shot to deafen her. Hiram Babcock slumped to the library floor, dead. And Jonas Babcock was waiting for her at Thornwynd.

*
Chapter 6

May 9, 1804   Morning

Bilby, Nottinghamshire

ISABEL AWOKE THE next morning to find sunlight flooding the room. Stretching, she realized that she had slept much longer than she was accustomed to.

Fear crashed into her.

She jerked up and saw that Brett was not in the room. The blankets he had used were folded neatly at the foot of her bed. She began to breathe again, although she found it disconcerting that Brett had been awake and possibly studying her while she lay in vulnerable sleep. Bad enough to expose herself once, but twice?

Quickly she got out of bed, the nightmare still very much with her, as was the feel of Brett's warm hands cupping her face, his taut expression, the imperative pull of his fingers as he made her look into his blue eyes. Never had she felt so vulnerable. Never had she wanted to trust a man as she did then. She felt herself to be in some danger.

Isabel froze halfway to the washbasin. In danger from an autocratic, disapproving earl? How idiotic! How terrifying. She had never before felt this mixture of longing and delight and fear, and it was all, she bitterly concluded, Brett's fault. Her emotions had never been so present with a man before. Her defenses had never been so weak. A change in strategy was clearly indicated.

She must rebuild the wall her nightmare had demolished last night. Safety was paramount. She must not yearn for a return to the camaraderie Brett had shared with "Jack." She must not be tempted into trust. "Harden your heart, my girl," she muttered, "and remember the life placed in your care."

She washed and dressed quickly, arranged her black hair, and hurried downstairs to the dining room where Jamie, in whiskers, was just finishing his breakfast. Brett, thankfully, was nowhere in sight.

"There you are!" said Jamie. "What a slugabed you are becoming, Granddaughter."

"I am sorry, Grandfather, I don't know what became of me," Isabel said as she took a seat and poured herself a cup of tea.

"What will you have?"

"I am not very hungry," Isabel replied. "Tea will do me admirably."

Jamie regarded her in some consternation. "Have you been having nightmares again?" he demanded.

Isabel sighed. " 'Twas only one."

"One is too many. What troubles you?"

"I think it would be wise if we adopted new roles in our charade," Isabel said with admirable calm. "You and I shall be brother and sister and Brett our uncle. The whiskers stand out from the crowd a trifle too much. And I do not want you playing the groom again."

Jamie nodded warily as he regarded her.

"I want you within my sight at all times from now on," Isabel continued.

"Very well," Jamie said.

He finished his coffee and Isabel her tea and together they went out to the yard where Brett—immaculate in tan breeches and a rust-colored coat of silk—was in conversation with Dawkins. Isabel stifled a bitter sigh. Why did the earl insist on growing more attractive with each new day?

He turned and, beholding them, quickly advanced on them. "I'm glad to see you got some rest, Mrs. Gollings. How do you feel?"

"Oh, I'm in fine fettle," Isabel replied, a bit unnerved by his honest concern.

"Have you eaten?"

"I'm not hungry."

"Isabel—" said Brett, beginning to adopt his tyrannical manner.

"Shall we go?" she said coolly.

"Obstinate female," Brett murmured. "Why did you tell Dawkins to make yet *another* exchange of our carriage?"

"I thought it would be safer," Isabel replied.

"Without even *bothering* to consult me?"

"I believe I am a good judge of safety, danger, *and* carriages. Dawkins thinks it an excellent chaise."

"Has it never occurred to you to solicit *my* opinion occasionally?!"

"No, never," Isabel retorted as Jamie helped her into the chaise.

The boy quickly followed and then Brett.

"Jamie and I have been discussing it," Isabel said as the carriage started forward and before the earl could utter a word, "and we have decided that it is time to once again undertake new characters in this play of ours. Jamie and I will be Arabella and Julian Porter, and you shall be our uncle, Hugo Pierpont."

"Your *uncle*?" Brett sputtered in outrage.

Isabel would not allow herself to be amused. The wall started here. "I assure you, Mr. Pierpont, that you are the *much* younger brother of our beloved mother."

"You mean to ruin all claims I may have to propriety, don't you?"

"You are a wholly respectable uncle."

"I do not enjoy capering about to your piping, madam! I find these continual masquerades deeply offensive."

"How could anything which insures Jamie's safety be

offensive?" Isabel demanded as she removed the wedding ring from her hand and placed it in her reticule with a barely suppressed sigh of relief. If only she and Brett were not now seated together in such close confines, recalling the intimacy they had known last night, she might know some peace.

"There are certain bounds of decorum which need not be overstepped to protect the boy!" Brett retorted.

"An uncle traveling with his nephew and niece is wholly decorous, I assure you, sir."

The earl regarded her with an expression she could not decipher. This was disconcerting, and even more so when he abruptly abandoned the argument to spend the next hour writing a letter to his sister.

"You are not, I trust, detailing our course to her?" Isabel inquired.

"You may credit me with some sense, madam," he retorted, not even looking up from his correspondence.

They drove into Blyth a little after one o'clock that afternoon and, as they were to change horses and carriage and dine, left Dawkins to the ostlers' care. After Brett had posted his letter, they inquired as to the best food in town and made their way to the King's Thorn, where they partook of a horrible boiled luncheon, Jamie and Isabel enacting their roles of nephew and niece to the hilt, for there was real pleasure to be derived from harassing the earl and it kept wayward thoughts at bay.

"Oh, but Uncle!" Isabel cried over their fruit and cheese, which at least were palatable. "You cannot mean for us to continue traveling the rest of this day! Why, there are so many pleasures to be had in Blyth. Just as we were driving into town, I spied the most *marvelous* millinery shop, and there in the window was a yellow hat with the prettiest ostrich feathers towering up out of it."

"You have quite enough hats, Arabella," Brett replied severely, clearly determined *not* to be their favorite uncle.

"Oh, but Uncle, this is such an *exquisite* hat," Isabel per-

94

sisted. "I will be the envy of all the girls in Plockton. *Do* buy it for me, Uncle, please do. You know I would look ravishing in it."

"You will look a perfect quiz in it, *Arabella*," Brett snapped. "That is quite enough."

"Uncle Pierpont, you wrong my sister," Jamie said, refusing to take the earl's far from subtle hint. "She'll be all the crack in that hat. And as for myself, as I was getting out of the carriage, I spied a bootmaker's with a most marvelous pair of half boots in the window. I protest I must have them, Uncle, or I shan't be able to show my face in town. Half boots are all the stare now. I cannot appear in public in *shoes*, even with these heels. I should be thought a complete greenhorn."

"*No one* could ever mistake you for a greenhorn," Brett grimly retorted.

"Oh, thank you, Uncle! I knew you would agree!" Jamie cried as he stood up. "I'll go buy them at once. Your purse, Uncle, if you please."

"I did not say—" Brett began.

"It will just take a moment, sir. I know how to deal with these country shop clerks. Come, give me your blunt."

The earl stared at Jamie a moment, and then, the suspicion of a smile quirking the corner of his mouth, he drew out his purse and handed the boy several coins.

"You will be careful where you go and to whom you speak," he said.

"Oh la, sir, I am the soul of discretion," Jamie assured him as he sauntered out to the street.

"Does he really mean to buy half boots?" Brett asked Isabel.

"But of course, sir. He said as much, did he not?"

Brett examined his purse. "You mean to see me ruined before the journey is out, don't you?"

"Why, sir, a gentleman of your position and responsibilities must have enough money to buy the few fripperies that will please his nephew and niece and save them from the ignominy of being out of fashion," Isabel replied.

He quirked an eyebrow at her. "Will you have the hat, then?"

"Perhaps. It was wonderfully hideous."

"Yes, that is the criterion Fanny uses whenever she visits a millinery shop."

"And yet you are still fond of your sister."

"Oh yes, I confess it," Brett said, taking a bite of cheese, "though Fanny is highly opinionated and delights in having her own way in everything."

"It runs in the family, then."

Brett glared at her. "'Tis a pity that during your training Monty did not impart to you some better manners."

"Monty always preferred the truth to the niceties."

"Good manners," Brett coldly intoned, "are a prerequisite for any civilized society."

"You think me a barbarian, then?"

"I think you a viper-tongued vixen!"

"Sir! How appallingly ill-mannered of you to say so."

Brett glared at her. "Clearly you were not thrashed enough in your girlhood."

The bile rose in Isabel's throat. She felt bloodless. "Jamie has undoubtedly had time to negotiate a price for the half boots. Shall we go?"

They rose from the table. She took the earl's stiffly offered arm and walked with him from the inn to the chaise-and-four.

"Well, Dawkins, where's the whelp?" Brett demanded.

"I haven't seem him, sir, since you entered the inn," Dawkins replied as he inspected the traces. "I thought he was with you."

Isabel's hand gripped Brett's arm. "He was going to a boot-maker's, Dawkins. Surely you saw him?"

"Well, miss, I was attending to the horses, and I might have missed him."

"Where is this bootmaker's?" Brett asked in a low voice.

"This way," Isabel said, pulling on his arm, nearly running in her haste.

The earl slowed her. "Remember your role, Niece. Remember the play you chose." He tucked her arm through his, as a devoted uncle would do, and patted her hand. "He was probably delayed in deciding between gold and silver tassels," he reassured her.

"Yes, of course."

Isabel led him to the bootmaker's, but three doors down from the inn. They entered into the rich aroma of tanned leather and found only the bootmaker.

"Good day to you, sir," said Brett. "I am looking for my nephew, a youth of seventeen. Have you seen him?"

"Nephew, sir?" said the elderly bootmaker, pushing his spectacles onto his forehead as he looked them up and down. "What was he like?"

"Oh, a little taller than my niece here, broad in the shoulder, brown hair and eyes. You would have seen him in the last quarter hour."

"No, sir, I've not seen anyone these last two hours," said the bootmaker.

Isabel began to tremble.

"Thank you," Brett said, quickly pulling her from the shop.

They stood outside, looking at each other.

"Where can he be?" Isabel said, knotting and unknotting her hands before her.

"And who could have diverted him from his chosen course?" Brett grimly seconded.

*

Chapter 7

May 9, 1804   Early afternoon

Nottinghamshire

THEY DIVIDED THE town between them. Brett was to take the northern half, Isabel the southern. Each moved quickly, though retaining an outer composure so that no one would think there was any alarm. But Isabel knew some difficulty in fighting the nausea that welled in her throat, in keeping the terror from her eyes and stopping her hands from shaking as she looked in shop after shop, scanning the alleys, the rooftops, looking behind and in carriages, searching clumps of people chatting together, and finding no one she knew.

Jamie was gone.

As each minute passed, her terror grew.

Jamie was gone and she had done nothing, *nothing* to protect him!

She returned to the inn and to Dawkins, who was holding the horses. "Have you seen him, Dawkins?" she whispered.

"Nay, miss, nary a sight," the grizzled coachman gently replied.

"And Mr. Pierpont?"

"Here."

Isabel turned to find Brett behind her. One look in his eyes told her all. "Dead or alive, he must be somewhere!" she cried.

Brett's large, warm hands cupped her face. "We will find him, Isabel, and he will be very much alive, I promise you."

She knew it was the height of folly, but gazing up into his determined blue eyes, she believed him. Her soul drank in his confidence. "We will search again," she said.

"Yes, of course."

Legs a little unsteady, she retraced her steps, openly asking now if any had seen her brother, describing him, excusing him with "He is always off on some lark or another, and my uncle is particularly anxious to get us back on the road."

No one had seen him. No one had spoken to him.

Oh, what had she done, playacting with the boy when she should have stopped him from ever leaving her sight?! She had failed him, failed Monty. The blame and the guilt were all hers. Jamie was taken, probably murdered, and she had sent him out to his death without a thought!

Isabel's dread increased to such a point that she jumped when she felt a hand on her shoulder. She whirled around to find Brett beside her. His expression was grim.

"I found him," he said before she could ask.

"Why is he not with you?" she demanded. "Is he . . . dead?"

"No," he said, squeezing her shoulders reassuringly, "very much alive."

The shock and relief were so great that Isabel actually sagged against Brett for a moment, grateful for his strength that kept her upright. "Why is he not with you, then?"

"He is in some danger. Come with me."

He took her hand. Somehow that warm clasp enfolded her in his strength as he led her from the main street, through a series of side streets, to the north end of town.

"He's in there," Brett said, pointing to a small ramshackle house surrounded by a broken fence and a yard of weeds strewn with debris.

"Who has him?" Isabel demanded.

"Two men I have not seen before. They are an unsavory pair. Come, if we are cautious, I can show them to you."

Moving silently, they crept around to the back of the house. Drawing near a filthy window, Isabel was able to peer inside and see Jamie seated on a high-backed chair, arms and legs tied, a welt on his temple indicating that force had been used in bringing him to this stinking place. A short, thin man stood at a table with a gun pointed at him, while a second man, bigger and more menacing, stood at a window looking out at the main street.

"When do we get paid?" said the man with the gun.

"I've told you: George and some of the others will be here to collect him in a few hours."

"But are you sure we've got the right boy?"

"There's no mistaking the description Brady gave us. Cracked head or no, he was certain this is the boy. Now just shut up and do your job!"

Isabel and Brett backed away from the house and, safely secreted, looked at each other.

"Damn the boy!" said Brett. "How could he land in so much trouble in so little time?"

"A family trait," said Isabel with a grimace. Now that she had seen Jamie alive and relatively unharmed, her old confidence had returned. "But you must own, Brett, that he *was* diverted."

"He thought of boots, not of caution, and that's how he was caught." Brett sighed heavily. "Well, what do we do now?"

Isabel glanced at the house and smiled. "Have you ever wanted to enact a Cheltenham tragedy?"

The Earl of Northbridge regarded her with growing horror.

"I will need no more than a quarter of an hour," she hurriedly continued before he could start raising the host of objections quivering on his lips. Jamie's life was at stake. The earl could defend his propriety on another date. "I ask that you change. You have a coat of blue superfine. Please put it on. It emphasized the breadth of your shoulders, and I particularly wish to impress your stature upon the gentlemen."

Before Brett could reply, she had hurried off down a side

street. She returned as promised a quarter of an hour later dressed in a yellow hat with huge ostrich feathers, a red wig, and a silver cloak that hid her gown.

For a moment he did not recognize her, and had it not been for the hat and the familiar mischievous gleam in her gray eyes, he would have overlooked her entirely. As it was, he could only stare.

"Come, come, Harcourt, you admired the hat, you know you did," she said.

Brett blinked. "What, are we husband and wife again?"

"For the moment," Isabel said coldly.

"Well, as such, you need a ring," Brett said, and drew the signet from his little finger. "You will oblige me by wearing this."

"As you followed my advice with the coat, I can but follow yours with the ring," she said, unable to hold back a slight tremor as he slid the ring onto her finger.

"What now?" said the earl.

"Why now, sir," Isabel said a trifle breathlessly, "you get to play the outraged husband."

Jamie sat far from comfortably in his chair, inwardly cursing himself, outwardly calm. If Isabel and Brett did not find him soon, he would need some plan of escape. Alas, his head throbbed so badly from the blow it had sustained that thinking was difficult. This did not bode well for his future.

Suddenly he and his two captors were arrested by a blood-curdling scream. In the next moment, a woman in an atrocious hat rushed into the room, shrieking at the top of her lungs.

"Help! Oh, help!" She threw herself into the arms of the man who had held the gun on Jamie, expertly tangling herself up with him so he could not move. "He's gone mad! *Help me!*"

In the next moment, Brett stormed into the room, shouting, "Unhand my wife, you blackguard!"

Before the sorely confused henchman was able to make any

sort of a reply, Brett tore Isabel from his arms and planted him a facer that laid him on the floor, unconscious.

"Oh, Harcourt, do not! Do not!" Isabel wailed.

Harcourt did not heed her. He turned, instead, to the startled man at the window. "How dare you abuse my wife in such a manner!" he bellowed.

"What the devil—"

With three sharp blows he laid the befuddled brigand on the floor as well.

Husband and wife, turned as one to find Jamie laughing so hard, tears streamed down his face.

"Oh, lord!" he gasped. "Oh lord, never had I hoped to see such nonsense. Harcourt, indeed!"

"Jamie, love, are you all right?" Isabel cried as she hurried to him.

"Never better. Don't fear, Isabel," Jamie said soothingly.

"How on earth did they capture you?" she demanded as she removed a knife from a strap at her ankle and cut at the ropes binding him.

Jamie flushed. "I was admiring a showy bonesetter when I was struck from behind. I never even made it to the boot-maker's." The ropes fell away. With a sigh of relief, he rolled his shoulders as he rose to meet the fulminating glare of the Earl of Northbridge.

"You should be whipped, James."

"Yes, sir, I quite agree," Jamie said equably.

The two henchmen began to come around. Without consulting Jamie or Isabel, Brett quickly tied and gagged them and left them on the floor.

"You will be found or you will not," he informed the two struggling men. "Come," he said to Isabel and Jamie, "let us leave while we have the chance."

They hurried from the house, down side streets, and back to their carriage.

"You will proceed at a good clip, Dawkins," Brett instructed his coachman as Isabel and Jamie scurried into the chaise.

Dawkins set the horses off at a quick canter. Blyth was quickly behind them.

Brett, Jamie, and Isabel regarded each other in silence for a moment.

"We have been found out," said Isabel, voicing their common thought. "The coach is no longer safe. Our disguise, the presence of a woman in the company of two men, is no longer a safe disguise."

"Agreed," Brett grimly replied. "At the next town, we will exchange this carriage for saddle horses."

"And I," said Isabel, "shall exchange my petticoats for breeches once again."

"I see no need—" Brett intoned.

"Have *you* ever ridden sidesaddle?" Isabel demanded. "Besides, petticoats hamper mobility—which is what we particularly need just now—and I, for one, refuse to do anything that will increase the danger to Jamie."

"I can accept, perhaps, the need to change your disguise as a woman, but I cannot and will not accept you playing the boy once again!"

"However did you come to believe that you have any say in *my* actions?" Isabel demanded. "It is Jamie's life I want to protect, not *your* rigid views of propriety!"

" 'Tis worrisome," Jamie said into the breach, "that my uncle's men should have been in Blyth."

"Very worrisome," Isabel agreed. She thought of Brett's letter, supposedly to his sister. No, it was impossible! He had helped her save Jamie. And yet . . . "The danger grows, it seems."

"Let us hope that stupidity does not," Brett said with a rebuking glance at Jamie.

"I shall not leave your side until we reach Ravenscourt, sir. I swear it," Jamie hurriedly assured him. "You will be heartily sick of me by the end of this journey."

"What makes you think I am not already?" Brett retorted.

"Dear me," said Jamie. "The accommodating gentleman grows weary of us, Isabel."

"I grow weary of your escapades, young James, not of Isabel's company. Although her hats—"

Isabel cast her eyes up and quickly removed the offending chapeau. "It is perfectly ugly, isn't it?" she said with an admiring gaze at the many feathers.

"Perfectly," said Brett with a wholly distracting smile.

"You are a handy man with a pair of fives," said Jamie.

"Jackson's has been most instructive," Brett said coolly. "Let us hope that there is no further need for me to undertake so ridiculous a charade and expend my pugilistic skills simply to rescue *you* from idiocy."

"*You* let me go," Jamie pointed out.

To his dismay, he quickly discovered that his guardian had a large vocabulary, including sapskull, cabbage-head, and cockle-brain, all of which he directed at Jamie with some vigor.

The road was uneven, their pace fast, the trip jouncing and jangling to body and soul. Conversation was kept to a minimum until they came to the town of Oldcotes, where Isabel, valise in hand, strode into the coaching inn. Dawkins exchanged the carriage for a new post chaise and team while Brett and Jamie selected three saddle horses and secured their own disguises.

"You will drive on with some caution, Dawkins," Brett instructed his coachman in a low voice. "We will rendezvous in Farnsfield within two days."

"I'd rather stay with you, sir," Dawkins replied. "Four guns are better than three."

"Things have not yet advanced to such violence. You have my orders; drive on."

Reluctantly the grizzled coachman climbed onto the box and started the team out of town.

But twenty minutes after she had entered the inn, Isabel joined Brett and Jamie, not as a woman, nor even as Jack

104

Cavendish, but as a simpering, perfumed tulip of fashion. She stood resplendent in blinding Hessians, yellow riding breeches that molded themselves to her legs, green-and-brown waistcoat, green riding coat with flowers embroidered throughout, a blond, beautifully coiffed wig upon her head, a quizzing glass raised to one gray eye, and a soft blush flooding her cheeks as the earl looked her up and down.

"I rescind my earlier objections," Brett murmured.

Damn the man! He was supposed to be outraged by this newest pose. "Oh la, Cousin," Isabel said in a languid voice, "are these shaggy beasts the best you could find?"

"We cannot be too choosy, *Cousin*," Brett retorted, a black wig upon his head, a cloak going a long way toward disguising the quality of his clothes.

"But, sir," she said, wrinkling her nose in distaste, "those bonesetters simply *reek* of the hinterlands."

"We are in the hinterlands, Cousin."

Isabel raised appalled gray eyes to the earl. "Yes, but, sir, must we advertise that fact to the world?!"

Brett's mouth quirked up. "You will mount your horse or I shall toss you up, and far from gently, *Cousin*."

With a weary sigh, Isabel climbed into the saddle.

Despite the danger, she was happy to be on horseback. To feel strength and speed beneath her. To feel the breeze on her cheek, to smell the new-growing things of spring. These were beloved pleasures long denied by their various carriages and the rain.

Besides, loath though she was to admit it, the danger of this journey *had* grown, not from Horace Shipley but from Brett Avery, Earl of Northbridge, with his speaking blue eyes, broad shoulders, strong, gentle hands, and continuing scrutiny. Any chance to avoid close confines with the earl was most welcome. Free of the intimacy of the carriage, she could draw a full breath again, her heart could maintain a calm, steady pace. She was safe. She could remember who she was, what he was, and that she must not trust him, must not rely on him, and most certainly must not let down her guard with him.

The fresh air cleared her mind. She could puzzle anew over the rotund man in Lennox and the two men in Blyth and why, though no one knew their course, Horace's men were yet able to find them. Had one of his men been following them since the Nave, informing others of every change in their course? Or was the informant among them?

Isabel glanced across at Brett, sitting so easily in his saddle. For all his protestations, did he mean Jamie harm or at least intend to keep him from Thornwynd until after the seventeenth? By all rights Jamie should have claimed his inheritance by now. Their journey across the Continent to Hamburg had been effected much more quickly than their current travel, and they had had armies to avoid, not just a few hired brigands.

Jamie suddenly pulled his horse up. Startled, Brett and Isabel reined their horses in beside him.

"What is it, lad?" Brett demanded.

"We've got company," Jamie said, studying their back road. "Militia."

"Militia?" Isabel exclaimed, scanning the road behind them and detecting the red coats, which could be clearly seen even though a mile away.

"I count a troop of six," said Jamie.

"And closing fast," Isabel murmured, utterly still in her saddle. "But do they come in response to our misadventure in Blyth?"

"Do nothing to draw their attention," Brett advised. "If they stop us, we are the Beasleys on our way home to York. Let us ride on with all the calm that befits one of York's best families."

"My, my," Jamie murmured, "aren't *we* inventive?"

"Remove your wig, Brett," Isabel advised. "We will be three blondes. Cousins. The Beasleys, as you said."

Brett gratefully followed her advice, placing the wig in his saddlebag.

They continued down the road at an easy lope. Six horses

came behind them at a gallop. A voice called out: "You! Riders, hold there in the name of the king!"

The three obligingly pulled up their horses once again.

"You will do nothing, Jamie," Isabel said in a low voice, "save to follow my lead. Offer no violence, no resistance. Let us see if we can talk ourselves out of this first."

The grim lieutenant leading the five men ordered his troop to halt beside the three travelers. "Gentlemen," he said, "if you will be so good as to dismount, I have a few questions for you."

Brett surprised them all. "What the devil do you mean by this?" he demanded, slinging himself off his horse in high dudgeon. "How dare you stop honest citizenry on a public road! I'll have your commission for this."

"I'm sorry, sir, but I have my orders," the lieutenant stiffly replied.

"There isn't a decently cut coat in the lot of them," Isabel said, quickly recovering from her shock at Brett's superb playacting. For all his protests, he was a gentleman of some ingenuity! She languidly dismounted and raised her quizzing glass to one eye to observe the disastrous work of inept tailors displayed before her. She shuddered. "What *is* this country coming to?"

"Well, *I* think they look splendid!" Jamie stoutly retorted as he jumped to the ground.

"Gentlemen," said the lieutenant, "I would like to ask you a few questions."

"You would like?!" Brett sputtered, rounding upon the hapless lieutenant who, though tall, still lacked a good three inches of the earl's imposing height. "Well *I* would like to know your name and the name of your commanding officer and the regiment you are with and what the devil you mean by stopping us!"

"I am Lieutenant Hardy, sir. I am under orders to stop all travelers on this road. We are looking for two fugitives: the Cavendish brothers."

"*Fugitives?*" Brett exploded. "You take *us* for fugitives? *Us?* The Beasleys of York?!"

"I'm sorry, sir," the lieutenant replied, taking a step back in the face of so much outrage. "I did not mean to insult—"

"I'll have you whipped for this! Of all the damned effrontery! Calling *me* a fugitive!"

"You mistake me, sir. I did not call *you* a—"

"Rupert," Brett commanded Isabel, "commit this man's name to your memory. I shall write to my good friend General Hammond the instant we get home. He'll have this fool flayed alive for his damned insolence!"

"I implore you, Cousin," Isabel said, rubbing her temples, "be not so disquiet. You know I am a bad traveler. My head aches from this swaybacked nag, and your thundering voice only makes the pain worse. Oh, *why* did I not bring any hartshorn with me?"

"As you plainly see," Brett witheringly informed the lieutenant, "we are not some murderous Cavendish brothers; we are the *Beasleys* of York. Well known to every good family in the shire!"

"Yes, sir, I'm sure that—"

"We do *not* make it a habit of shielding fugitives from the law."

"No, sir. I'm sure that—"

"We have supported every king and every good English law since Edward the Second's time, and I will not have some calfling lieutenant tell me—"

"I beg your pardon, sir," the lieutenant hastily interrupted. His head was also beginning to ache. "It's clear that you are indeed good honest folk and not the men we are pursuing. Good day to you."

The lieutenant retreated hastily to his horse, mounted, and led his men away at a canter.

Jamie burst out laughing. *"Very* well played, sir," he said to the earl. "You're developing a talent for this life. Monty would be proud."

" 'Twas a performance worthy of Kean," Isabel quietly

agreed, wondering whom the performance had been for: Jamie and her, or the militia?

Brett silently watched the six riders disappear down the road. They were not English militia. Their coats were all right, but their boots . . . No, it was all wrong. They were impostors. The question was, why? Why tempt jail with such a charade? Of equal concern, how had they known about the Cavendish brothers? Had Isabel and the boy, for all their disguises, been telling the truth after all? Did Horace mean their capture at least, or deaths at worst? Brett turned the problem over in his mind. Horace Shipley had influence on the Continent, it was true. But he had none in England. Nor had he enough money to purchase the services of six able-bodied and conscienceless men. Or did he? Suddenly Brett was not as certain of the world as he had been.

"Whoever are the Beasleys of York?" Isabel inquired as she swung herself back into her saddle.

"I thought only of one," Brett replied, "a pink of the ton. A second cousin on my mother's side who is the king of the dandies strolling up and down Bond Street. You are very like him."

"Sir! You honor me!"

Brett smiled even as his concern about the masquerading militia grew. Something was wrong here, something more than six brigands pretending to be the king's men. What was he missing?

"The danger seems now to surround us," Isabel said quietly as she studied him.

"Yes. That troop may realize their stupidity and our identities at any moment. We should avoid this road and Farnsfield at the very least."

"But we are to meet Dawkins in Farnsfield," Jamie protested.

"I will meet him there; you two will wait here for our return."

"But—" Jamie began.

"Brett is right," Isabel interrupted, to the earl's open astonishment. "Who knows what lies Horace has told to set a troop of militia combing the country for us. And who knows when they will realize just how badly they have been duped. It is more than possible that Farnsfield is not safe for *us*, while Brett may roam about with relative impunity."

"Oh, very well," Jamie said. "But at least let us stop at that tavern we passed a mile back."

"An unsavory place for any woman and boy," Brett pronounced.

"But—as it seems the rain is likely to begin again at any moment—it will at least keep us dry until you return," Isabel countered. "Besides, we are perfectly able to take care of ourselves, whatever the company."

Brett might have known her earlier acquiescence had been an aberration. It was just like Isabel to dash his hopes so quickly. He argued, vehemently, against the tavern and their ability to defend themselves from what was undoubtedly a host of scoundrels, but in vain. Jamie and Isabel set off for the tavern while he turned toward Farnsfield.

*

Chapter 8

May 9, 1804   Early evening

The Nag's Head, near Farnsfield, Nottinghamshire

NIGHT HAD BEEN fully ensconced for almost two hours. Isabel stared out a rainstreaked window as her fingers slid up and down the glass of ale before her. She had been assailed by doubts from the moment she had entered the Nag's Head, and she didn't want to doubt Brett. She didn't want suspicion to chill her heart and darken her mind.

But Monty had taught her to study each person she encountered for the secrets and lies they concealed, the purpose behind their words, the meaning masked by a smile. Brett was hiding something from them, something of import, something dangerous. She knew it in her bones. She failed both Monty and Jamie if she let her traitorous and growing regard for the earl deter her from a careful consideration of every moment he had spent in their company.

It was all she could do to maintain a pleasant conversation with Jamie as suspicion waged battle with instinct, doubts fought with a yearning to trust, and the memory of Brett's warm hands cupping her face plagued her. As the minutes ticked by, she made herself harden her heart more and more. Brett was late. She must be wary.

Finally, through the dirty, rainstreaked tavern window, she and Jamie saw Dawkins drive a team and carriage up to the tavern door. They hurriedly left some coins on the table and were out the door before Brett had even stepped from the chaise.

"You appear unscathed," he observed.

"How could you doubt us?" Jamie retorted with a grin.

"You are late, sir," Isabel said.

"I was detained."

"How?"

Brett seemed a trifle taken aback. "That troop of militia is maligning our names throughout the countryside. They have actually begun a house-by-house search for us. They pose a significant and immediate threat. And they have the help of Farnsfield's Sheriff Wilcox, a man of limited mental ability. Do you recall our gap-toothed friend from the day we first met? He calls himself Brady. He rode into Farnsfield just as I was about to leave and quickly convinced that idiot sheriff that you two tried to kill him. He has two impressive welts on his head to prove it. You are now wanted for attempted murder as well as fraud. A reward has been offered for your capture. We'd best be off, and quickly."

The three climbed with alacrity into the carriage.

"To Swanson Hall, Dawkins," Brett ordered.

"But it is not on Monty's itinerary," Isabel challenged.

"Hang Monty's itinerary!" said the earl with some heat. "We need a safe place to avoid that troop of militia and whatever search Sheriff Wilcox instigates. Swanson Hall serves our needs admirably."

Isabel longed to concede. But every suspicion of the last two hours stopped her. Why had Brett chosen Swanson Hall of all places? Had he laid some sort of trap? It seemed impossible, but she must consider it. Much had happened to keep Jamie from his inheritance, much of it in Brett's company. Too much to be laid to bad luck or chance.

"I must confess that I do not find it at all likely that the English militia should just happen to be looking for us," she said, trying to ignore the dull pain in her heart, "or that our gap-toothed friend should follow us to Farnsfield, or that two brigands should just happen to pluck Jamie off a Blyth street. Horace Shipley clearly had a hand in these matters. Perhaps you could tell us how he managed it, Brett?"

"I?" said the earl with a lift of his elegant eyebrows.

"You confessed some days ago to suspecting what scheme Horace Shipley has up his sleeve," Isabel said, holding the distrust in her heart like a shield. "This seems an appropriate time to share the wealth of your information."

It was not a request. The earl regarded her with shuttered blue eyes. "You still profess ignorance, then?"

"We are wholly in the dark," Isabel replied, her chest tightening. "Why do you suspect us?"

"Have you ever met your uncle, James?" Brett said instead.

"Never," said Jamie as rain drummed on the carriage roof. "We were occasionally in the same town together, but Monty refused to introduce me to, as he termed his brother, a despicable blackguard. He saw no benefit to me from the acquaintance and kept my uncle at bay."

"So he took some care with you after all," murmured the earl.

Isabel drew the knife from her boot and idly ran a finger over the slim blade. She felt encased in ice. "You appeared to us in the guise of Brett Avery. You then declared yourself to be the Earl of Northbridge. You are too young to be Horace Shipley, but you might well be in his pay. Are you?"

"No, Isabel, I am not!" the earl retorted.

"Then whence this secretiveness?" she demanded. "You are Jamie's guardian, sworn to protect his life, yet you withhold information vital to preserving that life. I cannot help but wonder why."

The earl's expression was grim. "Because another life also lies in my hands."

"Not mine, sir. I'm well able to take care of myself."

"I was not referring to you, Isabel. I meant a second James Shipley."

Jamie goggled at his guardian.

"Indeed?" said Isabel. "And where is the boy now?"

Brett's blue eyes bore into her. "Installed at Thornwynd in Horace Shipley's keeping."

"Ah. The clouds break and I see all." With the tip of her knife Isabel raised the ceiling trap. "Pull off the road, Dawkins, and stop," she ordered.

"What are you about now?" Brett demanded as the chaise lurched to a halt.

Isabel had only to glance at Jamie and he was up and following her out the door, jumping down into the mud as he put on his hat.

"We will leave you to your post chaise and estimable coachman, Lord Northbridge," Isabel announced, buttoning her greatcoat against the rain. "I trust you'll have a pleasant journey."

She slammed shut the carriage door, the only reflection of her anger she would permit, then went around to the back of the chaise to retrieve her and Jamie's valises. That she should have misjudged Brett so badly!

Brett, lacking hat and greatcoat, strode up behind her. "What the devil do you think you're doing?"

"Protecting Jamie," Isabel retorted as she tossed first one valise and then the other to the boy.

"By leading him out into this rain?" said Brett.

"By leading him away from *you*, my lord," Isabel snapped, finally turning to face the earl, shaking with barely controlled fury.

"You cannot honestly believe the boy to be in danger from *me*?" he gasped in open astonishment.

"Of course I can!" Isabel seethed, taking her valise from Jamie. "Look at the trouble we have already met in your company! Good-bye, sir. We'll meet again at Thornwynd."

"Isabel, this is madness," Brett said in exasperation. His blond hair was now plastered to his head. "Get back into the chaise."

"Madness?" Isabel cried, indignation and horror overmastering her at last. "Aye, 'twas mad of me to ignore the deceit you first practiced on us and the way you have studied us every minute of the last six days. You thought us the most despicable villains even as you lured us into your friendship. Good God, that I should have trusted Jamie's life to your company for six days!" It was all she could do not to weep from the bitterness assaulting her. He had made her want to trust him! "Get out of my way, sir."

"I'll do no such thing," Brett retorted, grasping her by her slim shoulders and holding her in place. "I grant you the right to be angry with me, but you carry it too far. How am I to know which is the true James Shipley? The boy at Thornwynd has the looks of a Shipley and the documents to back his claims. Your Jamie, I grant you, has his father's looks and history, but a skilled actor, as he and you have proven to be, could easily have carried off such a charade. Your Jamie lacks any identifying paper, even a baptismal record, to prove him the true heir, while the boy at Thornwynd has both proof of his identity and a blood uncle to substantiate his claim! Your Jamie even lacks a credible story. How am I to know the truth in this tangled skein?"

"Precisely, sir," Isabel said, wrenching herself free. "How are you to know? And how are you to act when the *villain* in your charge is threatened with murder? I cannot sit by to await the answer to that question."

"Until I know which Jamie is the true heir, both are under my protection," Brett pronounced.

"Perceive in me every qualm allayed," Isabel said witheringly.

"Remember to whom you are speaking!"

"Oh, I do, sir. I am speaking to a consummate blackguard. That you should suspect us—"

"How could I not?" the earl demanded. "You two have spoken of danger and detailed a most adventurous trek to England, but I had seen none of it. Much as I distrust coincidences, that

115

trio of brigands on the road to Little Bowden could have been just that and no more. I saw no trouble in Lennox. Blyth and the militia are suspicious, I grant you. But perhaps Horace is merely protecting the true heir from your villainy. Horace knows your Jamie is in England because I—in a rare blunder—told him so."

"You told Horace that Jamie is in England?" Isabel said incredulously, rain streaming from her hat.

"Yes."

"And did you, by any chance, mention that you were gone into Northamptonshire to meet him?" she grimly demanded.

"Yes, I'm rather afraid I did."

"God preserve me from all fools!" Isabel yelled to the heavens. "Come on, Jamie. Let's escape this . . . this *villain's* company while we still can."

She began stalking down the road, Jamie at her side, fury pounding in her veins.

"Whether the boy is the true heir or not, I will keep him safe!" Brett shouted after them.

They continued walking.

A wholly indecorous oath escaped the earl as he started after them. "Stop this nonsense at once!" he demanded.

They kept walking.

"Surely you must understand that it is possible Horace Shipley has tried to intercept this Jamie to protect the true heir?"

Silence.

"*Damnation*, you are the most infuriating female I have ever met!"

"Thank you," Isabel snapped, still a good ten feet ahead of the earl, Jamie at her side.

Brett was forced to increase the length of his stride. "Whether you have the real James Shipley or not, clearly you intend to present him at Thornwynd. *I* am going to Thornwynd. Could we not travel together in a comfortable, *dry* post chaise?"

116

The earl took an unconscious step back as Isabel whirled around on him. "And what will you do when we encounter further danger on the road?" she demanded.

"What I have done thus far, of course: my duty."

"Oh yes," Isabel sneered, "your *duty*. Was it your duty to lie to us every moment in our company? Was it your *duty* to pretend to believe that Jamie is the true heir?"

"Yes!" Brett growled, grasping her by her shoulders and refusing to let her go. "The life of a seventeen-year-old boy lies in my hands—"

"No, sir! In *my* hands!"

"And mine!" Brett shouted, shaking her a little. "I have sworn to protect that life with my own. Is this boy standing so gravely at your side the real James Shipley? I can't be certain. I won't be certain until we reach Thornwynd and bring the two boys together. Until that time it is my duty to try to discover the truth of the matter *and* keep this boy safe. I am a man of honor and you have my word, Isabel, that no harm will come to your Jamie in my company."

To the earl's surprise, that stopped Isabel. Now soaked to the bone, he could only stand in the middle of this bog of a road and watch the wheels turn in her mind.

She glanced at Jamie. "We cannot trust him."

"Agreed," said Jamie.

"I beg your pardon?!" Brett sputtered.

"But now that we are fully on our guard, we *can* ride with him," Isabel continued as if the earl had never spoken, "and insure at the same time that he does not betray us to your uncle."

"Of all the—" Brett gasped.

"Very well," Isabel pronounced as she began striding toward the post chaise Dawkins had drawn up behind them. "We will travel with you . . . for *now*, my lord."

"You are too good to me," Brett said grimly. "Truly."

"And if you have any more secrets, you will by God tell me them now, sir!"

"There's nothing else that comes to mind."

"Think of my relief," Isabel muttered as she grabbed Jamie's valise, tossed it up after hers, and secured both.

"I am to enjoy the continued pleasure of your company, then?" Brett inquired with admirable meekness.

"*Only* because I perceive the need for a second bravo to defend Jamie now that you have so brilliantly exposed us to Horace Shipley's machinations," Isabel snapped as she stomped back into the chaise.

"I trust you'll be more cautious in the future," Jamie said mildly, following his protector into the carriage.

Brett stared after them a moment, then glanced up at Dawkins, who had impassively surveyed the entire scene. "We will drive on, Dawkins. To Swanson Hall, using every back road you can find. With some haste, if you please."

"Yes, sir," the coachman said gravely.

Brett glowered at him and then climbed into the chaise. It rumbled back onto the road and then turned onto a side road as Brett pulled off his drenched coat of blue superfine and hung it from the pistol rack. His white shirt and yellow waistcoat were a trifle damp but comparatively comfortable. He wished he could say the same for his soaked breeches, but perhaps they were to be his penance. He chanced a glance at Isabel's grim face. The feminine protector would undoubtedly have preferred as penance a vulture attacking his liver. The earl thought he had got off remarkably well.

"Piquet anyone?" he inquired.

He met only silence as his fellow passengers stared out the rain-streaked carriage windows. The earl was unprepared for the pain that sliced into him.

118

Chapter 9

May 10, 1804   Dawn

Swanson Hall, Nottinghamshire

THE RAIN HAD stopped two hours earlier, and now a glorious Nottinghamshire dawn lit the sky.

Hidden behind a copse, guns drawn, Brett, Isabel, and Jamie watched as six men in red coats rode past them on a country lane leading to the village of Greeley. They said nothing. They scarcely breathed. Dawkins stood at the head of his team to keep them quiet. The sound of hoofbeats slowly faded on the cool morning air. When ten minutes had passed, Brett deemed them safe for now and ordered Dawkins to drive on. A quarter hour was all that was necessary to bring them to the carefully cultivated estate of the Marquis of Beaufort.

"Most impressive," Jamie said, breaking a silence that had lasted two hours.

"That militia is certain to search for us here," Isabel said grimly.

"Swanson Hall shall act as our fortress," Lord Northbridge assured her as they gazed at the Elizabethan manor three hundred yards before them. "No matter how well paid, no brigand would dare accost us in the Marquis of Beaufort's country home. Jamie and I will remain in the carriage while you collect your valise and change behind that thicket on our left."

"Change?" said Isabel, bristling. "Why should I change?"

"Because I will not have you parading about as a *boy* before the Marquis and Marchioness of Beaufort!" the earl retorted.

"Why ever not?"

"*Madam*, there are certain bounds of decorum which must not be overstepped."

"I assure you, Brett," Isabel frostily retorted, "I won't overstep a one of them as Dabney Langford."

"Who?!"

"I am her brother, Edward Langford," Jamie said with a grin.

The earl closed his eyes for a moment as if summoning divine support. "You may be *Deborah* Langford if you choose, Isabel, but not Dabney!"

"When ever did you develop the wholly erroneous belief that I would heed *your* command?"

"Beaufort is my friend, damn it!"

"Brett," Isabel said, draping his name in a frost she had never used before, "if trouble should follow us here, as seems more than likely, petticoats would only impede our escape. Nor would I be able to confer with you on a familiar basis if I were dressed as a woman. *Propriety* would prohibit such freedom, and I must have full access to both you and Jamie should anything untoward arise. You must see that."

"I cannot like it," the earl pronounced.

"That is your concern, not mine. Now I suggest we proceed before we are taken for trespassers." Isabel lifted the trap and ordered Dawkins to drive on.

As she had expected, Brett took full command of the situation the moment they stepped from their post chaise. He rapped soundly upon the front door and, when a startled young footman opened it, said in his most tyrannical manner, "You will deliver this note to Lord Beaufort at once, my man, while we await his reply."

"But, sir! The marquis is not yet awake!" the footman stammered.

120

"Then wake him."

"Sir, I dare not! The marquis left strict instructions—"

"And I," the earl thundered, "am countermanding them! I will take full responsibility for your actions, boy. Deliver the note and return immediately to me without speaking to another living soul. The marquis will thank you soon enough."

Servants of so notable a household are accustomed to the autocratic manners of both employers and guests, but the footman was young, the earl a good deal more than autocratic—tyrannical might be a better term—and so used was the footman to obedience that he haplessly led them into the morning parlor on their left, then ran all the way up a flight of stairs to the Marquis of Beaufort's bedroom.

"A charming room," Isabel pronounced as Jamie brought the fire in the grate back to life and the earl pulled open the drapes.

It was a comparatively small parlor for so large a hall. Light floral wallpaper and the blue and green upholstered furniture gave a note of spring to the room.

" 'Twill do," Brett pronounced.

Isabel quickly hid her smile. Damn the earl for reminding her of amusement when she had secretly sworn two hours ago to detest him for the rest of her life.

"Have you known Beaufort long, my lord?" Jamie asked.

"We were acquainted at Oxford," said the earl, "and have met on occasion throughout the years as our social duties demand."

"Oh, a bosom-bow, then," said Isabel.

The earl glanced at her. "Duty and social position go a long way toward surpassing any claims of close friendship, Mr. Langford."

The breathless and beleaguered footman hurried into the room. "I have given the marquis your note, sir, and he says he will attend you immediately."

"Excellent," said Brett.

121

"Gentlemen," continued the footman, "may I get you tea or coffee?"

"No," said Brett. "We do not require refreshment at this time."

"Yes, sir."

"Northbridge! Good God, what the devil is the meaning of this note and your presence at such an hour?"

The company turned to observe the Marquis of Beaufort standing in the parlor doorway. He lacked the earl's height by a good foot. His hair was brown and thin and already receding from his forehead. His face bore the ruddy complexion of a country gentleman. His figure was beginning to tend toward fat, and he wore the most atrocious dressing gown Isabel had ever been so unfortunate to see. It was a horrific combination of green and orange satin stripes that made its wearer appear bilious, or perhaps it was merely the hour at which he had been forced to arise.

"I am in some difficulty, Beaufort, and require your help for the next twenty-four hours," Brett said easily.

"Well—well, of course I will help you," said Beaufort. "But what's all the to-do?"

"There is a . . . *slight* possibility," Brett replied, "that a sheriff and perhaps a troop of militia are curious as to our whereabouts."

"What?"

"Oh, forgive me. I have not yet introduced my companions. Beaufort, this is Mr. Dabney and Mr. Edward Langford. They are in my charge for the next se'ennight."

Isabel and Jamie executed beautiful bows, murmured "Sir," and wisely forbore saying anything further. Brett had the situation well in hand.

"How do you do?" said the marquis distractedly. "What could a sheriff and a militia want with *you*, Northbridge?"

"It is a misunderstanding only," said Brett dismissively. He caught Isabel's eye and, with a faint smile, shrugged and

122

amended. "It seems, Beaufort, that my friends here are wanted for fraud and attempted murder."

The marquis tottered. His footman was instantly at his side, offering a supporting arm. "Murder?" their host quavered.

"Come, sit down, Beaufort," said Brett. "I realize it is early in the day to contend with such a story, and without your breakfast, too."

"Thank you," said the marquis dazedly as the footman helped him to a sofa.

Brett took the chair opposite him. Isabel and Jamie remained standing, flanking him. It took the earl but five minutes to concisely detail their adventures thus far.

"All I require from you, Beaufort," he concluded, "is a safe place to rest today and avoid what pursuers there may be. By dawn tomorrow, whoever is seeking us will have passed far along, and we may continue our journey with impunity."

The marquis, whose mind was not strong, was easily guided to Brett's desires. "Oh! Certainly, Northbridge. . . . It goes without saying. . . . B-B-But I do have a few houseguests just at present. Won't they—"

"Are there any who would know me at sight?"

"Oh no! They're just some of mother's émigrés."

"Her what?"

"The Duc and Duchesse de Montville, their son and two daughters. They escaped the Revolution some years back and have been living off the *haut* ton ever since."

"Does your mother accompany them?"

"Oh yes, but I do not think you have ever met."

"Fortunately no," said Brett. "I foresee no difficulties in any event. This footman shall act our valet and servant until tomorrow morning, supplying us with whatever we need and," he said with a glacial glare at the shaking footman, "will say *nothing* of this to anyone for any reason. It will be our secret, boy."

"Yes, sir! Of course, sir!" the footman stammered.

"Excellent," said Brett. "Have you three rooms we can use until the morrow, Beaufort?"

"Oh, certainly!" said the Marquis. "Gad, there's a thousand rooms to choose from in this pile of rocks."

"Thank you. We will leave you now to bathe and rest and appear before your guests this afternoon as Sir Howard Langford and his nephews Dabney and Edward. Remember that, now, Beaufort. I am Sir Howard Langford."

"Oh, yes, yes, yes. You may count on me, old fellow. Stewart," he said to the footman, "escort Sir Howard . . . er . . . Langford and his nephews to the Blue Suite on the second landing.

"It should be quiet there," he informed his impromptu guests, "and allow you to rest undisturbed. I'll shoo away anyone who comes looking for you."

"Thank you, Beaufort. I knew I could count on you," said Brett.

The marquis flushed with pleasure. "I'm always happy to oblige you, Northbridge."

With a curt nod Brett strode from the parlor, Isabel, Jamie, and the footman scurrying after him. "We will require baths, breakfast, and complete refurbishment of our travel clothes, which you will find in my coachman's care," Brett informed the footman as they mounted the stairs.

"The Earl of Northbridge," Isabel murmured in Jamie's ear, "terror of the north counties."

The earl acknowledged the Blue Suite to be suitable to their needs, assigned Jamie and Isabel to their rooms, and issued a long list of orders to the hapless footman. An hour later, Brett, with undisguised pleasure, had bathed and partook of a well-deserved breakfast. Then, with strict orders to the footman, Stewart, to wake him in no more than four hours, he laid himself down upon a tolerably comfortable bed and promptly fell asleep.

Four hours to the second later, he awoke at Stewart's first word and was up and dressed in newly laundered and pressed clothes within a quarter hour. The Earl of Northbridge did not believe in dallying before his mirror. He then set out to awaken Isabel and Jamie but found that they were already up and in company. Horror washed over him.

He hurried down to the first landing and entered the main drawing room where he found, somewhat to his chagrin, a charming scene that wholly belied the scandalous scenarios that had been blooming in his brain. The Marquis and Marchioness of Beaufort were seated at a card table with an elegant couple in their forties who must surely be the Duc and Duchesse de Montville. They were playing at whist and were wholly engrossed in their cards.

Jamie was seated upon a gold-and-tan upholstered settee with a pretty brunette of perhaps fifteen years who dimpled and blushed and heartily encouraged the mild flattery and flirtation with which Jamie was waxing poetic.

Isabel, looking every inch the respectable young man about town in white pantaloons that lovingly molded themselves to her shapely legs and a blue-green frock coat that did fascinating things to her eyes, stood at the opposite end of the room conducting a conversation—entirely in French—with a young man of perhaps one-and-twenty years, brown hair, blue eyes, decent figure, and reasonable taste in clothes, and a pretty young woman of perhaps nineteen, who was doing her level best to capture what she perceived to be Dabney Langford's heart.

The earl felt it incumbent upon him to stop this appalling charade at once but was forestalled when Isabel looked up and, catching his eye, called out, "There you are, you slugabed!"

The earl winced.

"Uncle Langford, you must come and let me make known to you the most entrancing people I have ever met." She walked arm in arm with the young woman and man and presented them to Brett. "Allow me to introduce Adelle and Hilaire Saville. *Mes amis*, this is my uncle, Sir Howard Langford."

The three exchanged the requisite bows.

"I hope my nephew has not been boring you with his prattle," said the earl, with a most forbidding glance at Isabel.

"Mais, non!" declared Adelle with a pretty laugh. "Your nephew is a wit and most *charmant*."

"I am relieved to hear it," said Brett with the utmost honesty.

"And this divine little creature beside Jamie," Isabel said, a hint of frost back in her voice, "is Julienne, who secretly wants to elope with a poet—as yet unchosen—and act his muse to the benefit of English literature. *C'est ça, Julienne?*"

Julienne dimpled up at Brett. "If I do not choose to marry Monsieur Edward first!"

"Let me assure you, my lady," Brett said gravely, "that I could not permit such a match, for Edward, I fear, is very far from being your equal."

"Ah, but Uncle Langford," Jamie said wickedly, "her smile could raise me to the heights!"

"Now, of course," Isabel intervened, "I must present to you, Sir Howard, the Duc and Duchesse de Montville."

Brett made his bows and greetings and then turned to his exquisitely dressed hostess and raised her hand to his lips. "My lady, I must thank you for your largesse in allowing us to intrude so suddenly on your house party."

"Sir Howard," murmured the Marchioness of Beaufort, a beautiful woman with lush auburn hair, "it is always a pleasure to see you, *however* you appear at our door. I hope you will be able to stay with us a few days at least."

"No, I'm sorry, Marchioness. My nephews and I must leave with the dawn."

"Oh no!" pouted Julienne, clasping Jamie's hand and pressing it protectively to her budding breast. "You cannot take the delightful Edward away from me so soon."

"I am afraid, my lady, that the delightful Edward is required elsewhere."

"That is too bad, for I suspect you will miss out on a capital piece of fun," said the marchioness with a bland expression.

126

"We've had the most extraordinary visitors today! First there was some country sheriff covered from head to foot in dust and looking for two escaped murderers. Can you imagine! And then came knocking a ragged troop of militia with an officer who insisted upon searching the house and grounds for someone named Cavendish, or Beasley, he wasn't entirely clear on the point. As if *we* would ever harbor fugitives from the law! The idea! Our butler, Lawton, was so distressed that he had to retire to his room."

"And I must needs sleep through all the fun," murmured the earl with an appreciative gaze down at the marchioness. It was widely acknowledged in the ton that it was the Marchioness of Beaufort who had the brains of the family. The marquis had been known in his youth as a rakehell, a bad driver, and a worse hunter. His taste in light-skirts had been outrageously expensive. Since his marriage, however, he had become a model of decorum and almost sensible conversation, and his wife was given all the credit.

The four at the card table returned to their game and Jamie to his flirtation, while Isabel called Brett to her side to join in her conversation with Adelle and Hilaire Saville. Concluding that Julienne was relatively safe in Jamie's company, Brett returned to Isabel's side. He had not anticipated that Jamie and she would plunge so gleefully into acquaintance with the Beauforts' guests. He had hoped they would be sensible enough to keep a low profile.

That, he realized now, had been utter foolishness. Whatever role they had taken on in his company, they had played it fully, and now was no exception. Even he, knowing who and what Isabel was, found her wholly convincing as Dabney Langford. She made no misstep, by word, action, or even look. And she held her own in this French conversation, speaking the language as if born to it and meeting her social betters by modifying her superior intellect to theirs.

It was not what he had expected, this seamless portrayal of a young member of the ton. He had earlier been unable to conceive of Isabel in such a setting, yet here she stood, at her ease and perfectly at home, as if born to the life! Her etiquette was sublime, her conversation irreproachable, her occasional jokes fit for the mildest company.

How was this possible? How could one woman cross the rigid bounds of class without causing a ripple? He had never seen it done before. He had never thought it possible before. But then, he had not known Isabel before.

He should be appalled. The Earl of Northbridge was convinced that he should be appalled at such able deceit. But he was not, for he was now not entirely certain that this was deceit. The pleasure Isabel took in this exuberant discussion of horse racing was as real as the pleasure she had once taken in bantering with him. The appreciation she expressed at the superb wine a footman was offering to the Beauforts' guests was as real as the appreciation she had shown an innkeeper for the plain dinner he had provided.

Had he ever appreciated all that he had as Isabel appreciated how little she had?

Had he ever enjoyed himself as Isabel was doing now? He looked at all thirty-five years of his life and found them gray and dull and dry as dust. He had permitted no absurdity to grow there, no laughter to color his world, no *fun* to lighten his heart. Only a se'ennight ago he had thought of himself as rich and powerful. Looking at Isabel now, hearing her low gurgle of laughter, he felt himself a pauper. All that he had valued—his position, his wealth, his duty—seemed somehow a prison.

Could he have been wrong all these years?

O happiness! our being's end and aim!

He had studied all of Pope's works and somehow had missed entirely that exultant cry. Happiness. He with his estates and his incomparable stable and grand house and overbearing valet had yet known nothing of happiness, while Isabel—who lacked home, family, and any accepted form of stability—had leapt almost gleefully into every role she played and derived every ounce of happiness she could from life.

She actually liked these masquerades of hers with the challenge they posed and the fun they offered. Time and again at the beginning of their acquaintance she had tried to lure him into that fun, and he had held himself back . . . at least until recently. A smile quirked the earl's lips. Playing the outraged Mr. Beasley berating that malignant lieutenant had been thoroughly . . . delightful.

The earl's eyes widened in surprise at this startling acknowledgment. Perhaps he was not entirely beyond salvation.

The marquis was called away to meet with his estate agent and the marchioness entreated Sir Howard to partner her at whist. He obligingly took his place at the table, but his mind was not on the cards. As he escorted the marchioness in to dinner a few hours later, she sunnily rebuked him for his lack of attention and her subsequent loss to the duc and duchesse of two hundred pounds.

"But North . . . I mean, Sir Howard never loses at cards!" the Marquis of Beaufort exclaimed behind them.

"I was so distracted by your wife's beauty, Beaufort, that I could not keep a clear head," Brett said smoothly.

"That's why Kate and I make such good partners," the marquis said jovially. "She's so damned distracting, our opponents never know where they're at. I've won twice the blunt with her that I lost in my bachelor days."

"To the gratification of your heirs, no doubt," Brett murmured as he handed the marchioness in to her chair.

"You have become a wicked man since we last met, Sir Howard," she said with a mischievous smile.

He sat on her right, Lady Adelle was on his other side, and his duty dictated that he attend and entertain them both. This the Earl of Northbridge wholly failed to do, for his thoughts were distracted, his mind at work trying to unravel several heretofore unexplored concerns.

A bark of laughter brought his head up. The Dowager

129

Beaufort, a spray of rubies in her white hair, sat opposite him, jowls jiggling with laughter. Beside her sat Isabel, mischief in her gray eyes as she whispered an undoubtedly scandalous tale into the dowager's ear. The dowager had been country bred and raised. Like her son, she was not very clever. Double entendres were Greek to her. Isabel had captured her heart with a tale about a Sussex man so determined to win a local horse race that he had kept his four-legged contender in the morning parlor, for the barn was drafty. The dowager had chained Isabel to her side ever since, and Isabel seemed perfectly happy to be there.

No one, the earl believed, could be perfectly content in the dowager's company for more than a quarter hour, and he gave Isabel full credit for entertaining the old battle-ax. Jamie, on the Dowager's left, now claimed her attention, and Isabel turned to their hostess on her right.

"Your mother-in-law informs me, ma'am, that you made the marquis pursue you a full year before agreeing to marry him."

"Of course I did!" the marchioness replied, laughter in her hazel eyes. "I would have said yes to his proposal after the first week of our acquaintance, but I thought it wise not to appear too eager. Gentlemen like a well-fought campaign, and I wanted him to appreciate having me."

"He could not fail to do so, ma'am," Isabel assured her. "But come, do you mean to tell me you set your cap for him? Is this the old tale of chasing a man until you let him catch you?"

"Now, who told you that feminine secret?"

"My uncle has been most instructive on the ways of the world," Isabel murmured, flashing a glittering glance at Brett. Did she intend to make this meal his further penance, he wondered. "Had you chosen the marquis for your husband?"

"Certainly," the marchioness replied. "He was so different from my many beaux, you see."

"He was richer?"

130

The Earl of Northbridge blanched over his asparagus.

"No, you wretch!" the marchioness said on a delightful gurgle of laughter. "I had a vast dowry of my own. I could have married a pauper and been comfortable. Besides, at one time I had a duke, two earls, and a viscount all dangling after me. Even the reserved Earl of Northbridge danced with me twice in one evening at Almack's."

"No!" Isabel murmured. "And you didn't snap him up then and there?"

"He didn't offer."

"He was a fool ma'am," Isabel assured the marchioness in all seeming sincerity. "A fool."

"Yes," she tartly replied, directing a laughing glance at Brett, who could not help but smile in turn. "He was. But I don't think I would have had him, in any event. He was so terrifyingly self-sufficient, you see. He didn't need me and I like to be needed."

"Hence the Marquis of Beaufort?"

"He was quite at sea in the world, poor lamb. And he adored me. It was a heady combination. You mark my words, Mr. Langford: Few women can resist being needed and loved. I would have thrown myself at his feet if I hadn't kept my wits about me."

"I hope, Marchioness, that you made *him* throw himself at *your* feet!"

"Of course I did, Mr. Langford. Any suitor must prove himself worthy of the woman he wishes to marry, otherwise he is not satisfied with his prize."

"You must have been a holy terror on the Marriage Mart."

The marchioness burst into a musical ripple of laughter. "Oh, I was, Mr. Langford. I was!"

"But the antics of our hostess," the earl blithely broke in, "were nothing to your determined deviltry, *nephew*."

The marchioness raised her fan and leaned toward Isabel. "And how long has Sir Howard been your uncle, Mr. Langford?"

131

"It seems like forever," Isabel muttered.

The marchioness chuckled and insisted on pouring Isabel some more wine while Brett considered this entertaining pair.

The former Lady Katharine Huntsford had been a charming creature, even as a girl. He had indeed danced with her at every ball they attended together, had called on her a few times, dined with her (and a good dozen others) often. She would have been, he realized with a start, an eminently suitable wife and Countess Northbridge. Why had he not seen it before?

Studying her now as she directed an affectionate comment to her husband at the opposite end of the table, Brett began to suspect that he had perceived her suitability during her London Season. Perhaps his claim of waiting for a suitable wife had been a sham. Perhaps he had been not seeking but avoiding marriage, or more likely avoiding the intimacy that the Beauforts shared. Had he married Lady Katharine Huntsford, he would have made her miserable, for he would have denied her what she seemed to need: mutual affection and intimacy.

It had never occurred to the earl that he would make a lamentable husband. But then, he had never before realized how wholly he had failed to make Lady Katharine laugh as Isabel had done tonight. He had never inspired this particular gleam in her hazel eyes. He had never brought her to speak so easily in his company.

The dowager had reclaimed Isabel's attention by declaring that the country was the only proper place to raise a family, and she was grateful that her daughter-in-law had the sense to agree with her. She continued her monologue from there. Brett's attention was reclaimed by Lady Adelle, but he, it must be confessed, gave her but half an ear. He had much to think on.

At meal's end, the gentlemen—including Isabel—rose to journey to a nearby salon to enjoy their port and cigars in peace—when Julienne voiced her dissent.

"No, no, no! You must not desert us!" she cried. "If we are

to have the company of the Langfords for this one night only, you cannot be so cruel as to take them away from us now."

"What do you propose, poppet?" her brother demanded with an indulgent smile.

"I want to dance with Edward," was her reply. "I may never see him again in this life, and I want to dance with Edward tonight."

"I could play the pianoforte if anyone else is interested in an impromptu ball," Isabel volunteered.

The scheme was quickly termed delightful. Brett, to his chagrin, found himself claimed for the first dance by the Dowager Beaufort. The couples promenaded back into the drawing room. There, Isabel seated herself at the pianoforte as if she really knew what she was doing, and a moment later Brett found that she did. She played not as a schoolgirl or even as one of those flirtatious debutantes forced to present some musical talent to potential husbands but as a skillful musician with a love of the instrument.

Jamie, too, was skillful . . . at the dance. Indeed, it was his enthusiasm and talent that kept them happily at this makeshift ball far longer than many were accustomed to. His delight was infectious; his pleas for just one more dance—and one more after that—were impossible to refuse. Even the earl could not recall a more enjoyable evening.

Nearly three hours after they had begun, the dancers at last loudly proclaimed themselves wonderfully exhausted, applauded their pianist, who offered them a grave bow, and called to the servants for refreshments. The overheated party then settled back into conversation and cards.

The dowager soon excused herself—stating that she was un-accustomed to such high jinks and it was time for her to claim her bed—and at last left Isabel free of company. She took this opportunity to step out onto the balcony and enjoy the humid spring night air. Moving casually through the room, Brett fol-lowed her.

"You performed admirably this evening," he said, reaching

133

her side and gazing with her at the lush back gardens. He felt more than saw her stiffen beside him.

"I have always enjoyed the pianoforte."

"That, too, but I meant in particular your performance as Dabney Langford."

"I have not put you to the blush?" she coolly inquired, turning to him.

"Dabney Langford has not put me to the blush," Brett corrected.

"Dabney is weak with relief," she retorted. There was a pause. "You are a skilled dancer. Do you hold many balls at Ravenscourt?"

"None. I am not a social man. My duties—"

"Keep you much too busy to partake in anything so frivolous as a ball," Isabel concluded for him. "Yes, I know. Do *you* even know what pleasure is?"

"Oh, I have known some pleasure in my past."

"I meant diverse forms of pleasure, sir, *not* sexual pleasure."

He gasped and glared at her. "No woman should say, let alone think, such things!"

"Fiddlesticks! Women discuss such things all the time, and men know it! How many wagers, after all, have been paid not with coin of the realm but with a woman's bed?"

The earl opened his mouth to make a cutting retort, then stopped and considered her a moment. "You say such things just to shock me, don't you?"

"But, sir, you are so easily shocked!" Isabel murmured wickedly.

"Why do you delight in tormenting me so?"

"Oh sir, I *tease*, I do not torment."

"Madam," he said fiercely, "you will allow me to use the adjective of my choice! I said torment and I *meant* torment." His eyes, his expression were impassioned as he stared down at her, and Isabel could not help but tremble.

"I only seek to remind you that there is some fun to be had

134

in life, if you are willing," she said, hurriedly looking back to the gardens.

"What? Have you made it your mission to redeem my soul?"

"That black vessel? No, indeed!"

Brett sighed. "I have suffered the stings and arrows of your discontent all day. Will you never forgive me for not telling you of the second claimant to the baronetcy?"

"What could an earl want with a vagabond's forgiveness?" Isabel demanded, her heart beginning to beat a little faster.

"Do not denigrate yourself," Brett commanded. "Whatever your true name and history, our association has revealed your many . . . admirable qualities."

Isabel gasped and stared up at the earl. "Do you . . . no longer find me quite so objectionable, sir?"

"It is damnably difficult to object to someone of your wit, intelligence, courage, and beauty, *Dabney*."

Isabel flushed with pleasure. "And it is impossible not to desire the approbation of so superior a gentleman."

"I said nothing of approbation."

"Oh." Isabel stared at her shoes. "I beg your pardon."

Brett's fingers tilted her chin up so that she must look at him. It was all she could do not to tremble at the heat coursing from his fingers to her entire body.

"I cannot like the many masquerades you undertake," he said quietly, holding her captive in the night with his blue gaze. She forgot to breathe. "Nor can I like the danger to which you expose yourself with each day you remain Jamie's protector. But I must admire the skill you display in each of your masquerades, and the courage you vouchsafe with each day you remain Jamie's protector, and the love which guides you to do what you deem right by the boy."

Isabel could not say whether her body was flushed from the heat of his touch or the wonderful glow of his words.

"I must apologize," Brett continued, "for my earlier churlish

135

behavior when I first learned your true sex. It was a shock and I acted badly."

"It was no less than I expected, sir."

"Then you believed me to be a rigid, judgmental old slowtop?"

"You are the most irritating man," Isabel complained, a little amazed that Brett should be bantering with her about himself like this. "How could you not be angered by our deceit? You were unaccustomed to such betrayal."

"And how do you know that?"

"Your character is writ on your face, sir."

"And yours in your eyes, I think." Brett studied her as if delving beneath an ocean wave. It was all Isabel could do not to shiver from such delicious scrutiny. "I think I have hurt you more than angered you, Isabel, and for that I am truly sorry."

Staring up at him, she believed him. It wasn't a wish or a dream in her heart; she actually believed him. Perhaps it was the intensity of his gaze, the sincerity in his voice, or the knowledge that this earl had apologized to very few people in his life.

"You didn't intend to hurt me," she said slowly. "You meant only to protect the two boys in your charge. I understand that now."

"And will you forgive me for acting as I thought my duty demanded and not telling you of the second claimant? Your Jamie is safe with me, Isabel. I swear it."

"I know it," Isabel said softly. She took a deep breath and met his gaze. "And I forgive you."

"Thank you." His smile faded. He was leaning toward her, almost . . . intimately. She had to tilt her head back to look up at him and was instantly caught by the unfamiliar light in his blue eyes. Oh, she could melt into that light! "Isabel, I—"

"Yes?" she whispered.

He abruptly pulled away. "It is time we rejoined the others."

It took a moment for Isabel to regain her equilibrium and quell her disappointment. "Certainly, sir." She almost put her hand on his arm for him to lead her inside. She blinked. When had she ever forgotten that she was playing at being a man?

She hurriedly walked back into the drawing room, Brett following her.

Chapter 10

May 11, 1804   Early morning

Swanson Hall, Nottinghamshire

IT WAS NOT yet dawn when Stewart, the footman, brought Brett, Isabel, and Jamie their breakfasts. Nor was it yet light out when he helped Isabel into her coat, presented Brett with a freshly laundered and ironed neck cloth, and gave a final dusting to Jamie's clothes.

Having said their good-byes to the Beauforts and their guests the night before, Brett, Isabel, and Jamie now bid good-bye to Stewart. Brett pressed a few guineas into his startled hand, and then the three went silently downstairs and out the front door to the stable yard. There Dawkins had one of the Beauforts' carriages and a team of blacks in its traces waiting for them.

"Prompt as always, I see, Dawkins," said the earl as the first pale blue and pink tendrils of dawn began to light the eastern sky.

"Promptness may not be what we're needing, sir," said Dawkins.

The three gave him their utmost attention.

"Is there trouble abroad?" Brett inquired.

"I've been talking to some of the grooms, my lord. It seems that a troop of militia spent last night in the village of Greeley, just five miles from here. That young lieutenant has been declaring that the fugitives he seeks are in the neighborhood. Stirred up quite a scare, he did. People have even taken to locking their doors."

"A most persistent lieutenant," said Isabel, her fingers drumming on a back wheel of the carriage.

"Yes. If he was in the king's pay, we might not have to worry so much about him."

Isabel's head came up. "If not the king's, than whose?"

"Perhaps Horace Shipley's," said Brett. "That troop of militia are impostors. They seek Jamie and no one else."

"And just when were you planning to inform us of the duplicity of this militia troop?" Isabel demanded.

"Why, when it became necessary, of course," Brett blandly replied. "And it is now necessary."

"Do you think our faux lieutenant suspects the Beauforts?" Jamie tactfully intervened.

"It's possible," Brett conceded. "Since trouble has not passed us by and suspicion may well settle on Beaufort as my known acquaintance, a diversion seems in order."

"Let Dawkins act the decoy?" Isabel inquired.

Brett smiled at her. "Exactly. We three will venture out on horseback. I need only leave a note for Beaufort. We will return the horses to him in good time."

"So we go cross-country while Dawkins takes the road," said Jamie. "A pretty scheme."

"Yes," said Isabel expansively. "Brett grows more adept at this adventurous life with each new day."

"Was that intended as a compliment?" the earl inquired, blue eyes twinkling down at her.

"Oh, of the highest sort, sir."

"Very well," said Brett decisively, "we have our diversion and the beginnings of a plan. Let us add to the lieutenant's confusion by returning to the carriage that he will already have inspected and passed in . . . Slaidburn, I think. . . . Oh, with your permission, Isabel!"

Faith, for all his elevated position and many duties, the earl was well on the road to being a rascal. "Slaidburn will do admirably, sir," she said composedly. "It is on the itinerary Monty gave us."

"I am happy not to quarrel about the rendezvous. Very well, Dawkins," said Brett, "you need effect no disguise. I suspect the lieutenant would now see through it easily enough. You will drive this carriage and team to Slaidburn at an easy pace and wait for us there. We will undoubtedly do a bit of wending and winding through the countryside. Do not expect us for, I would say, two days."

"And if that wooden-faced blackguard of a lieutenant should stop me, sir?" Dawkins inquired.

"Why, you are merely transporting one of the Beaufort carriages and teams to Ravenscourt, where the Beauforts will soon come for a house party."

"Very well, sir," said Dawkins with a gruff tug at his forelock. "I'll be off, then."

He climbed onto the carriage box, gathered the reins, and with a soft crack of his whip set the team trotting out of the Beaufort stable yard.

"The marquis, for all his inadequacies in the saddle, keeps a decent stable, I believe," said Brett. "Come along, *nephews*. Let us find suitable mounts."

A chestnut mare for Isabel, a bay gelding for Jamie, and a large black thoroughbred with a white star on his forehead for Brett were quickly saddled and bridled. Brett scribbled a quick note of explanation to the marquis and pressed it into the hand of the head groom, whom he had just roused from a sound sleep.

Then the three mounted and, Isabel in the lead, left the stable yard at a decorous trot, no more than ten minutes behind Dawkins.

The general pleasantries of travelers no longer at odds with each other were soon given over to silence, thought, and watchfulness. It would be best if they spied the militia before the militia spied them. Ever alert, Isabel now had ample opportunity to examine the thoughts that had plagued her the whole of last night, for Swanson Hall had dealt her a leveler.

More accurately, the Marchioness of Beaufort had brought Isabel to think of herself in ways she had never allowed herself to contemplate before. She had lain in bed the whole of last night marveling over and over again to herself how rich and broad and varied Lady Beaufort's life was. Here was a woman only a year older than herself who was blessed with an adoring husband, four doting children, important household and social duties, and a wide cadre of friends with whom she shared her laughter and her troubles.

Isabel's life seemed narrow and barren in contrast. Unlike the marchioness, she had admitted no one into her heart these last thirteen years save Monty and Jamie, and now there was only Jamie. She had no former beaux to help her recall past pleasures, no friends with whom to share her heart and her confidences, no adult to love her, no children to need her. For all the hundreds of people she had met in her lifetime, she was on intimate terms with no one.

Here she had taken Brett to task more than once for the rigid and unhappy life he had made for himself, when in some respects her own life was just as bad, if not worse. True, she had the skill, which he lacked, to find the fun in life. But she, like Brett, had no one to share that fun with. She had told herself for so many years now that it was not safe to let anyone into her heart and her thoughts. And indeed, that was the truth. But having witnessed the bounty of the Beauforts' lives, safety was fast losing its appeal.

In the past, her thoughts and plans had always been geared to what she could have, rather than what she wanted. But really, was it so impossible that those two should become one? If she but broadened her perception of what was possible, what was possible just might bump into some of her dreams.

In that moment, Isabel was numb to the strong wind blowing against her, the warmth of the sun on her skin, even the movement of her horse beneath her. Old dreams, dreams she

141

had hidden away so long ago, had suddenly swamped her heart with yearning.

An hour after leaving Swanson Hall they entered into Yorkshire. Though she would reveal it to no one, Isabel was in her home county and knew the area well. For the first time in thirteen years, she disobeyed Monty's instructions. She led Brett and Jamie on a serpentine course that avoided the towns of Plockton, Birstall, and Wadsworth Moor.

They followed a West Riding road that was in Isabel's memory only. She had ridden these hills daily in her girlhood and still knew the way to the Birstall River. Slaidburn was but twenty miles upstream after that.

It was just after noon when she at last heard the song of a reed warbler. Allowing herself but a slight smile of satisfaction, she silently led Brett and Jamie down a steep hill to the slow-moving Birstall River. At the riverbank, she slid off her weary horse and led him to drink, which he did greedily. Brett and Jamie also dismounted and led their horses forward.

"Where the devil are we?" Jamie demanded.

"We are approximately twenty miles from Slaidburn," Isabel replied. "With luck, we'll rendezvous with Dawkins tonight. You should be at Ravenscourt and safety in two days."

"If Ravenscourt *is* safe," Jamie amended. "What will the earl do with me if I am proved the villain he believes me to be?"

"Oh, string you up by your thumbs, no doubt," Isabel lightly replied, but her heart sank at the question.

"Perhaps he will turn me over to my uncle instead."

"Neither option appeals, whelp," Brett retorted. "You may yet be a rogue, but unaccountable as it seems, I've developed a liking for your company. Perhaps I'll put you to work as a stable boy."

"Oh, come, a groom at least!" Jamie protested.

"You will have to earn that elevated rank."

"And what of Isabel?" Jamie demanded with a grin.

"That requires more thought. If you are an impostor, then she must be not merely your accomplice but your mentor."

"It goes without saying," Isabel agreed equably.

"The greater crime would be hers, therefore, and her punishment consequently greater," Brett concluded.

"I have always fancied myself as a dairy maid," she offered.

"*Far* too romantic for such villainy," Brett riposted. "You will be a scullion at most."

Isabel wrinkled her nose in distaste. "A complete waste of my talents, sir. Best to make me governess to your future progeny. *I'll* give them an education to haunt you the rest of your years."

Brett leaned against his horse and laughed.

Isabel gaped at him. The Earl of Northbridge was *laughing*! Warm sunshine and rich glee wrapped up in contagious hilarity enfolded her. She conceived in that moment a lifelong ambition to make Brett laugh every day for the rest of his life.

"The perfect revenge!" he said admiringly. "You have a devious mind, Isabel."

"And if I am proved the true heir," Jamie said with a grin, "what of Isabel then?"

Brett opened his mouth to reply, but Isabel hastily intervened. "Why, then I may choose my own fate, just as I have always done. Come, the horses have rested enough, and we still have a long journey before us."

She pulled her reluctant horse away from the water, led him up the riverbank, and swung herself into the saddle. She again led Brett and Jamie on a trail that existed only in her memory. It was amazing to her that she could be so calm in such familiar country. By all rights, she should be tortured by painful memories, shivering with the terror of her childhood, thinking of the noose Jonas Babcock was making for her. Instead, she drank in the beauty of this place and the pleasure she derived from scanning the woods for a pine marten or a stoat, or watching a hawk on the wing.

Had she seen this beauty as a girl? Perhaps she had. Perhaps it was this beauty that had given her the strength she had needed to survive the tortures of Hiram Babcock's household. Perhaps that was why even now, thirteen years later, she could guide her horse so unerringly through woods that had grown and changed over the years and yet were still intimately known to her.

At several points she found herself almost turning in her saddle to tell Brett how she had found this spot in her girlhood or taken shelter from the rain under that large tree. This unaccountable desire to share her love of this country with the earl was wholly unnerving. She remained mute.

Finally they came to a broad green valley of dappled sunlight and a few lazy cows. A cow track led off to the right. Isabel sighed. She was reluctant to leave this relative safety and peace. But they must pass through Colne if they hoped to reach Slaidburn by nightfall.

She led Brett and Jamie onto the cow path. Half an hour's further ride brought them to the more direct and obvious path to Colne. A sharp turn in the road suddenly brought the village into view, and there, at the entrance to the town, were six men in red coats, on horseback.

"Damn!" said Brett.

"Persistent, aren't they?" Jamie commented.

"Why are they waiting for us?" Isabel demanded.

"The Beaufort groom may have been bribed into betraying us," Brett said grimly.

"Hoy!" shouted the lieutenant. "Stop in the name of the king!"

Intending no disrespect to George III, Brett nonetheless wheeled his horse and set off at a gallop down the road, Isabel and Jamie flanking him.

Once beyond Colne, they left the road and spurred their horses to gallop across country. The ground was soft, occasionally marshy, making the going difficult. Glancing over her shoulder, Isabel spied six men on horseback coming at them with good speed.

"Brett!" she cried.

"I see them," he said.

Spurring their horses, they raced on.

After nearly an hour of hard riding, their horses were lathered and blown. They had to pull them up to a slower pace if they hoped to keep them in any shape for the rest of their journey.

On their left was a checkerboard of green fields separated by hedges that would have to be jumped one by one if they chose that path. On their right was a wood. Isabel pulled a compass from her pocket and studied it and the country around them.

"We can hide better in the wood," she said, "but it will slow us even further."

"We will be too exposed in the fields," said Brett.

"Yes. If there is to be a pitched fight, I'd much rather have some protection," said Jamie.

"Let us hope we can avoid the fight, pitched or otherwise," said Isabel, and turned her horse into the woods.

As there was no path, they could move only at a trot through the trees. Riding abreast of each other, they were silent for the next half hour. Finally reaching open ground, they pushed their horses once again to a gallop.

Topping a small rise of land, Isabel suddenly wheeled her horse. As the chestnut danced beneath her, she scanned the woods and field over which they had come.

"They're closing on us!" she said. Wheeling her horse once again, she raced off, Jamie and Brett in close pursuit.

Suddenly, Isabel's horse screamed and fell to the ground with a sickening thud, legs thrashing. Isabel rolled and was on her feet before she quite knew what she was about. She stared at the horse writhing on the ground.

Jamie and Brett had pulled to a stop and quickly joined her.

"She caught her leg in a rabbit hole," Isabel said, drawing her pistol. "It's broken."

145

Without another word, she place the muzzle to the poor beast's head, closed her eyes, and pulled the trigger. All was silence.

"Quickly, Isabel, behind me!" Brett said, holding out his hand.

She grasped it and swung up behind him. Wrapping her arms around his waist, they were off.

"We've come too far, Brett," Isabel said as they sped over fallow ground. "Your horse cannot carry two for long."

"I know it," said Brett. "We have another five miles to Barnaldswick, where we might be able to hide. He will have to do until then."

The sun had abandoned them long ago. They entered into a new park that made the night even darker.

"I hear them," Jamie panted.

"Yes, they make enough noise," Brett said. "We won't be under any illusions as to their proximity."

"Brett," Isabel said reasonably, "if you leave me here, I can easily hide and fend for myself and you can get Jamie to Barnaldswick."

"Do not even think it."

"But—"

Grim was not an adequate description for the set of the earl's jaw. "If you even try to get off this horse, I will bind and gag you and throw you over his withers. Is that clear?"

"Yes, my lord," Isabel muttered.

They came out of the woods and onto a road, their horses lathered and already blowing. Brett leading the way, they galloped down the rutted path, across a wooden bridge, and into the tiny village of Barnaldswick.

"Off your horse, Jamie, and set it free!" Brett cried as he and Isabel slid from his exhausted gelding.

Slapping them, they set their horses down the main street of Barnaldswick at a run.

"What now?" Isabel said.

"We hide," said Brett.

"But where?" Jamie cried.

The sound of six horses pounding across the wooden bridge left no opportunity for reply.

Brett, catching Isabel's hand in his, set off at a run.

"Split up! Mort and Charlie, check the livery. Sam and Bill, check the inn. We'll search the main street. Look sharp now; we've got 'em!"

Brett, Isabel's hand still clasped in his, and Jamie moved stealthily down the wooden sidewalk, turning quickly from the main street into an alley, and from thence to a side street. Behind them they heard the heavy, rough breathing of two men.

They looked wildly around. There was nowhere to hide.

"On your hands and knees, Jamie," the earl commanded.

"What?!" Jamie gasped, and was roughly shoved to the ground.

Brett shook out his cloak and sat on Jamie, the cloak making it seem as if he were seated on a tree stump rather than a stunned youth. In the dark of the unlighted street, he quickly pulled Isabel onto his lap. He drew the cloak around her and with it his arms. In the next moment, he kissed her.

Isabel's "Yip!" of surprise became a soft moan as Brett's mouth moved hungrily over hers. She had kissed men before—strictly in the line of duty, Monty's duty—but never had she felt this inferno that roared through her, burning away all thought, all sense of danger. Her arms, of their own accord, wrapped around the earl's neck as she returned his kiss with equal hunger, luxuriating in the fire he had ignited. *"Yes,"* she said to herself over and over again. This was what she had wanted for so long.

In the next moment, a large hand gripped her shoulder and roughly shook her. Dazed, Isabel pulled away from Brett and stared up into a surprisingly ugly face covered with sweat. The red coat was a shock.

"Have you seen a boy and two men come this way?" he demanded.

She took a gulp of air. "Canna tha' see we're busy?" she retorted in a broad Yorkshire accent.

"Get tha' hand off her," Brett said in a similarly rough accent. "Tha'rt a cheeky beggar to go maulin' my girl. Shove off!"

The interrogator growled, but he shoved off.

Brett and Isabel watched them go, and only when they were fully out of sight did Isabel scamper off Brett's lap. Jamie, still beneath the earl, began to shake and choke with laughter.

"Get off!" he gasped. "You weigh a ton!"

Brett got off. "My apologies, young sir."

For her part, Isabel was grateful for the darkness of the night that hid a blush of monumental proportions that heated her from head to toe. Her heart was thundering as she looked up at Brett. She was certain the whole town must hear it. It was only when his eyes met hers that she quickly looked away.

"They've already searched the livery stable," she said breathlessly. "I suggest we hide there."

"Agreed," said Brett.

Moving cautiously, edging along the sides of the few buildings they passed, they crept into the livery and were glad to find no livery man, no stable boy, just one ancient, swaybacked horse and a good deal of dusty hay.

"I will survey the terrain," Jamie said, and began to thoroughly and methodically search the stable, pistol at the ready.

"I think we've eluded them for now," Brett said stiffly, not looking at Isabel.

She didn't know where to look or how to contend with the sudden pain stabbing through her. How could he be so indifferent? He had kissed her as if . . . as if he had meant it. Tears started into her eyes and she hurriedly blinked them back. "You should *not* have kissed me, Brett!"

"Desperate situations call for desperate means," he replied testily.

"You are a man of some intelligence," Isabel snapped, taking refuge in anger. "I trust you will find some other *means* if any further desperate situations arise."

"Yes, of course," Brett said, moving another step away from her. "I apologize for so rash an act. It shan't happen again, I assure you."

The anger drained out of her. She knew only pain and embarrassment as Jamie hurried up to them.

"It's all clear," he said. "I suggest we hide in the loft. We don't want anyone stumbling in upon us by accident."

Isabel led them up the ladder, Jamie followed, and Brett stayed below.

"I think I shall play the scout," he said. "We must know what we're up against."

"Brett!" Isabel hissed. "Don't be a fool! They may find you."

"Yes, but they're looking for three, not for one. And they're looking for Jamie. I can hardly be considered a stripling. And I lack the Shipley nose. I am armed. I shall be careful; be at ease." He slipped silently out of the stable.

"Idiotish, muttonheaded *dolt*," Isabel muttered. She began to plump hay together in the outlines of a bed, sneezing violently as dust billowed around her.

Half an hour later, the Earl of Northbridge slipped quietly back into the stable. " 'Tis me," he called softly.

"I know," was Jamie's equally soft reply. "If it hadn't been, you'd have a bullet between your eyes."

"Oh my." Brett climbed up the rough ladder, somewhat impeded by a plump burlap sack. Reaching the hayloft, he found Jamie seated near the ladder, a pistol resting in his lap. Isabel was sleeping on the opposite side of the ladder, her pistol at her fingertips.

"What's all this?" whispered Jamie.

Brett tossed him the burlap sack. "Here, puppy, your newest role. I am sorry to inform you that you've come down in the world. You shall be a tenant farmer's son."

Jamie wrinkled his nose as he pulled the clothes from the

sack. "I don't mind being a farmer's son. But surely, sir, wouldn't I be a farmer's son with better taste?"

Brett chuckled. "It was all I could find, I'm afraid. Barnaldswick is not a wealthy town."

"Oh la, sir, beggars can't be choosers. These will do very well. Thank you. You are quick on your feet."

"Coming from you, young James, that is high praise indeed."

Jamie grinned at him. "What news?"

"The supposed militiamen have all ridden on," Brett replied quietly as he sat down beside him, "after knocking on every door in town. They are convinced that we only passed through Barnaldswick and did not stop."

"Thank God for that."

"Yes. They'll find our horses soon enough and assume we've continued on foot. They should be spending a fruitless night searching the country for us. I think that we may rest tolerably well tonight. You go ahead and sleep; I'll stand watch."

"Of course you will," Jamie retorted as they both began to change into their new clothes. "Isabel and I had already agreed that since you were so singularly foolish to rush out after my uncle's men, you should stand the first watch if you made it back alive and relatively unscathed. We'll take turns so that we all get some sleep. And don't you dare try to coddle Isabel. She insists on pulling her fair share. Besides, she can sleep through the noisiest battle—and has—but she wakes up on the stroke of the hour she agreed to."

"You love her very much, don't you?"

Jamie's expression softened as it always did when he spoke of Isabel. "How can I not? She has been friend, sister, and mother to me."

"And now protector."

"Yes," said Jamie. "Monty chose well."

"I hope you *are* the true heir."

Jamie cocked his head. "Do you? Why?"

Brett smiled. "I've developed a liking for your rag manners and the way you speak of Monty."

"And how do I speak of him?"

"With unqualified love and admiration. I believe Monty to have been deserving of both."

"He was and is, sir," Jamie said quietly. "On my honor."

He stood up, walked across the loft, plumped a bit of hay, sneezed once, and lay down. He pulled his coat over himself and within a minute was soundly asleep.

Brett gazed at the slumbering youth. Never had he wanted anything so much as for this boy to be James Shipley. And if he was not? "Pray God it will not come to that," he murmured.

Reluctantly he turned to gaze at Isabel sleeping so near him. A quizzical smile touched his lips. Indeed, for the whole of his watch he found it difficult to fulfill his assignment—watching the town from the livery window—when she slept so peacefully just a few feet away.

He pulled off his cloak and gently settled it over her. She sighed contentedly in her sleep. Smiling, Brett reached a hand out to brush a wisp of hair from her cheek, then froze.

What was wrong with him? He sank back into the straw with a groan. This unattached and unprotected young woman was in his care! Every sensibility should be outraged! He glanced at her again and groaned once more.

She looked no more than twenty, sleeping there as if she hadn't a care in the world. That she had endured every danger, every pain, every discomfort on this journey without a word of complaint told him much of the life she had led and the woman it had made her. That the love and devotion she felt for Jamie had never wavered during costume changes, adventures, and danger also told him much.

This love that Isabel and Jamie felt for each other, this loyalty they expressed, was oddly affecting for the earl. He had never known the closeness they shared. He had never seen it in anyone before. Or perhaps his eyes had not been opened enough to see it before.

151

For the first time in his thirty-five years, the Earl of North-bridge felt envy and was even, he realized with a start, a little jealous of Jamie! *He* had Isabel's love, while the earl was blessed with her suspicions, her sharp tongue, and her rapier wit. What he wanted . . .

Brett bitterly damned himself for a fool and turned to stare out the livery window. What was wrong with him? Who was this man dressed in shabby clothes, seated in a dusty old livery far from the comforts of his valet and chef? How could he be thinking of the pleasures of Isabel's company, rather than of his duty to her as a gentleman? *Why* could he still feel her sweet mouth on his?

What had happened to him? For years his every thought and action had been centered around his position in society, but now something had shifted him. The familiar boundaries he had long cherished were gone. That God Duty he had always depended upon was fading rapidly. His world seemed without form. He could not find himself in it any longer.

All the old reassuring words he had used to define himself the whole of his life seemed empty and meaningless now. Had they been a sham? They had certainly kept him safe from these wayward thoughts and a host of emotions that would not let him be. He couldn't seem to stop *feeling*. Would Ravenscourt put an end to this heretofore unknown problem? Would he re-turn to himself once he was home, or was he returning to him-self now?

With a start, he heard the church clock tower at the opposite end of town faintly toll the hour and realized that somehow three hours had passed. He watched in some amusement as Isabel's eyes flew open. She sat up with every semblance of being wholly alert.

"Good evening," he said gravely.

"Good evening, sir," she replied with equal composure. But then, she had not had any nightmares. She glanced with sur-prise at the cloak that covered her. He thought she blushed but couldn't be certain in the dim light. "Thank you."

"You're quite welcome."

She stood up and stretched and pulled a few wisps of straw from her black hair, avoiding his gaze all the while, her body stiff, her manner cool. Then she noticed the change in Brett's habiliment. "Have you been struck with poverty since we last met?" she inquired.

"Having apprenticed with two masters of disguise, I thought I would add my poor mite. Here you are," Brett said, handing her the now far less plump burlap sack.

"What's all this?"

"Your new raiment, my lady. I'm afraid I could find you nought but women's clothes, and rough women's clothes at that."

Isabel shook her new wardrobe from the sack and looked it over with a practiced eye. "Oh, these will do very well, sir. I commend you. For a gentleman who has such an aversion to masquerade, you have taken to it admirably."

Brett hung his head. "I have been corrupted."

Isabel smiled for the first time since they had entered Barnaldswick. "You certainly look very different from when we first met."

"It seems like eight years ago, rather than eight days, doesn't it?"

"Yes," Isabel replied, not quite meeting his eyes. "Much has happened."

"Certainly more than I ever expected." He paused a moment. "Am I a cold man, do you think, Isabel?"

Her eyes flew to his. "Oh no, sir! Not at all! You have a large heart and a warm regard for those near to you."

"Have I?" Brett said, flushing with unexpected pleasure. "My family would not agree with you, I think."

"That is only because you have sat in your stately home as the Earl of Northbridge, rather than tramping the road with them as Brett Avery. You've the love of adventure in you, my lord. You just never had the opportunity to express it before."

"I thought I loved a steady, quiet life."

"You were wrong."

The earl was startled into a laugh. "Are you never shy about expressing your opinions?"

"Occasionally, sir. At least those opinions that are not fit for public communication."

The earl considered her a moment and knew some satisfaction when she looked away. "I think you have too many secrets, Isabel."

"That is only because they put you at a disadvantage and that is something you are not used to," she tartly replied.

"I do like to be in charge."

"So I've noticed."

Brett found himself smiling. "Have you never considered even *trying* to flatter me?"

"When your worth is apparent to all? It would be redundant of me."

The earl stared up at her, seeking something unknown even to him in her gray eyes. "What? Do you value me, Isabel?"

"Why certainly, sir!" she said lightly. "You make an excellent bravo."

This was not what the earl had hoped for.

"You also make a most impressive farmer," Isabel continued, looking him up and down, "albeit one just ending a sudden growth spurt." His shirtsleeves reached only the middle of his forearms. His trousers came only to midcalf. To avoid strangulation, he had had to leave the top four buttons of his shirt undone. "Will not the former owners of these habiliments find their loss a grievous blow?"

"I left them enough guineas to fit up a new wardrobe."

"I might have trusted to your honesty and generosity. 'Tis a pity about the dress, but for a dress it's not too bad." She cast him a frosty glance. "You were never happy with me as a boy."

"No, the woman is far more admirable. I'm afraid I could find you no shoes," he blithely continued in the teeth of her rosy blush. "You will have to remain in the boots."

"Hm," said Isabel gazing at her feet. "Hessians don't quite suit the gown, do you think, sir?"

"Not quite, no. You will have to renovate them, I'm afraid, to make them more suitable to your new situation in life."

"Alas, my poor Hessians. I loved them, Brett. I loved them well."

The earl laughed.

"Well," Isabel said, seeming a trifle distracted, "enough of this pleasant chatter. It is my watch, I believe."

"I am not at all tired," Brett replied. "Why don't you get what rest you can? I'll stand the watch."

Isabel, arms akimbo, looked derisively down at him. "A fat lot of good you'd be to us half dead from lack of sleep. It is *my* watch, Brett."

How could any woman look so magnificent in such decayed surroundings? "You've a touch of the duchess about you, you know."

"I wouldn't know," said Isabel. "Unlike you, I do not usually associate with the *haut* ton, and count myself lucky, I can tell you."

"There's a rapper if ever I heard one," Brett riposted. "According to your own stories, you've associated with every titled man, woman, and child in Europe—if they had enough money to catch Monty's interest!"

Isabel's smile was sheepish. "Well, perhaps a few," she conceded. "To your bed, Brett."

"But I am not tired."

"Piffle!"

The earl's eyebrows shot up at this. "I beg your pardon?"

Isabel sighed heavily. "When will you learn that that lord-of-the-manor tone makes no impression on me? To sleep, man, or," she said, raising the butt of her pistol with bloodcurdling intent, "I shall assist you."

"Oh, very well," Brett said. "Goodnight . . . my lady." He moved to where Jamie was resting, plumped a bit of hay, lay down, and, somewhat to his chagrin, found himself falling asleep within five minutes.

Grateful to escape the earl's further scrutiny—if only she would not keep reliving his kiss!—Isabel changed into her new clothes and then arranged herself near the tiny window overlooking the main street. She surveyed the scene carefully. The moon was still obscured by clouds, but she could see the shapes of the other buildings and the street below. Nothing was stirring, not even a stray dog looking for scraps. It was not long before she found her gaze turning again and again to the handsome features of the Earl of Northbridge.

His suspicion, sardonic humor, and tyrannical manner were abandoned in sleep; the gentleness he had periodically extended to her throughout their journey was revealed now for anyone to see. Perhaps she had wronged him earlier. Perhaps he had avoided her after their kiss because he had embarrassed himself with his impropriety. Perhaps she had attached too much import to both the kiss and his subsequent coolness.

It seemed she could no longer feel anything harsh toward the Earl of Northbridge, or at least she could not maintain it for more than a few minutes. She didn't have to look far to find the reason why. She had never had a close friend before, but somehow, without her looking, and for all his outraged posturings, Brett had become her friend. Her first friend—despite the danger and his continuing suspicion—her friend.

She felt the iron bands that had so long constricted her heart loosen. She sighed with contentment. She had the most insane longing to confide every secret to Brett. She wished he were awake so they could banter together. She had laughed more in one week with Brett than she had the whole of last year. How gratifying to have reclaimed the respect he had first given to Jack Cavendish. How satisfying to savor the peace and safety she knew simply by being in his company. It mattered not that Horace Shipley wanted them dead or that a hangman's noose awaited her. In Brett's company she had discovered a safe harbor. How ironic! She had always thought she'd find the

156

safe harbor she longed for in a place—a country, a town, a house—and instead it reposed in the tall, muscular frame of a golden elf king.

And what had she found in the kiss that still burned on her mouth?

It took a moment for her lungs to reclaim some badly needed oxygen. Her hands flew to her burning cheeks.

Oh God, she loved Brett! He was still suspicious of her. He still doubted Jamie . . . and it didn't matter! She, at seven-and-twenty, she who had never considered marriage, she who knew at firsthand the selfishness, insincerity, and cruelty of men, had in only a week tumbled irrevocably into love with a man! And not just any man. She loved the great, the proper, the duty-bound Earl of Northbridge!

"Oh, this cannot be! It must not be so!" she said violently. But her heart, as she gazed upon his face, gave the lie to such determination. She longed to sleep beside him, enfolded in his arms. She wanted to spend the rest of her life bringing laughter and happiness into his. She wanted to feel his mouth pressed hungrily to hers every day and every night.

She loved the man.

Isabel could conceive of no greater evil befalling her. Not a wisp of a dream of future happiness entered her head. As there was no possibility of uniting a nobleman with a murderess, she thought not of a possible future with the man she so foolishly loved but only of how she could conceal this disastrous weakness from its creator.

Dissimulation was to be her watchword. She would continue as she had done thus far and escape the earl's company at the first opportunity. Her breath caught at the thought and she shuddered slightly. Soon, if she was able to get Jamie safely to Thornwynd, she would lose not only the boy she loved and had helped to raise but the man she now hopelessly and passionately desired and loved. To lose one was bad enough; to lose both seemed impossible to her.

"But I must not think of that," Isabel said to herself.

"Perhaps I shall be killed by Horace's men or arrested at Jonas Babcock's behest, and that will set everything right."

With this rather grim note of hope, she resumed her survey of the street, though her thoughts were of the man with the expressive blue eyes, infectious laughter, and gentle smile lying just behind her. Her traitorous thoughts kept placing her beside him, his arms enfolding her, his heart beating against hers, his lips warming her own.

*

Chapter 11

May 12, 1804   Early morning

Barnaldswick, Yorkshire

BEFORE DAWN HAD broken, Brett, Isabel, and Jamie had slipped out of the stable. Moving cautiously through the town, they searched in vain for three horses of reasonable composition that they might borrow, leaving behind a suitable sum to be found and understood by the owners. Alas, it was a small, poor village and they found nothing.

"So, we are to tramp the highway," said Jamie.

"Tramp?" Brett gasped. "But walking in these clothes, people will think we're . . . we're . . ."

"Vagrants?" Isabel inquired. "It won't be the first time . . . for some of us."

She burst into a hiking song that made the earl groan and Jamie smile as they proceeded afoot. The day was bereft of clouds and unseasonably warm. The trio, lacking both food and water, keenly felt these deprivations as the May sun rose higher and higher in the sky. The rutted, marshy road toward Slaidburn climbed relentlessly uphill through the West Riding. The three, after a few hours, abandoned conversation to the weary task of putting one foot in front of the other and keeping dried throats from becoming parched. They shied like skittish horses at the sound of any rider or cart but found to their vast relief that all passed them by with either a cheerful doff of the hat or a cold scrutiny that clearly told them they were not fit to be traveling on the same road with a well-mounted gentleman or a fashionable family in an equally fashionable barouche.

This was yet another new experience to add to the long list the earl had begun upon entering Isabel and Jamie's company. He had known only admiring or deferential or flirtatious glances in his life. To be treated like a common and despised vagabond cast him into the larger pool of humanity, and he found it most discomfitting—and instructive.

Just after eleven o'clock, a farmer driving a team of huge drays was passing them and inquired if they might like to ride rather than walk. They accepted his hospitality with alacrity and, with many a heartfelt sigh, settled themselves in his wagon. Though they jounced and bounced and tumbled about a bit in the back of this rustic vehicle, their feet were exceedingly grateful for such kindness.

Brett took up the lion's share of the conversation with the farmer, blaming their misfortunes to a lame team and an uncle in Slaidburn who had commanded their presence, for though they were poor, he was considerably well off and it behooved them to make every sacrifice to attend him whenever he requested.

The earl scarcely noticed how easily the lie came to his lips.

He and the farmer proceeded to discuss the weather, the crops, the war, the high prices, the shocking reports of aristocratic high jinks that filtered up from London, and various other matters. Isabel and Jamie remained quiet—an unusual occurrence. Brett glanced back to find Jamie indulging himself in a nap while Isabel's gray eyes carefully averted his gaze, as they had done all day.

They reached Slaidburn an hour later. They bid their substitute coachman a fond and grateful adieu, the earl noting that Isabel took care to leave behind several guineas in the wagon as token of their thanks.

Then they began to search out Dawkins. This was not easily accomplished, for the town was large and Dawkins, a cagey

160

customer, had hidden himself well. It required almost an hour's search before he was discovered comfortably installed at the Golden Scythe, a tavern of dubious reputation. He welcomed them heartily to his table, loudly called for drinks all around, and then addressed Brett in a hushed voice.

"On your guard, sir. There was a troop of militia in town this morning. If they were militia. Which I doubt."

Brett swore under his breath. "We must avoid the main road if we can. Can you find your way through the West Riding, Dawkins?"

"Why, blindfolded, sir!"

Brett grinned and was forestalled from disputing so rash a claim, for their drinks came and with them lunch. They all fell upon the feast with an appetite that assured the tavern a good profit that day.

Less than an hour later they rose, paid for their fare, and hurried to the livery where Dawkins had hidden the Beaufort carriage and team. Not even taking time to change from their rough garments into the clothes Dawkins had saved for them, they bundled into the carriage and were off.

Dawkins could not drive quickly, for the road he chose was rough and required all his concentration and skill. The tension of his passengers increased with each passing hour, for such slow travel left them vulnerable when the supposed militia was combing the shire, every road, every hamlet. The sun began to set over the western horizon before them.

"I still say," said Jamie, continuing an argument of some hours' duration, "that we would all be much safer if we split up here, went out on horseback, and met at Ravenscourt."

"No," said Isabel firmly. "Monty consigned you to my care, and in my care you shall remain."

"Ditto," said Brett.

"But hang it," said Jamie, "they know we're three! They know that we have used disguises. We're found out. How can we be safe together?"

161

"Who ever said we would be safe?" Isabel inquired. "Danger was apparent from the beginning."

The carriage lurched to an abrupt halt with such force that Isabel was thrown into Brett's arms, a most pleasurable experience for his lordship until she begged his pardon and drew her pistol. It took a moment for Brett to realize that the pistol was not meant for him. He might have known some relief had he not heard shouts and the gruff orders to Dawkins to keep his team still or suffer a bullet through his heart.

"What's the to-do?" Isabel whispered.

"A robbery?" said Jamie.

"No," Brett grimly replied. "It is a search of all travelers on this road in the name of the king. I recognize that voice. It is the militia, or I should say, the show of one."

"You there, in the coach. Come out with your hands raised. In the name of the king!"

Brett glanced at his calm companions, opened the carriage door, and stepped down to the road, his arms raised as commanded, his swift gaze taking in the six men in red coats, armed and on horseback. Two guns were trained on Dawkins, who glowered at the men with undisguised venom. Three guns were pointed at Brett and now at Isabel as she slowly emerged. Finally Jamie stepped down.

"You led us on a merry chase, my lord Earl," the lieutenant sneered. "But you'll not escape us again. That's the lad that brings the gold," he said, pointing his gun at Jamie. "Tie him up, boys."

"What about the other two?" asked his sergeant.

"What do you think?" their leader demanded harshly.

"But that one's an earl!" one of the men protested.

"They bleed just as easily as the next man," the lieutenant declared.

While he and the sergeant kept their pistols trained on Isabel and Brett, two of his men jumped from their horses and advanced on Jamie, ropes in hand, delighted smiles crinkling their faces, for they were about to become rich men.

162

But when they came within a foot of Jamie, he suddenly leapt forward in a furious missile, knocking them both to the ground as Isabel dived to one side and fired her pistol from a front pocket of her dress. The bullet spattered into the dirt before the hooves of the horses belonging to the two men guarding Dawkins. The horses promptly screamed and reared.

Dawkins needed no prompting. He slashed his whip at his team and drove them straight at the two red-coated henchmen.

Infuriated by this unexpected trouble, the lieutenant raised his gun and fired just as Brett threw himself at his horse, causing the animal to rear and unseat his rider. The earl could not see Isabel or Jamie or the other men. There was only this murderous lieutenant.

Brett dragged the lieutenant to his feet and hammered at him, relishing the contact of his fists against flesh and muscle and bone. Then his stomach turned over as he heard several shots behind him and sharp human cries.

"Jamie!" Isabel screamed just at Brett rendered the lieutenant unconscious.

He turned to find Jamie slipping to the ground, blood spreading across his shirt.

Brett knew terror for the first time in his life.

Two of the shots had felled two of their opponents, both of whom had been advancing on Jamie. They were not dead, but they were most decidedly out of the fight. Isabel, an opponent's sword in her hand, was fighting off the sergeant while Jamie, white and bloodied, groped for and found his second pistol just as the sixth brigand raised his sword and began to drive it home. Jamie fired. His assailant fell back, stunned, gasping, and dead before he hit the ground.

Isabel furiously slashed and lunged at her opponent, drawing blood again and again until the sergeant dropped his sword, turned tail, and ran . . . straight into Brett, who rammed his fist into the man's face as if he would drive it through his skull. The man dropped like a stone.

Brett looked quickly around and saw that Dawkins now held a shotgun on the two men left standing.

"Jamie!" Isabel cried, tossing her sword aside as she ran to the boy.

" 'Tis not mortal, I assure you," he gasped, leaning against the rear wheel of the chaise.

Isabel said nothing as she drew her knife from her boot and quickly cut away his shirt. She gazed at the blood pouring freely from his shoulder.

Brett ripped the shirt off an unconscious henchman and handed it to her.

"Thank you," she said, not looking up.

She wiped enough blood away so they could both see clearly the ugly hole in Jamie's white shoulder. Quickly she pressed against the flow of blood, Jamie groaning at the contact. She pulled him against her a little bit and pressed more cloth to the exit wound in his back.

"Well, child," she said, her voice shaking only slightly, "it looks like the bullet missed the bone entirely and went clean through. You'll live."

"Yes, but do I want to?" Jamie moaned.

Brett smiled as he began to rummage through his portmanteau tied to the back of the chaise. Was there anyone in England who could match this pair?

"How bad is it?" Isabel asked.

"Well," Jamie managed, "it's not as bad as sailing the North Sea."

"Oh, well, I won't worry about it, then."

Jamie laughed, his face contorting with pain at this sudden movement. "Goose!" he gasped. "You will worry about it six months after it's healed."

"Yes, of course I will," she said. "I'm your protector, aren't I?"

Brett knelt at Isabel's side and silently handed her a flask for Jamie, a canteen of water for her to clean his shoulder, and several of his own silk shirts to staunch and bind the wound.

With practiced skill and speed she cleaned away the blood,

pulled the flask from Jamie's lips, and, with a stony face, poured half the contents into the wound. As it was brandy, Jamie shrieked with abandon. Isabel's face convulsed for only a moment before she handed him back the flask, and while he drank eagerly, she quickly staunched and bandaged his wound, using a ripped square from one of Brett's white silk shirts as a sling.

Seeing that she had things well in hand, and suspecting the curt set-down he would receive if he tried to intervene, Brett went to examine the six men who had pursued them so relentlessly. One was dead, two unconscious, the others under Dawkins's guard. Using the ropes their attackers had intended for Jamie, he knew a deep satisfaction as he tied up the five left living in painful knots.

Then, talking softly, he was able to gather three of the horses that had scampered off during the battle. The other three, it seemed, had more sense than to stand around watching people try to kill each other. They had emigrated to more hospitable climes.

"I require your help, Brett," said Isabel.

He quickly tied the horses to the back of the chaise and strode to her side. Together they raised Jamie to his feet and helped him into the carriage. He sank gratefully against the cushions while Isabel and Brett and Dawkins held a council of war at the door.

"Very well," Brett began, "is this the end of our troubles or a turn for the worse?"

"Surely Horace's pockets are not so deep that he can hire more men to pursue us?" Isabel said.

Brett was silent as he considered the possibility of other dangers on their road.

"What's come before will come again," Dawkins bleakly prophesied. "We'd best keep our powder dry and hope for the best."

"Wise counsel, Dawkins," Isabel said with a fond smile at the dour coachman.

"Very well," Brett said, "we've got weapons, saddle horses, a carriage, and our own wits to sustain us. We may see Ravenscourt yet."

"We must continue to rely on Dawkins's capable service for now," Isabel cautioned. "If we put Jamie on horseback, the wound will continue to bleed. He could die."

"Agreed," said Brett, studying the road before them. The sun had set. The moon had not yet risen. "We've little choice. We must keep driving. There will be no stops. I doubt if there is even a safe farmhouse between here and Ravenscourt."

"Agreed," said Isabel. "Dawkins, we are in your care."

She climbed into the carriage. Brett followed. Gently, Isabel sat down beside Jamie and, with but a little urging, got him to lie with his head in her lap. He was soon asleep. Isabel stared at the blood that stained her clothes; traces of it were still on her hands. She looked up at Brett.

"That was a trifle too close for comfort," she said composedly.

"Yes," he said. " 'Tis a pity Jamie was forced to kill one of them."

"A pity?" Isabel gasped. "They meant our deaths!"

"Yes, but it is impolitic to leave corpses along the road," Brett pointed out, "particularly when we are already unpopular with some representatives of the law. Now we may have the *real* militia pursuing us, or at least every sheriff within a hundred miles looking for us on charges of murder. It was a spot of bad luck; there's no two ways about it. We've got nearly two days between us and Ravenscourt if we continue at this pace."

"Much can happen in two days," Isabel said soberly. "Much has happened already."

"Yes," said Brett. "If we can get through the rest of tonight and tomorrow alive, we'll have to put Jamie on horseback. I have the most uncomfortable feeling that the closer we get to Ravenscourt, the more our danger increases. That Jamie should nearly be killed . . . You were not hurt in our skirmish, Isabel?"

"No, my lord. The blood is all Jamie's, not mine. And you?"

Brett's mouth tightened into a grim line. "Unscathed, though I have discovered that I am not at all the gentleman I thought myself. The blood lust was in me. I wanted only to kill those men."

Isabel's eyes locked on his for the first time that day. "I very much fear, Brett, that you will have ample opportunity to do so . . . however impolitic it may be."

Chapter 12

May 13, 1804   Early morning

Between Barnaldswick and Marsdon,
West Riding, Yorkshire

WITH THE DAWN, which colored the clouds pink, Brett ordered
Dawkins to stop. While Jamie slept, Isabel and he descended
the carriage.

"It is time for me to undertake a new role," Brett said. "That
of coachman."

"Sir?" his retainer said, bristling.

"Dawkins, I want you to take one of the saddle horses and
ride ahead on the road as a scout. We need someone to give us
warning of any further danger awaiting us. We cannot keep
running into trouble at our enemies' whim."

"Very good, sir," said the coachman, jumping to the ground.

"You will be careful, Dawkins," Isabel said.

He flushed at her concern. "Yes, miss."

"And *you* will forbear tossing us into a ditch," she archly instructed the earl.

"I am known," said Brett in mock outrage, "for the best pair
of hands in the ton!"

"Can a man of such respectability be a noted whip as well?"

Brett smiled. His finger brushed against her cheek for a moment. "I can be whatever it is you need me to be, Isabel," he
replied. Then he turned and climbed onto the box.

Isabel, heart hammering painfully in her breast, climbed back into the carriage.

She sat gazing at the slumbering Jamie a moment and then, with an angry shake of her head, pulled herself from her reverie. Scavenging through her valise, she pulled off her bloodstained clothes and replaced them with buckskins, shirt, and riding coat, pulling her black hair severely from her face and tying it behind her with a blue ribbon. Her Hessians, though disreputable in appearance, were still in good enough condition to carry her into Lancashire. She cared not about disguise; there was little reason to hope that any disguise would succeed now. She thought only of traveling in comfort and ease. They would be riding soon.

She stuffed her bloodied clothes into the valise. It was then that the morning sunlight glinted on Brett's signet ring on her left hand, recalling it to her consciousness. Once again. She should have returned it to the earl long before this, but she kept pretending she had forgotten it was on her hand . . . because she could not part with it. Not yet.

It was odd. She had never thought to wear a man's ring. She had never thought she would want to lean on a man, to trust him. She had long believed that her history had denied her such pleasures, such luxuries. But then, she had never had to reckon with the temptation of Brett Avery before.

They continued to drive for another two hours. The morning sun, moving in and out of the clouds, was not too hot. Suddenly Brett pulled the team to a stop. Instantly Jamie was awake, groping for his gun. Isabel already had her pistol in hand. She lifted the trap.

"Brett?"

"Be at ease. It is Dawkins returning."

Jamie and Isabel released equal sighs of relief. Isabel climbed down from the carriage, pistol still in hand, just in case.

Dawkins was nearly as lathered as his horse as he rode up to them. "It's bad, sir," he said without preamble. "Very bad. There's a barricade just outside of Marsdon. Sheriff Horton and a good dozen so-called deputies are searching every carriage. They say they're looking for the ringleaders of a band of Luddites that tried to incite rebellion in Oldcotes. But I noticed they were only interested in the striplings. They'll stop us, sir. They'll search us. They won't hesitate to take Master James."

"So Horton is a hired hand, eh?" said Brett calmly. "An interesting piece of information. I had not known it."

"We cannot remain with the carriage, Brett," said Isabel, gnawing on her lower lip.

"No," he said, turning to her with that gentle smile that always reassured her, no matter the trouble. "I'm sorry, Isabel. Jamie cannot have even this day to recover. He will have to ride."

"And I shall," said Jamie, stepping out of the carriage. He was a trifle pale but steady on his feet. "I am not some baby you must wrap in cotton wool, Isabel. I shall do very well."

"You have always done very well, Jamie," said Isabel with a fond smile. "But don't push yourself."

"I mean to push myself only as far as Thornwynd, and then I shall sleep a hundred years."

"We will change places, Dawkins," Brett said, jumping down from the box. "We shall not see each other for a few days, I think. I want you to drive to Ravenscourt. We know not what path we will take, so you cannot meet us again. But some precautions may still be taken. Alert the Ravenscourt staff. Mason should be of some help. See if you can organize a cordon of safety. At this point, I wouldn't be surprised if someone tried to attack us in my own house."

"I'd like to stay with you, sir," said Dawkins. "Four guns are better than three."

"No, Dawkins. I won't have you risking your life in this matter any further. You've done more than any man could expect. You will obey me. Drive to Ravenscourt and raise the alarm."

"Very good, sir," Dawkins said stonily.

"Dawkins," said Isabel, placing a hand on his arm, "I am

grateful for everything you have done for us." She kissed his grizzled cheek.

"It's been a pleasure, miss," Dawkins said gruffly, flushing up to his scalp, "and an honor knowing you."

"Thank you, Dawkins."

"And you, young whelp," said the coachman to Jamie, "don't you go putting yourself in front of any more bullets, do you hear?"

"Your sage advice speaks to my heart, good Dawkins," said Jamie. "I shall avoid bullets as I would avoid my Uncle Horace."

With a nod Dawkins climbed onto the box. Brett stepped up to him, keeping his voice low.

"I have one more job for you, Dawkins. I want you to find what connection exists between Isabel, Yorkshire, and Jonas Babcock. Ask Sir Henry Bevins for help. Look for something that happened ten to fifteen years ago. I'll need that information the instant I arrive at Ravenscourt."

"I don't like spying on the young lady," Dawkins said squarely. "She's a good 'un."

"I do not want your opinion, only as much information as you can gather by the seventeenth," Brett said icily.

"It ain't right, my lord, and it ain't like you."

"You have your orders, Dawkins. Drive on."

The dour coachman glowered at his master for a moment and then set the team off at a trot.

Isabel took Dawkins's horse before Brett could argue with her. Brett led the two other saddle horses up to Jamie. Disdaining any aid, Jamie climbed into the saddle with surprising ease. Brett quickly followed his example.

"Now that we are on horseback," he said, "it will be safer to travel at night, I think. So the first order of business is to find a good place to hide."

"The Forest of Bowland has succored the occasional bandit, or so I've heard," said Isabel.

"An excellent suggestion," Brett said. "You know this

171

country well it seems, my mysterious expatriate. The forest is west of us by about ten miles and well on our way to Ravenscourt."

"We are off then," said Jamie.

Though billowy clouds obscured the sun now and then, and a soft breeze blew the perspiration from their brows, the day was still warm and Jamie still weak from loss of blood. They had to move slowly. Jamie slumped more and more in his saddle as the first hour passed and then the second. Isabel rode beside him and casually began to talk of their adventures on the Continent to distract him from the pain and his weakness and the sun.

Just as Jamie began to privately believe he could go no farther, they entered the cool shade of the Forest of Bowland single file: Brett, in the lead, scanned each tree and shrub in case their enemies were hiding there; Isabel, bringing up the rear, carefully ascertained that they were not followed; while Jamie, between them, concentrated solely on staying in his saddle.

They continued for nearly half a mile before Brett found a shady glade with thick soft grass on which Jamie might lie. This Jamie felt fully capable of doing. Getting out of the saddle, however, was another matter entirely. Dimly he was aware that someone stood at his side.

"It's all right, lad, I've got you," he said.

Trusting that voice, Jamie let go and slipped unconscious down into Brett's arms. The earl caught him easily and gently laid him down.

Isabel knelt quickly beside him and removed Jamie's sling and bandage. "It's as I feared," she said. "The wound has opened again."

"Take this canteen. I'll see if I can find some more water," Brett said as he lifted an empty canteen from his saddle.

Working quietly, Isabel put a new dressing and bandage on Jamie's left shoulder, created a fresh sling for his arm, and frowned slightly as her hand felt his warm forehead. Her fingers checked his pulse and found it a trifle rapid. Brett came silently up behind her.

"How is he?"

She sat back on her heels, badly worried and trying not to show it. "Not very well, Brett. He can't travel anymore today, and by that I mean he cannot travel tonight."

"We must camp, then," Brett said, handing her the now full second canteen, "and this is not the place to do it. It's too exposed. I'll find us a safer hiding place."

That brought Isabel's head up. "Brett?"

He stopped and looked down at her. "I found evidence that others have been here before us. Several horses, maybe five, six. The prints were blurred. They passed recently. Within the last twelve hours, I'd say."

"The Forest of Bowland is not safe, then," Isabel said.

"The whole of the north of England is not safe, Isabel," Brett wryly retorted.

"True," Isabel said with a smile. "You will watch your back, Brett."

"And you, Isabel, will do the same, if you please."

She smiled and pulled her gun and went back to sit beside Jamie. With a lazy salute, the earl strolled off.

She watched him go, the sun glinting on his flaxen hair. Faith, 'twas a nonesuch indeed. She didn't even mind that he had changed from bravo to leader of their little band. The role suited him and he performed it well. And she trusted him. "Oh, Jamie," she whispered, "how I wish things were otherwise."

Brett walked into the glade two hours later to find a pistol aimed unwaveringly at his heart. "What? Is this a robbery?" he inquired.

With a smile, Isabel lowered her gun. "Merely caution in troubling times."

He smiled in turn. "I found a place for us to hide. It's neither as comfortable nor as commodious as this lovely glade. But it is far safer."

Isabel glanced at Jamie.

"Have no fear," Brett said. "I can carry him easily."

"He is hardly a lightweight, sir."

"No. But then, neither am I." Kneeling beside Jamie, Brett lifted him into his arms. Jamie moaned only once and remained unconscious.

"Lead on, sir," said Isabel.

Brett did so. "I found more evidence of someone passing nearby within the last day," he said. "It might have been poachers."

"But then again," said Isabel, "it might not."

A half hour's brisk walk brought them to the hiding place of Brett's choosing. Isabel surveyed it admiringly. It was on a slight rise in the midst of a rock outcropping. Not a cave, but certainly a rather large hole surrounded by rocks and shrubs. It gave them shelter from sun or rain and, better still, provided them with a view of the surrounding forest. They would have ample warning should anyone come looking for them.

"You were born to an adventurous life, sir," said Isabel.

Brett grinned at her. "This had better be the true heir, Isabel, or I will be decidedly peeved at being put to so much trouble on his behalf."

"La, sir, this is a lark compared to the trouble he will cause you when he is officially your ward."

"I begin to rethink the many charms of duty," Brett retorted, which made her chuckle, as he had intended. The troubles *she* had already endured, and now this newest concern for Jamie's health, were taking their toll. He saw it in her shadowed eyes and the tension in every inch of her body.

He carried Jamie up to their new hiding place and laid him gently down on the ground. Isabel squeezed in beside Jamie as Brett camouflaged the entrance to their hole with a variety of shrubs and twigs he had gathered. Then he squeezed in beside Isabel, felt the heat of her body beside his, heard her soft breath. For a moment he forgot all about the danger surrounding them.

"I think we should rest as much as possible," he said

abruptly. "Who knows when we will have the chance to sleep again?" He brushed her cheek with his fingertips and heard her sharp intake of breath. "I shall take the first watch, if you please, Isabel," he said gruffly.

"Oh, now, Brett—"

"Madam, you will be so good as to allow me to be chivalrous at least once in our acquaintance."

She smiled. "Oh, very well. But you will wake me before nightfall or I'll know the reason why."

"I am quaking in my boots," he assured her.

Isabel cocked her head, a new smile playing on her lips. "I doubt if you have ever quaked in anything, Lord Northbridge."

Then she lay down beside Jamie and in the next moment was asleep.

"Why, there's a wench!" Brett murmured, gazing down at her. He brushed a few wisps of dark hair from her cheek, his fingers resting against her warm skin for a moment.

As he had promised, he woke her just as dusk was seeping through the forest. She came instantly awake, her hand on her gun, the pistol half raised before she understood from Brett's quick "It's all right" that there was no immediate danger. Shoulder to shoulder, they gazed out into the darkening forest.

"Any sign or sound of trouble?" she asked.

"Nothing. Birds have twittered, animals have skipped past, the sun has shone, and no human has blighted the serene landscape."

"A most satisfactory report."

"Aye." Brett grinned at her and Isabel smiled back. Their gazed held. Their smiles faded.

Isabel's eyes dropped first. "Sleep now, sir. I'll keep watch."

"And be sure you eat," Brett said as he handed her the small packet of what remained of their food. "You won't be any bloody use to us if you faint from hunger."

"Yes, sir," Isabel said dutifully.

He shook his head at her, clearly unconvinced by this

avowal, stretched out as much as their cramped space allowed, and was instantly asleep.

Isabel gazed down at the tall gentleman for a moment and then resolutely turned her eyes toward the forest and was vigilant.

It was just after midnight, judging by the position of the moon and stars, when she first heard them. They were not exactly subtle. This told her that these were not poachers crashing through the forest but men unused to woods and stealth. In a moment she saw their torches. She judged them to be a good three hundred yards distant. Between the faint light of the torches, the obscured moon, and their voices, she thought them to be ten or a dozen men. Her hand rested lightly on Brett's shoulder. She had not even to call his name before he was awake.

Jamie slept on as, with a few hushed words and her hand pointing out the various objects of interest in the night, she explained the situation.

"They are too many for us," said Brett, holding her gaze with his own.

"I know it."

"We'll need Jamie when the time comes, but not just yet I think."

They both checked their weapons as the searchers drew closer.

"Can they track us at night like this?" Isabel whispered.

Brett shook his head. "This is a blind search, methodically done, but a blind search nonetheless. They don't know where we are. They only suspect we are somewhere close at hand."

After that they were silent, careful not to let any voice or sound of theirs carry in the night air as the men drew nearer and nearer, their torches illuminating their faces now. Isabel shivered inwardly. They were a hard crew. Scarred, grizzled, shabbily dressed, lethally armed. There would be no mercy at their hands.

"Hey!" shouted a voice in the distance.

The ten men with torches stopped and turned toward the glade where Jamie and Brett and Isabel had first rested.

"Horses! I found horses!" called the first voice, thin over the distance.

"Bailey and Childers, see what he's found," said one of the ten.

Two men separated from the group and ran toward the glade.

"Damn!" Brett said in a low voice.

"Horses, all right!" came a shout. "Well rested."

"Spread out," commanded their leader. "They must be near. Not even they'd be foolish enough to leave their horses and try to reach Thornwynd on foot."

The nine remaining men dutifully scattered, torches raised high as they scanned the wood.

Isabel moved to wake Jamie, but Brett stopped her. She looked at him inquiringly. Her heart began to hammer in her breast as she saw the new and wholly unexpected light in his blue eyes.

"In case we do not survive," he whispered as one hand slipped to the back of her head and pulled her to him.

Brett's mouth on hers was hard, demanding, and she gave without hesitation, moaning as his tongue slipped into her. She felt as if her blood were on fire. Her heart was pounding so fiercely, she was certain it must explode.

And she didn't care. She didn't care that death was so close or that this was an earl and she an adventuress. She felt and knew and wanted only Brett and this kiss that seemed to last forever and only a moment as it burned the world away and left her gasping for breath when Brett finally pulled back and they stared into each other's eyes.

Heart thundering in her breast, she first became aware of the blush burning in her cheeks, and then how bruised and aching and hungry her lips felt, and then of the shouts of the men below. Blindly she turned to stare at their pursuers.

Three men began picking their way up the rise, sending rocks tumbling down.

"Here! Watch what you're doin'!" came an angry voice from below them.

The three paid him no mind. They continued their search.

With one hand on Jamie's mouth, Isabel gently shook the boy awake. His fever had passed. It took but a moment for him to become fully alert. She handed him a gun and kept one finger on his mouth for another moment. He nodded.

Using his long hands, Brett indicated who should have which target. They nodded. He held up two fingers and again pointed. They had their targets for the second wave that would undoubtedly assault them.

And still the three men scrambled upward, muttering at the rocks and the terrain and the brambles.

Isabel's eyes and ears were painfully strained following the progress of these three who sought their deaths. It had taken but a moment for her to calculate that if she and Brett and Jamie discharged each of their pistols with perfect accuracy, they could take down only six. That left five more and the serious question of whether they could reload in time and the very probable answer that they could not.

The three men scrambled up the rise. She saw clearly now the first man: an old, greasy hat on his head, most of his teeth missing as he grunted and panted his way nearer and nearer, a torch in one hand, a gun in the other, two guns stuck into his belt. His compatriots were equally bloodcurdling. One had a scar that ran from his forehead down through his cheek and his throat to hide within the filthy rag of a shirt he wore. The third man was razor thin, his face sharp and vicious.

The first man, with the battered hat, had come within three feet of their hiding place and reached out to move aside the bushes shielding them. It was Jamie's man and Jamie, his hand steady, raised his pistol. But Brett closed his fingers tightly around his wrist. Jamie glanced at him in surprise. Brett shook his head.

"Yeow!!" screeched the man as he jumped back from the

thorny bushes, clutching his hand to his chest. "Jesus Bloody H. Christ! What a place to look for your fortune."

He walked away from them farther up the rise.

The others searched around him and with him. After a quarter of an hour, the scarred man shouted, "There's no one up here!"

"All right, then," came their leader's voice. "Come on down."

The three started to scramble down the rocks. It was only when they had moved a good hundred yards away from them that Isabel realized she had not been breathing. Her fingers ached from the tense grip they held on her pistols.

"God!" Jamie breathed.

"Yes," said Brett. "That was . . . close."

"We are safe for now," said Isabel. "But will they search for us again in the morning?"

*

Chapter 13

May 14, 1804   Early morning

The Forest of Bowland, West Riding, Yorkshire

DAWN CAME SLOWLY, heralded by the cacophonous shrieking of a myriad of birds inhabiting the woods. In the midst of this feathered chorus, Isabel, Brett, and Jamie, straining their ears to the utmost, were gladdened by the complete absence of any human sounds. For now their pursuers had moved on, and they thought it wise that they do the same.

Despite the tension of the last twenty-four hours, the enforced rest had done Jamie a world of good, and he was able not merely to avoid holding Brett and Isabel back but to keep up with them in good form. Isabel insisted that they rest a few minutes after each hour's walking, but outside of that, Jamie required no further attention.

They walked through the Forest of Bowland, all senses straining to detect any observers, any followers. There were none in the morning. They walked single file, Brett in the lead, Jamie in the middle, Isabel bringing up the rear. They did not talk. They moved carefully to avoid making any unnecessary sound.

At noon they stopped beside a small stream, drank their fill, and ate what little remained of their rations. The forest, not yet blessed with summer's warmth, could provide them with no berries, no nuts, no fruits. As for animals, there was, of course, a plethora of birds and wild game, but the dangers of a cook fire were apparent to them all. There could be no smoke; there could be warming light to guide their pursuers to them.

As Brett had expected, neither Isabel nor Jamie made any complaint. They accepted the privations of this journey with a matter-of-fact calm that never wavered. Yet he could not help but worry. Jamie, though stronger now and as resilient as his youth and natural good health could make him, still required rest and nourishment to fully recover from his wound. And Isabel had had little sleep and less food in the last twenty-four hours. How were they to walk the fifty miles between them and Ravenscourt?

Two hours after their meager luncheon, as they were walking through a stand of elderly evergreens, a horse's faint whinny stopped Brett cold. His eyes met Isabel's. The same fear lurked there.

There was no convenient outcropping of rock, not even plump bushes to hide behind.

"There! Up ahead!" came a jubilant shout. "I saw someone, a boy I think!"

"Shipley?"

"Aye! After him, lads!"

Eleven men on horseback were crashing through the forest toward them. Less than two hundred yards away.

"Run for it!" Brett cried.

As one, he, Isabel, and Jamie turned and plunged farther into the forest, the crashing of horses and the shouts of men sounding as if their pursuers were already at their heels.

"How did they find us?" Jamie gasped.

"I don't know," Isabel said. "Dumb luck. A tracker. I don't know. Run, Jamie, run!"

They ran, gasping for breath, muscles burning with their hopeless effort. They covered one hundred yards. Two hundred. The men on horseback, though impeded by the thick woods, drew closer.

"We're in for it, Jamie!" Isabel panted.

"I know," said the boy. "But I mean to take several with me!"

"As do I," said Brett. He spun around and, holding still for just a moment, raised his gun and fired.

An agonized yelp filled the air and brought everything to sudden silence for a moment. But only a moment. Then Jamie fired. A stream of curses pierced the air.

"I'm hit!" were the first coherent words they heard. "My God, I'm bleeding all over the place!"

"Come on," Brett said, "reload!"

They ran and reloaded their guns as they slid downhill through the trees.

"How many do you make it, Brett?" Isabel gasped.

"As many as ten, as few as eight. Still too many."

"Brett! To the left!" Isabel cried. "A ravine!"

"I see it!"

Fifty yards away lay the only chance they had of keeping their lives. It seemed like fifty miles.

The pounding of horses' hooves on the ground thundered in their ears. Their pursuers were shouting to each other. "You get the girl! I've got the boy dead to rights!" Two pistol shots rang through the forest, and still Brett and Jamie and Isabel ran, the pounding hoofbeats and human shouts drawing closer.

As one, they threw themselves into the ravine, scrambled through briars and branches back up to the edge, and fired.

Two men dropped from their saddles. A third, clutching his shoulder, barely stayed on his horse as the terrified animal careened away through the woods. The two who had fallen scrambled to hide behind the nearest trees and fired their own guns.

Bullets chucked up dirt at the ravine's edge.

Hurriedly reloading, Brett looked up and gasped as Isabel wormed her way through the ravine in a flanking action. To call to her and order her back was to reveal their position and bring their certain deaths.

182

Under cover of their pursuers' yells, deafening gunshots, and the whinnying and neighing of frightened horses, she crept forward until, a horse almost upon her, she rose suddenly. Startled, the horse reared up, unseating its rider. She aimed and fired her gun at the same moment she grabbed the horse's reins, ignoring the hooves slashing at her. Numb with horror, Brett fired at the men nearest him, hoping to create a diversion as Isabel threw herself up into the saddle, the horse quivering beneath her.

There were five men still unharmed and on horseback, two quite near her. Maneuvering her horse so that she was partially hidden by a tree, she cried out in a loud, gruff voice: "There they are, lads! To the east!" she pointed them away from Brett and Jamie. "They're heading for the road! After them!"

The two men raced off.

"Isabel!" Brett shouted desperately.

She wheeled her horse and fired her second gun. A man they had wounded earlier fell almost at her horse's hooves. She had no time to reload. Drawing her sword, she forced her horse at a gallop into the midst of their pursuers, slashing at anything she could reach.

"Isabel, no!" Brett shouted.

He heard the bark of a gun. Isabel's horse screamed and went down from under her. She barely kicked free in time. With a groan she forced herself to her knees just as Brett charged from the ravine toward her.

The world dropped from his feet. There was only Isabel on her knees and the scar-faced man of the night before standing triumphantly behind her.

"I've got him!" the man shouted as he swung the butt of his pistol down on her head.

She slumped lifelessly to the ground.

Brett didn't have time to reload his guns. Reaching Isabel's attacker a second too late, he furiously threw himself against the man, knocking him to the ground. Brett snatched the gun from the man's slack fingers, rolled to his feet, and fired at point-blank range. There was no time to feel any pleasure in revenge or even discover if Isabel still lived. Two men were riding down on him.

Picking up Isabel's sword, he ran at them, shrieking and yelling like the Celtic warriors of a more barbarous age. The horses, already nervous from the rigors of the fight, were frightened by this unholy noise and the flash of the sword. They screamed and reared. One rider fell. The other dropped his gun to cling to the animal's mane as it charged off at a hysterical gallop through the woods.

The man who had fallen, like Isabel, had only reached his knees before Brett brought the hilt of his sword down with murderous rage against the man's head. He slumped unconscious to the ground.

He heard another gunshot and a sharp cry. He picked up a gun that had fallen to the ground and spun around.

"Jamie!" he yelled.

"I'm fine, Brett!" the boy shouted. "Behind you!"

Brett turned and fired, the sword in his other hand slashing up, not knowing what he would find. The shrill cry of a man who a moment earlier had had a gun trained on his back was his answer. The man fell to the ground, sobbing.

Brett wheeled around to meet whatever enemy came at him next but found in the groans of the men who had fallen and his own harsh breath that there was only one other left standing and that one was Jamie.

"Are you all right, lad?" he said.

"Yes," Jamie gasped, stumbling toward him. "Isabel?"

"I don't know."

Isabel lay unmoving on the ground beside the man Brett had killed.

Reaching her first, the earl threw himself beside her and pulled her into his arms. "Isabel!" he groaned, cradling her, rocking her as his shaking fingers searched desperately for the pulse that should have been at the base of her slender throat.

"She lives!" he gasped as Jamie knelt beside him.

"How badly is she hurt?"

"I don't know," Brett said, staring, horrified at the bloody hand that had cradled her head. "And we haven't time to find out. The two men that she sent off to the farm road may realize the deception and come back for us. We have to move, and now. Gather what weapons you can and follow me."

He tenderly lifted Isabel into his arms.

"Where to?" Jamie said, still panting for breath. His face was white and beaded with perspiration.

"I know this country. There's a hunting lodge about eight miles to the west of us."

"Won't they look for us there?"

"No, at least not until morning," Brett said grimly. "Squire Beechem prefers the shooting to the north of us. That hunting lodge has been deserted for more than a decade. Few will remember it. Can you catch any of the horses?"

"I haven't Isabel's skill, but I'll succeed," Jamie replied. "You walk on. I'll get the horses and follow you."

It took twenty agonizing minutes of patient coaxing for Jamie to capture two of the frightened horses. Then he was in the saddle of one and, holding the reins of the other, jumped forward at a gallop.

Brett, hearing him moments later, whirled around, his gun in his hand, Isabel carried in but one arm. In the next moment he would have fired had Jamie not called out his name.

"Hand Isabel up to me. I'll carry her," Jamie said, drawing beside Brett.

"No, your shoulder is still weak. I'll take her."

With a little help from Jamie, Brett was in the saddle of the second horse, Isabel cradled in his arms. Jamie reclaimed his horse, and in the next moment they were off at a gallop.

*

Chapter 14

May 15, 1804   Noon

The Forest of Bowland, near Holden, Lancashire

WITH A GROAN that came from her heart, for everything ached, Isabel tried to open her eyes and failed completely.

"Hush now, it's all right," a gentle voice said as a cool cloth was laid across her throbbing brow.

Trusting that voice, she fell back into the welcome, painless black depths. But after awhile they would no longer claim her. In fact, they began insistently pushing her out into that throbbing, wracking, searing pain and heat that seemed to envelop her. She swore bitterly.

A low rumble of laughter beat back some of the pain, and she was able to open her eyes for a moment. But her eyelids, impossibly heavy, fell shut again almost immediately.

"Brett?" she said, but it came out as much less than a whisper.

She felt herself raised a little, and then her head was resting against something broad and inexplicably comforting. Warm lips pressed against her forehead. A sigh broke from her. She felt a glass pressed to her lips, and from somewhere far, far away heard a gentle command.

"Drink."

With great difficulty she opened her mouth and then felt something cool and sweet and tangy slide over her tongue and down her throat. The cup was pulled from her lips.

"Oh, that was wonderful!" she said, and this time it *was* as loud as a whisper.

"Compliments are always welcome," said that warm, soothing voice as she was gently lowered again.

Irritated at not being able to stay in that comforting place, Isabel opened her eyes and this time kept them open. Focusing them was another matter entirely.

"Brett?!"

"Still here."

He looked exhausted, as if he hadn't slept in days. There were shadows beneath his blue eyes; his face was pale and taut with worry.

"What . . . happened?"

"You drank some wine."

Isabel thought so little of this response that she freely cursed Brett with all of the venom her throbbing head could conjure.

"Very well," said Brett, chuckling, grinning down at her in utter delight. "You were so singularly foolish as to have your head split open."

"Oh," she said, and frowned, trying to remember. Suddenly her eyes widened. "Those men—"

"It's all right," Brett said soothingly, taking the cloth from her forehead. "They're long gone. We're in no danger."

Isabel didn't think this at all likely. "I may be aching in every millimeter of my body," she retorted, "but I'm not a *baby*!" Suddenly her heart clenched. "Where's Jamie?!"

"It's all right, Isabel. Trust me," Brett said, placing another cool cloth on her forehead. "He's out fishing."

"Fishing?" Isabel shrieked, sitting straight up. This was a mistake. The room danced drunkenly around her. Invisible blacksmiths seemed intent on pounding her brain into mush. With a groan she fell back against the makeshift bed.

"It was his turn," Brett said reasonably.

"If I weren't on the brink of death, I would strangle you," Isabel retorted, and then paused. "What do you mean, his turn? Where are we? What time is it?"

"We are at the former hunting lodge of Squire Beechem. The time is a little after twelve o'clock in the afternoon but not on the day that you imagine. This is the day after we were attacked, Isabel."

"What?" Isabel ejaculated, and for a moment almost rose up again. Fortunately she thought better of it and stared pleadingly up at the earl. "You're joking me, aren't you, Brett? I've lost an entire day?"

"A whole unremarkable day," Brett affirmed with a tender smile.

Isabel uttered a bitter laugh. "A fine protector I am."

"Now, now, I won't have you disparaging yourself. You acquitted yourself very well in the battle, except, of course, for the singular stupidity of having your head split open."

"Thank you," Isabel said witheringly.

Brett's low laughter warmed the room. "Come, have another sip of wine. It seems to have a most beneficial effect upon you."

He slipped his arm behind her and began to help her up.

"I am perfectly capable of sitting up and drinking some wine by myself!" she snapped, despite the renewed pounding in her head.

"You are the most odiously stubborn woman," Brett said with a sigh. He did not release her. "Can you not just relax and let someone else take care of you for a change?"

Her gaze flew to his and instantly she was caught. "I am used . . . to doing for myself," she faltered.

"Clearly. But there is equal pleasure in being cared for by another now and then," he said softly. "Drink, Isabel."

Heart hammering in her breast, Isabel took a sip from the cup pressed to her lips.

Brett gently released her against the cushion behind her and set the wine back down. Then he began to caress her forehead and temples with his long fingers. Isabel hadn't the strength to fend off the delicious sensation curling from her head to her toes.

"How does your head feel now?"

"Better, thank you," Isabel murmured, her eyes drifting closed as she luxuriated in his touch. With both his hands massaging her temples, she could pretend for a moment that he held her in his arms, safe, enfolding her in his strength and heat.

"It's a miracle you weren't more seriously wounded," he said.

"I've always had a very hard head."

Brett chuckled. It rumbled deliciously up and down her spine. "Yes, and I used to think it a curse."

"You just disliked meeting your equal."

"No longer, I assure you, Isabel. Just don't expose yourself to so much danger again."

Isabel's eyes drifted open. "Were you worried about me?"

"Worried?! You were doing your level best to throw your life away yesterday, and there was nothing I could do to stop you!"

"I thought I was trying to save Jamie's life."

"There are other means to accomplish that end. Don't you dare frighten me like that again, Isabel."

"Yes, Brett."

He smiled down at her, and the most delicious heat suffused her body. "If I'd known a bump on the head would make you so docile, I'd have purchased a cudgel long before this."

"The Earl of Northbridge would never be so rag-mannered."

His warm fingers caressed her cheek. "But what of Brett Avery?"

"Oh, *he* is capable of anything!"

Brett laughed softly and pressed a warm kiss to her forehead. Isabel's toes curled beneath the blanket that covered her.

In the next moment a door crashed open, setting the blacksmiths to pounding at her head with appalling vigor. A hearty voice cried out, "Success! We shall lunch like kings!"

189

"Did no one ever teach you how to enter a room quietly?" Brett demanded of Jamie. "You have shattered what remain of Isabel's nerves."

"What? Is she awake?" Jamie cried, and was instantly kneeling at her side. "Isabel! Isabel, are you all right?"

Slowly Isabel turned her head and glared at the boy whose life she had sworn to protect. "The minute I can get up, I am going to throttle you."

"Hooray!" Jamie cried. "Oh, Isabel, I've been so worried!"

Her eyes closing against the robust tone of his voice, Isabel cringed. "If you were so worried, why are you bellowing like a water buffalo?" Suddenly her eyes opened. "And why are you still here? Thornwynd! You've got to get to Thornwynd! You've only . . . Oh, God, I can't think! How many days do we have left?"

"Two, Isabel," Brett replied soothingly. "We have two days and thirty miles and horses to carry us. Do not worry. What you need to do is rest and get well so we can continue our journey."

"Oh, why am I surrounded by imbeciles?!" Isabel moaned. She glared up at the earl. "You will oblige me, Brett, by putting Jamie on a horse and yourself on another horse and taking him to Thornwynd *now*. I am fine; you said so yourself. I will do very well here."

"She's fine!" Jamie scoffed. "A bump on her head the size of a melon, and she says she's fine!"

"Jamie," said Isabel, "if you have any regard for me, you will go to Thornwynd now. Brett will see you safely there."

"Brett will see us safely there in a day or two," the earl replied. "We will not desert you, Isabel. There is time, we have horses, and we are a day's ride away from Thornwynd at most. Now, I suggest you rest while Jamie and I prepare a little lunch."

Despite the irritation of nerves and the worry she suffered on Jamie's account, Isabel's throbbing head convinced her that

190

resting was a very good idea. She gratefully closed her eyes and was soon fast asleep.

When Isabel awoke again, the blacksmiths had settled down to a steady, light, almost musical drumming inside her head. She found that she could open her eyes without difficulty and keep them open, although she did blink at the domestic scene before her.

Brett stood at a fireplace, thoughtfully stirring the contents of a black pot while Jamie sat at a rickety table, a wooden cup filled with spring flowers at its center, repairing what seemed to be some sort of snare. By turning her head slightly, Isabel was able to perceive that her bed was actually an antiquated sofa of lumpy design. The room that all three inhabited was lit by a single candle near Jamie and by the fire in the grate. She saw a door and two windows, each covered with heavy curtains. She dimly remembered Brett saying something about a hunting lodge and someone by the name of Squire Beechem, but who Squire Beechem was and how they had come to his hunting lodge she did not know and did not think it necessary to find out at this moment. She was still a little amazed at this scene of domesticity.

Brett suddenly turned and smiled at her, a smile of such warmth that the blacksmiths agreed to lower their drumming to a mere murmur inside her head.

"Ah, good, you're awake," he said.

Jamie looked up at her and smiled, too. "And looking *much* better."

"Oh dear," said Isabel. "If I'm looking much better and I'm feeling this bad, I dread to think what I must have looked like a day ago."

"A ghost," Jamie supplied.

"A wraith," Brett corrected.

"Lovely," Isabel muttered.

Brett scooped some of the contents of the black pot into a wooden bowl and carried it to her.

191

"Here," he said, "let me see if I can help you sit up."

"I am fully capable—" Isabel began.

"No," Brett countered, "you're not."

Somewhat to her chagrin, Isabel found that she was not. Lifting her gently under her shoulders, Brett brought her into a seated position and then handed her the bowl and a spoon.

"Here," he said, "you need this."

She regarded the wooden bowl warily, sniffed at the contents, and found that it smelled suspiciously like . . .

"What is this?" she demanded.

"Rabbit stew," Brett pronounced.

She stared up at him. "Rabbit?"

"In our continual pursuit of new roles to play, Jamie and I have become poachers. Eat up."

Isabel blinked. The thought of the convention-bound Earl of Northbridge turning poacher was so astounding to her that she actually goggled at the man!

"You aren't going to turn your nose up at my culinary efforts, are you?" he inquired.

Isabel recalled herself to the immediate situation, filled a wooden spoon of recent manufacture with the rabbit stew, raised it to her lips, and delicately sipped at it. She had never been fond of rabbit, but the extraordinary—not to say incomprehensible—effort expended on her behalf required recompense.

"Why, it's not bad," she managed.

"You are too kind," said Brett with a bow. "A chef is always happy to have his work praised."

Isabel stared up at him in utter amazement. "You're enjoying yourself!"

"Of course I am. I've never had to cook before, you see," he said simply.

"He's quite good with fish," Jamie supplied. "*I* found the wine."

"Did you indeed?" said Isabel distractedly. "How enterprising of you."

Jamie flushed and Brett laughed.

"There was a root cellar," Jamie said, "which had an assortment of rather disgusting odds and ends but also a bottle or two of decent wine, which have come in handy."

"Lovely," Isabel pronounced. "A *drunken* water buffalo. Are we really in no danger, Brett?" she pleaded.

"For the moment," he replied. "Jamie and I have been on continual watch. No one has come near the place."

"This is the evening of the day I first awoke?"

"Yes."

"And we still have two days left to us?"

"Yes!" said Jamie. "Don't worry, Isabel. Everything is fine."

"Ha!" said Isabel with a scowl. "The boy who took a bullet in his shoulder two days ago and is two days away from losing his inheritance says everything is fine."

"Eat your stew," Brett said.

Isabel glumly complied. She found that she had a decent appetite and was able to finish the bowl without gagging and drink half a cup of wine. When Brett and Jamie had completed their meals, she announced: "We leave tomorrow morning."

"Isabel—" Brett wearily began.

"You say we are a day's ride from Thornwynd and Ravenscourt. Who knows what could happen in that day?" said Isabel. "Look what has already occurred!"

"I don't like it," said Brett.

"Neither do I," said Jamie.

"You have my deepest sympathies," Isabel retorted. "We leave tomorrow morning."

The gentlemen argued, but in vain. Isabel had a streak of stubbornness in her that would, when necessity demanded, brook no opposition. Brett and Jamie consoled themselves with the thought that on the morrow, when Isabel tried to get up and realized how difficult it was to do, she would recant.

193

Brett then declared that it was his watch and, checking his guns, walked out the door.

Isabel stared at that door for a good minute.

"I'm so glad you're feeling better, Isabel," Jamie said softly.

She fondly regarded the boy. "What, were you worried about me, child?"

"Scared to death. I don't want to lose you, Isabel. Not ever."

Isabel hesitated and then said, "I promised to get you to Thornwynd, and I mean to do so."

Jamie regarded her for a moment but asked merely if she wanted a little more wine or water and then urged her to go to sleep.

Isabel, tired from the exertions of the evening and warmed by the food and wine, readily agreed to this scheme and was soon fast asleep, Jamie watching over her.

Brett awoke the following morning to find that Isabel had risen before him; she had refurbished her wardrobe, and her black hair was brushed and tied neatly behind her head. Judging by the dishes on the table, she had also breakfasted.

"You are an obstinate female," he pronounced as he rose from his pallet on the floor. Jamie, he observed approvingly, was still on watch outside.

She turned to him and smiled brightly. "Yes, I am. Jamie has already eaten. When you have breakfasted, sir, we may go."

She seemed steady enough on her feet, but she was still so pale and . . .

"How is your head?" Brett demanded.

"But half the size it was yesterday."

"A decided improvement," Brett agreed, "but still, don't you think—"

"No," said Isabel, "I don't."

The earl considered her a moment. Had she ever agreed with anything he proposed?

They were on horseback a half hour later. As there were but two horses, Brett insisted that Isabel ride with him, and despite her protests, he lifted her up and placed her in the saddle. He sat behind her and wrapped his arms around her waist to, as he innocently informed her, make sure that she did not fall out of the saddle fifteen minutes after they had begun. Isabel delivered something suspiciously like a growl but made no further protest.

They moved at a fast walk to keep their horses as fresh as possible should further danger arise. Brett insisted that they stop every hour on the hour so that Isabel could rest for ten minutes before continuing on. Had she not quickly discovered that she needed these respites from the saddle, Isabel would have objected vehemently to such coddling. As it was, she remained mute and grimly upright in the saddle, fully conscious of Brett's arms around her, the throbbing in her head, and the treacherous desire to lean against Brett and let him hold and support her on what was becoming a tortuous journey.

Avoiding all roads and any hint of civilization, they rode through the morning, took an hour for lunch, and then were back in the saddle and riding westward once again. Her head feeling twice the size and weight of a cannonball, Isabel wished with every breath for a soft bed and drapes drawn against the brilliant afternoon sunlight.

To her relief, just after four o'clock they entered the shadowed coolness of a thick wood.

"Where are we?" she asked. "How far is it to Ravenscourt?"

"We are on Ravenscourt land now," Brett replied, his voice low, his mouth near her ear. It felt oddly . . . intimate. "But another five miles will see us to the house."

Twenty minutes passed, and then thirty. Isabel felt the excitement stirring in her belly. They were so close! They were so close to safety, to Jamie's inheritance, to an end of this nightmare. To Jonas Babcock. And to the end of her time with Jamie and Brett. Excitement died into misery.

"Hold there!" a voice shouted. "One move and we shoot!"

Chapter 15

May 16, 1804   Late afternoon

Ravenscourt, Lancashire

ISABEL JERKED UPON the reins. Her horse stopped, tossing its head angrily at this rude behavior. Her hand was on her gun, but Brett's hand closed over it, warm and sure.

"Be not so hasty," he said, "I recognize that voice. Mason, is that you?" he called.

"Yes, sir!" came a happy shout. "And right glad to see you safe and sound!" A tall, barrel-chested man stepped out from behind some trees, a shotgun cradled easily in his arms. "We've been expecting you these last two days and more, sir," he called.

"We were unexpectedly delayed," Brett said.

Other men now showed themselves. Isabel counted six. All were armed with shotguns.

"What's all this?" Brett said.

"Ah, sir, it was Dawkins. He insisted we surround the house and so we've done. We've trussed up half a dozen men in the last three days. They claim they were hikers; one even said he was a poacher. We took leave to doubt them all. They're housed, far from comfortably, in the Scorton jail."

"Well done, Mason!" said Brett.

"No, my lord, it's Dawkins you should be thanking. He

doesn't say much, but he's a cagey old fellow and seems right taken with your . . . companions."

"As he should be. Onward to clean clothes and a decent meal!" Brett declared.

Isabel longed to sag with the relief coursing through her. They were safe! They were at Ravenscourt! But to relax in her saddle was to relax against Brett, something too tempting to contemplate. She nudged their horse forward, the earl's men falling into a cordon of protection around them.

"Just in case, my lord," said Mason.

Isabel liked him on the spot.

They emerged from the cool of the park onto a gravel drive that swept in a circle up to a huge, gothic mansion, its white stones reflecting the sunlight. Spires seemed to reach to the sky. Isabel counted four stories, not including the garret or any underground rooms.

"Good God, it's as big as Blenheim!" she exclaimed.

"No, no," Brett assured her. " 'Tis but half the size. It has only three hundred rooms."

Isabel turned in the saddle to stare at him in growing horror. "No wonder you are so high-handed," she said without thinking. "I'm amazed I wasn't reduced to hitting you with a tackling block."

With Brett pressed close against her, she felt more than heard the low rumble of his chuckle.

More of the Earl of Northbridge's men came out of the woods to greet him and welcome him home and surround the trio as they moved up the drive to the stately front door.

Isabel, though she was loath to admit it, was badly shaken. To find that Brett was so rich as to possess such extensive lands and so vast a house had quite overset her scarcely recovered nerves. She remained mute on that walk up to the front door. She silently accepted Brett's aid as she slid from the horse. But she shook off his supporting arm when she reached the ground and held on to the saddle instead as a formidable-looking butler and liveried footman descended the front steps.

"Welcome home, my lord," the butler intoned.

Home? Isabel tilted her head back to stare up at the edifice. This was a home?

"Thank you, Gregory. It's good to be back," Brett replied. "I require rooms for my friends, baths for us all, clean clothes, good food and wine. Anything like that in the house?"

"Yes, my lord," the butler replied with some severity.

They entered the hall. It was a good five times the size of Squire Beechem's former hunting lodge. Black and white marble tiles made up the floor; a huge chandelier glowed above them. A broad stone staircase swept upward on their right.

"Has Miss Fanny arrived, Gregory?" the earl inquired.

"Yes, sir," the butler intoned. "She is installed in the Peacock Room."

"Oh, nonsense," a feminine voice countered. "Why would I be in that huge drafty room when I can be watching the most amazing procession I've ever been privileged to witness?"

The company turned to find a plump little woman in an Empire gown of brown-and-gold muslin emerging from the parlor on their right. Her blond hair and long straight nose linked her irrevocably to the earl. She was also a good six months gone with child.

"Fanny!" Brett cried. His voice deepened with affection as he strode up to her, taking both her hands in his. "My dear sister." He kissed her on both cheeks. "How good of you to come on such short notice."

Lady Fanny Clotfelter stared up at her brother in open amazement, her expression wholly comical. "Brett, are you . . . quite well?" she faltered.

"I have just spent a momentous fortnight, and I will tell you all my adventures later," he said, tucking her arm through his. "Come, you must meet my friends. This," he said, leading her to Isabel and Jamie, "is Miss Isabel—"

"Seton," Isabel hurriedly supplied.

"Indeed?" murmured Brett, cocking an eyebrow at her.

She scowled at him and then turned back to Fanny. "How do you do, Lady Clotfelter?"

"I am glad to meet you, Miss . . . Seton," Fanny said. She was clearly dumbfounded by Isabel's wardrobe but working hard to take everything in stride as she took Isabel's hand in hers. "Have we met before, do you think? You seem so familiar to me."

"I shouldn't think it likely, Lady Clotfelter," Isabel warily replied. "I have lived most of my life abroad."

"I believe, Fanny," said her brother, "that you will find Miss . . . Seton a diverting companion. I hope you will become good friends."

Both women stared at him in the utmost astonishment.

"And this whelp," the earl blithely continued, "claims to be James Shipley, heir to Thornwynd."

"I make no such claims," Jamie retorted. "I *am* James Shipley and I *am* heir to Thornwynd. How do you do, Lady Clotfelter?" he said, gracefully raising her hand to his lips.

"I believe that I am . . . agog," Fanny dazedly replied. "Yes, I *am* agog. Brett," she said, turning to her brother, "what *is* all this?"

"I will explain everything in good time, Fanny," the earl replied. "But first there are some practical matters to attend to. We have had a long journey and are in need of baths and a change of clothes and some refreshments. And Miss . . . Seton must rest, for she has not yet fully recovered from her injury."

"My dear Miss Seton!" Fanny cried, turning to Isabel. "Are you hurt?"

" 'Tis a bump only, my lady," Isabel assured her. "Your brother exaggerates the case."

"But Brett never exaggerates anything!"

"And I haven't now," the earl intervened before Isabel could make her own retort. "You will rest, Isabel."

"Oh certainly, my lord," she gravely replied, gray eyes twinkling with mischief. She turned to Fanny. "He's so wonderfully masterful, don't you think?"

Fanny gaped at her.

"I beg you, Isabel," Brett said wearily, "do not corrupt the awe in which my sister holds me."

Now Fanny stared at *him*! Had the world run mad without her noticing?

"Gregory, send Dawkins to me," Brett stoically continued. "I want a word with him before my bath. But first, be so good as to escort my friends upstairs."

"Certainly, my lord," Gregory said with the stiffest of bows. Isabel received the distinct impression that he was accustomed to dealing with more elegant guests. "If you will follow me, sir," he said to Jamie, "and"—he looked at Isabel twice—"miss."

Before they could journey upstairs, the air was rent with the piercing cry of "Master James! Miss Isabel!"

They all turned to see a tiny little man, his hair a tuft of gray, his sharp face alight with joy as he hurried into the hall.

"Dick!" Jamie shrieked, and hurled himself into the old man's arms. "Dick, you old buzzard, it's good to see you safe and well!"

"I could say the same of you, Master James," Dick replied, hastily drying his eyes. "And you, Miss Isabel."

"Oh, Dick, we missed you so," Isabel said, fiercely hugging the little man.

"You don't know what I've been through these last months, Miss, worrying about you night and day. I lost two-thirds of my hair just thinking of all the mishaps you might encounter."

"And you never had much to begin with," Jamie said fondly.

"Just you mind your tongue, Master James," Dick tartly retorted. "Well, it's plain I worried for naught, for here you both are safe and sound and none the worse for wear."

"None at all," Isabel said with a suspicious grin. "Oh, Dick, I am so glad you are here and well. I have so much to tell you."

"Just you wait till you've cleaned up a mite and had a bit of food," Dick advised. "There's time enough now for tale telling."

"Dear Dick," Isabel said, pressing a kiss to his balding head.

Twenty minutes later, she was submerged in a bathtub of scalding hot water and bubbles, her mind reeling with the sudden change in her circumstances. Was it only yesterday that she had been eating rabbit stew on a lumpy sofa in a moldy hunting lodge? This huge room of emerald green drapes, two ornate marble fireplaces, and (she squinted up at the ceiling) murals of Artemis bathing in a forest glade was the stuff of fantasy. The blow on her head must have been more severe than she had thought. Her wits were addled. It was the only reasonable explanation.

Then a pert little maid enveloped in a starched white apron bustled into the room and laid out a gown and underclothes upon the massive carved oak bed.

"Here's some clothes, miss, for when you're done with your bath. His lordship thought you might like to change from your traveling clothes."

"You are . . . Eliza?" Isabel managed.

"That's right, miss," said the maid as she bustled over to the bath. "Is the water still hot enough?" She inserted a hand into the bubbles. "Ah, good. Would you like me to wash your hair, miss?"

It occurred to Isabel that she would love to have her hair washed. The offer confirmed everything in her mind. This was definitely a concussion-induced fantasy.

Working gently, Eliza proceeded to shampoo Isabel's black hair, nimble fingers slowly massaging her scalp until the pounding on her brain became little more than a faint hum.

"You are the most wonderful fantasy I've ever had, Eliza," Isabel murmured.

201

"Thank you, miss," Eliza said as she poured clean warm water over her head.

She then wrapped a towel around Isabel's hair and quietly left the room as Isabel settled back into the bath with a contented sigh. Whoever had told Brett about her innermost dreams had certainly got the details right. Thinking on the pleasures of a hot bath, clean clothes, and something other than rabbit stew for dinner later, she slowly drifted asleep.

"Miss?"

"Hm?"

"Miss?"

"Hm?"

"Miss, it's time to dress for dinner."

The gentle but insistent shaking of her shoulder finally forced Isabel to open her eyes. She found herself gazing up into the somewhat anxious face of her maid.

Her maid?

Isabel woke up with a vengeance.

"Dinner?" she said rather stupidly.

"Yes, miss. They're all waiting for you."

Fantasy collided with reality. Isabel hurriedly stood up in her lukewarm bath. "What time is it?"

"A little after seven, miss," Eliza replied, wrapping a towel around her mistress. "You fell asleep, and I didn't like to disturb you after all your trials and tribulations."

Isabel glanced down in considerable alarm at the maid. "What do you know of my trials and tribulations?"

"Oh, nothing, miss! Only that you've had them."

"Aye, I've had them," Isabel murmured, stepping out of the bath with Eliza's steadying hand on her forearm. "I wish to God there weren't more coming."

Curiosity drove her to the bed. Somebody had superb taste. The dress was a lovely concoction of sky blue cotton with puffed sleeves and satin trim.

An amused smile curved her mouth. "Does the Earl of Northbridge usually keep women's clothes lying about?"

"Oh no, miss. It was Miss Fanny that brought them."

"Miss Fanny?"

"Lady Clotfelter, miss. The earl's sister. Her what married Sir Robert Clotfelter some three or four years back."

"Yes, we've met . . . I think. But she isn't my size," Isabel said, holding the gown against herself and seeing that it would be a perfect fit.

"Oh no, miss. She's a plump little thing, just like her mother. Pretty as a picture, of course, but not at all like you."

"Then how comes this gown?"

"I don't know, miss. She just handed it to me and told me to bring it to you."

" 'Tis a riddle that requires an answer." Isabel studied her towel-draped figure in the large gilt-framed mirror near the wardrobe. "I don't suppose I am at all ready to meet company in my present state."

"*No*, miss," said Eliza firmly.

Thirty minutes later, however, and that opinion was revised. Isabel dressed quickly, but her hair required a good deal more attention, particularly when it had to conceal the bump on the back of her head that was now the size of a duck egg. Gazing at the finished product in her mirror, Isabel found herself hard pressed to recall the sword-wielding Valkyrie she had been but three days earlier.

The blue dress flowed deliciously down her body, the square bodice hinting at, rather than displaying, what lay beneath. Matching gloves were on her arms, blue kid slippers on her feet; her shiny black hair gleamed in the candlelight. It was the most awful thing, but she was glad that Brett would see her at least once in all the elegance and pomp she could muster when not fighting for her life.

"You are a wonder, Eliza," she pronounced.

"Thank you, miss," the maid replied with a blush and a curtsy.

Eliza led Isabel on a serpentine course down passages lined with Chinese and Arabian carpets of sumptuous artistry, family portraits, and works by old and new masters gazing down at them from the walls. The sound of laughter, at first faint, grew louder as they passed the staircase leading to the main floor. They continued down the first landing until they reached a room framed by an open double door. Light and laughter poured from within.

"Thank you, Eliza," Isabel murmured as she stared into the drawing room. It was huge. Large medieval tapestries covered the walls. A fabulously carved wooden ceiling was above her. An enormous white marble Renaissance fireplace boasted a brilliant fire big enough to roast an ox. The furniture was early Georgian and contemporary, somehow both lush and understated at the same time.

Brett and Jamie had also bathed and were dressed now in the first state of elegance. Brett's double-breasted coat of dark brown superfine molded itself to his broad chest and shoulders. His fawn-colored breeches and white stockings seemed only to emphasize the length and power of his legs. Black slippers were on his feet. His neck cloth was a work of art, beautiful and yet without the ostentatious posturings of a Mathematical. His hair was soberly arranged, gleaming with gold in the chandelier light. He looked as if he had never stepped foot out of this mansion, let alone knew what dirt was. It was a shock for Isabel to see Brett standing so at ease in his element. She could imagine no other master for this house.

He stood now at the side bar, refilling his glass of port as he talked to the plump little woman in pink on the sofa beside Jamie. Isabel had liked Fanny Clotfelter on first sight and saw no reason to revise that opinion now. She was bubbly and warm, and the laughter dancing in her blue eyes led Isabel to think there was a touch of the rogue in her as well. What a trial she must have been to her proper older brother!

The room's other occupant was a man Isabel did not know. He was not quite as tall as Brett but a good hundred pounds heavier. His beefy body strained his fashionable clothes to their utmost. His hair was gray, his eyes, which had a shrewd look to them, were black. He laughed as heartily as Fanny and Jamie at the end of Brett's tale, but Isabel suspected that his mind was busy cogitating on everything that seemed to lie below the surface of this gathering.

Suddenly Brett turned and his blue eyes met hers. Isabel felt her heart lurch and her breath leave her lungs in a *whoosh*! His gaze scorched her from head to toe, and she was unrepentantly grateful she had taken the full thirty minutes to dress. She felt suspended above the floor, every inch of her skin aflame. Oh, never in her wildest dreams had she imagined Brett could look at her so!

An appreciative whistle broke the heated spell, and Isabel, with a barely suppressed gasp, turned and stared at Jamie.

"Now that," said the boy, "is what I call dressing for the occasion, and well worth waiting for."

"Thank you," Isabel said, forcing herself to recover quickly. It seemed one occasionally had to fight for one's life in evening dress after all.

Brett materialized at her side. "You are beautiful, my . . . lady," he said in a low voice. Looping her arm through his, he pulled her over to the sofa. "You see, Fanny, she *does* clean up well."

Roused from the warm haze the earl's first words had generated, Isabel gasped and promptly jabbed him with her elbow.

"She's as lovely as I suspected," Fanny retorted, her blue eyes brimming with laughter as she met Isabel's gaze.

"I have you to thank, I believe, for this beautiful dress, Lady Clotfelter," Isabel said demurely.

"It's thanks enough to see you in it, my dear Miss Seton," Fanny replied, her blue eyes twinkling. "You are quite beautiful, you know. I'm glad to see that Brett did not mistake your coloring or size."

"Somehow I knew Northbridge had a hand in this," Isabel muttered, striving to keep a blush from her cheeks.

"I only wrote my sister to ask her to fetch you a few clothes and act your chaperon," Brett said innocently.

Isabel burst out laughing and was quite helpless to stop it. The others stared at her in the greatest surprise.

"I'm sorry!" she gasped. "But the idea of my needing a chaperon after the last fortnight is just too ridiculous!"

"Nerves overset," Jamie opined.

"Mentally disordered," Brett said, nodding sagely. "Perhaps some wine?"

Jamie shook his head. "Only make her worse."

"That is enough, the both of you," Isabel said, getting herself in order. "The furnishings alone should inform you that we are no longer in Squire Beechem's decrepit hunting lodge. A little decorum, if you please," she said to Jamie, "and a better example from *you*," she said grimly to Brett.

Fanny looked on with growing amazement. Who *was* this woman?!

"I beg your pardon," Brett said with a bow, but the laughter was dancing in his blue eyes.

And when had Fanny ever seen laughter there? 'Twas Armageddon and no one had told her!

"Allow me," Brett continued to Isabel, "to present you to Sir Henry Bevins, the magistrate for northwestern Lancashire. Sir Henry, Miss Isabel . . . Seton."

"How do you do, Miss Seton?" said Sir Henry as he heaved himself to his feet and shook her hand. "It's a pleasure meeting a gal of such courage and ingenuity. The fop in Oldcotes was quite brilliant."

"Why, thank you, Sir Henry," Isabel replied, and then cast an inquiring glance at Brett.

"I have told Sir Henry all, for reasons I shall explain later," he replied. "But for now, let us go in to dinner. I am famished."

"That is usually Jamie's line," Isabel said as she took his proffered arm.

"I merely reiterate what he has been saying this last hour."

"The chastisement was subtly wielded. I'm sorry I was so late coming down. I fell asleep in my bath."

Brett's step faltered for a moment. "A charming picture. Any gentleman would be glad to excuse the most blatant tardiness after such a confession."

"I am going to have to box your ears before the evening is out," Isabel stated.

Laughing, Brett led her into the family dining room.

It was, Isabel saw with some relief, but half the size of the drawing room. A cozy apartment, in fact, when compared to the rest of the house. She could almost allow herself to forget the grandeur lurking just beyond the door.

Brett sat Isabel on his right, Fanny was opposite him, and Jamie and Sir Henry were on his left. Throughout the meal Brett devoted most of his conversation to her, and Isabel found herself taking double pleasure in this for he did not look at her as he had done in Lennox or Bilby or even at Swanson Hall. There was no suspicion in his blue eyes, no surreptitious watching to see if she made some misstep in table manners, conversation, or decorum. Rather, his warm blue gaze seemed to enfold her, to make her a natural part of this luxurious room and sumptuous meal. In response, Isabel found herself acting not as Charlotte Hampstead or even as Miss Seton but simply as herself, as she had been on the road with Brett, on the Beauforts' balcony with Brett, and in Squire Beechem's hunting lodge with Brett.

Often he would lean toward her to share a private comment or a joke, and she would meet him halfway, their heads nearly touching, their breaths mingling almost with the intimacy of a kiss.

Isabel had never known such happiness.

Two hours after they had begun, the covers were removed, crystal decanters of brandy, port, and claret were placed upon the table, and the five diners leaned back in their chairs with contented sighs. Isabel's sigh was particularly heartfelt. There hadn't been a smidgen of rabbit in any of the twenty-four dishes that had passed before her.

"Well," said Brett, holding his brandy snifter between his hands and rolling the amber liquid slowly around the glass, "I suppose it's time I told you of the plans I've laid."

Isabel went still all over. "That would be nice," she said.

Brett smiled knowingly at her. "The most important matter, of course, is to meet the terms of the Thornwynd legacy. On the morrow, therefore, we shall repair to Thornwynd, where we will be joined by Sir Henry, Squire Babcock, Lord Farbel, and the Reverend Dillingham. They fill the roles stated in the legacy, to wit: the attending magistrate, the current squire, the bordering neighbor, and the local clergyman. Oh, and Nigel Clark must attend as well."

"Absolutely necessary," said Sir Henry, "to have the second male heir acknowledge the succession of the new Baron of Thornwynd."

Jamie and Isabel exchanged glances. Reading Isabel's caution, Jamie held his tongue.

"And what of Horace Shipley and his faux Jamie?" Isabel mildly inquired. "Will they not object to the proceedings?"

Sir Henry shifted uncomfortably in his chair. "We have as yet no proof that the boy at Thornwynd is not the true heir. Your Jamie, Miss Seton, must prove himself beyond all doubt to Babcock, Farbel, Dillingham, Clark, and myself, of course."

"And *when* that is accomplished, what then?" Isabel demanded. "We have many injuries to redress." She watched the earl and Sir Henry exchange glances.

"As to Horace Shipley," said Brett, taking a sip of brandy, "I have discussed our recent adventures with Sir Henry in great detail, and we have both reached the conclusion that we cannot charge Horace with Monty's murder."

The color flew into Jamie's face. He opened his mouth to protest, then suddenly closed it. He had seen Isabel's hand rise slightly from the table. His eyes were riveted to her face.

"And how is this, sir?" she calmly inquired.

"There's no proof," Brett said quietly.

"Not enough evidence," amended Sir Henry, "to incarcerate a fellow for murder done on foreign soil at any rate. Besides, a jury won't like seeing one of Lancashire's best families in court."

"And so Horace is not to be charged with Monty's murder," Isabel said, gazing at Brett's signet ring still on her hand. Her fingers slid up and down the stem of her wine goblet, rhythmically, almost idly. "What of the trifling matter of the fraud he now attempts to practice on his nephew's estate by championing an impostor?"

She felt Brett's eyes boring into her, but she would not look at him. She could not. It was all she could do to keep herself in her chair.

"Horace has covered himself nicely there as well," Brett said quietly. "His story has always been that Monty *sent* his Jamie to him for safekeeping. If your Jamie is proved the true heir, Horace has only to claim to be this second boy's dupe and that is the end of that. The courts can't touch him, Isabel. But I shall, I promise you. This adventure must have driven him into debt. I shall see to it that he is beggared. The rest of his miserable life shall be his punishment."

"And that, of course, redresses everything," Isabel said.

"I cannot go against the law," Brett said quietly.

"Particularly when so many doubts still plague your mind!"

"Justice will be served, Isabel, I swear it."

"I am very much afraid, my lord, that your idea of justice and mine are vastly different."

Brett forced her to meet his gaze. "Perhaps not so different as you believe."

"British law and British justice are not one and the same, Brett!"

"Miss Seton!" Sir Henry protested.

She forced her anger underground as she turned with a smile to the magistrate. "I'm sorry, Sir Henry. I did not mean

209

to offend. Philosophical debates often leave the truth behind in pursuit of victory. I should really study poetry more. Have you a favorite poet, Sir Henry?"

The party remained in conversation for another hour, discussing poetry, the muses, and German philosophers. All the while Isabel thought only of Monty, and Horace, and the sword stabbing out Monty's life.

At ten-thirty, Fanny Clotfelter rose from her chair and announced in a voice that would brook no opposition that the adventurers must surely be exhausted from their travels and longing for their beds. She was always happy to see Sir Henry, but it was time for them to retire. Calling her a naughty puss and chucking her under the chin, Sir Henry rose somewhat laboriously from his chair, opined that Sir Robert Clotfelter must be glad of this brief respite from such a martinet, and bid them all adieu.

Fanny drew Isabel's arm through hers and began to lead her down the hall, Jamie and Brett following behind. "If you don't take a firm hand with men," Fanny confided, "you'll never get anything accomplished."

"Words to live by, my lady," Isabel replied somewhat grimly.

"Now, now, you agreed to call me Fanny, remember? Why, from everything Brett has told me of you, I feel as if we were practically *sisters*."

Isabel barely kept in step with her escort. "You are very kind . . . Fanny."

"Tut, tut, I'm a plainspoken woman, like yourself, the bane of both my parents, my brother, and occasionally my husband. But Sir Robert is such a lamb that he never gets cross at any of my odd starts. Brett, on the other hand, always used to look at me in the most appalled manner. He is so very different now. Why, I scarcely recognized him today, he has changed so dramatically since the last time I saw him."

"When did you see him last?" Isabel inquired.

"In March."

Isabel blinked. "Well, they say that adventure can change a man."

"A woman may also change a man. Here we are, my dear! I'll bid you goodnight."

Fanny stopped Isabel at her bedroom door, kissed her on both cheeks, and then pushed her into the room before Isabel could scarcely make her adieus to Jamie and Brett. She found, with the door closed firmly behind her, that Eliza was waiting for her, a nightdress and dressing gown laid out on the bed.

"Will new clothes continue to magically appear, or is that the lot of them?" Isabel inquired as she advanced into the room.

"I've hung the rest of the clothes Miss Fanny brought for you in your wardrobe, miss," Eliza replied, "along with the clothes Dawkins saved from your travels."

"Which wasn't much, I'm afraid," Isabel said with a melancholy sigh. "There was this one atrocious hat that I dearly wish I had kept."

Chatting innocuously, Isabel allowed Eliza to help her change into her nightdress and brush out her hair. She got into bed and was firmly tucked in before Eliza blew out the candle and tiptoed out of the room.

Isabel would have been grateful for such consideration if she had planned, as she dearly wished, to sleep. But she could not sleep just yet. Throwing the bedcovers aside, she got up, pulled on her dressing gown, and in bare feet began to slowly walk the room. Occasionally she glanced into the carefully banked fires in the two fireplaces or gazed through one of the tall windows of her room that looked out over the thickly wooded park. She listened as the house grew more and more still. Pulling the curtains once again, she lit her bedside candle and waited.

Just as the clock on her mantle began to strike midnight, her bedroom door opened cautiously and then closed without a sound.

"We have to talk," said Jamie.

"Yes," Isabel said, "we do."

*

Chapter 16

May 17, 1804   Noon

Ravenscourt, Lancashire

THE NEXT MORNING was overcast and threatening. It seemed as if at any moment the slate sky would open up and dump torrents upon the somber-hued countryside. But Isabel saw little of the morning. She did not wake until after ten and did not appear in company until noon, when she walked into the dining room. Masculine charges of keeping city hours and a feminine inquiry if she had slept well were courteously addressed as she took her seat.

Her head was feeling its regular size again. The lump at the back of her head had been reduced to a barely noticeable bump. To her vast relief she was feeling fit and ready for action. At the moment action consisted of sampling the many dishes laid before her and keeping up an innocuous conversation with Fanny about the newest improvements to the pianoforte, an instrument to which they were both devoted, while every ounce of energy was dedicated to erecting and maintaining a wall that the lord of the house would not be able to breach that day.

By the time lunch had ended, rain poured out of the heavens and down the dining-room windows in sheets that obscured any view. Thunder could be heard in the distance. Isabel took little notice of the storm save to be grateful for the excuse it gave her to wear the cloak Fanny had thoughtfully provided in the wardrobe she had brought to Ravenscourt.

Isabel's thoughts, her spirits, and her heart were depressed. She would lose Jamie on this day, one way or another, and Brett. And the safety of secrecy she had known these last thirteen years.

She wondered if she would survive her coming meeting with Jonas Babcock and the accusations that must follow. For much of last night and now through lunch, she wrestled with whether or not she should tell Brett about the outstanding warrant for her arrest. Better for the news to come from her than from Squire Babcock.

And she wanted no more lies or hidden truths between them.

But there were two impediments to the confession: first, she hadn't the heart; and second, Jamie's rightful succession came first. If she told Brett now about the crime in her girlhood, his devotion to duty might demand he have her arrested before Jamie reached Thornwynd. And Jamie was counting on her help.

So she sat through lunch, gaily chatting with Fanny and inwardly miserable.

The earl glanced at his watch and stood up. "We should start for Thornwynd, I think. This rain is bound to make the roads slow-going."

"I want to change my coat," Jamie said, frowning at a sleeve of blue superfine. "This isn't quite suitable for the event."

"And I must get my cloak," Isabel said, forcing herself into the role—her last—that she must now play in Brett's company.

"Very well," Brett replied. "We will rendezvous in the Great Hall in fifteen minutes."

Isabel's return to her room was a study of careless ease. Once she had ordered Eliza out of the room, however, she hurriedly changed her clothes, frenetically checking and rechecking herself in the mirror to make sure that no tell-tale bulges could be seen in the thick cloak she drew around herself. She practiced walking and sitting until she could do it easily and unselfconsciously.

A quarter of an hour after she had risen from the dining table, she appeared in the Great Hall. Jamie had preceded her. He wore a dark blue many-caped greatcoat that enveloped him from chin to ankles. Fanny was also ready despite Isabel's hints throughout lunch that the succession ceremony would be wearying to any woman in her delicate condition.

"Stuff and nonsense!" Fanny had retorted. "I'm as healthy as an ox. Only ask Sir Robert!"

As Sir Robert was not at hand, and as Fanny clearly was in the first state of health, Isabel had finally given up trying to detour her hostess from the coming events.

With Dawkins once again upon the box, the four of them rode together in a dark green chaise-and-four, the Northbridge crest in gold upon the door, four magnificent chestnut thoroughbreds leaning into their traces. A dozen of his lordship's men on horseback surrounded the coach and acted as escort.

To convince their companions that nothing had changed in the night, Jamie and Isabel kept the conversation in the carriage on a light plane, telling Fanny some of their adventures with Monty on the Continent and arguing between themselves whether the gaming house in Brussels or the gaming house in Vienna had been more popular with the upper echelons of Continental Society.

"Your journey is ended, James," Brett said quietly.

Startled, Jamie craned his neck and gazed out the window just as they passed under a black iron arch bearing the Thornwynd crest.

" 'Tis a pretty park," he said softly, "even in the rain."

The mature trees on either side of them slowly gave way to extensive formal gardens, the colors muted in the gray day. Finally the road curved to the left, and there before them stood Thornwynd Manor, a handsome and surprisingly massive Tudor building of gray-white brick.

"Home," Jamie said softly.

215

Tears flooded Isabel's eyes and, horrified, she forced them back. She would not grieve that Monty had been unable to return to his home; she would not grieve that Jamie had been denied his own home until now; and she would certainly not grieve that she would not have the home and family this manor represented. This wasn't the time for grief. It could come later.

"Think you can live up to all this grandeur?" she demanded of Jamie once she could trust her voice again.

"It's going to be a pleasure," he replied with a grin.

"I've always been fond of Thornwynd," Fanny said with a wistful little sigh. "So stately and elegant, and yet there's just a touch of the pirate ship around the edges."

Yes, Isabel thought with a smile, it would have suited Monty admirably.

Dawkins drew the chaise to a stop before the front steps. Brett was the first out. He handed down Isabel and then Fanny. Finally Jamie stepped down onto the brick walk and stood gazing up at his ancestral home.

"Good luck to you, sir," said Dawkins.

"Thank you, old friend," Jamie said with a grin at the dour coachman. "I'm going to like it here," he announced as, leading the way, they walked through the rain to the front door.

Before Jamie could pull the bell, the door was opened by a butler of comfortable girth, his bald head shining in the lamplight. The butler looked Jamie up and down in a most imposing manner and then allowed the barest hint of a smile to touch his mouth.

"This is much better. Welcome home, my lord," he intoned. "I am Griffith, your butler."

"Not old Blood and Guts Griffith from my father's adventurous boyhood?" Jamie exclaimed.

"The same, sir," the butler replied without a blush.

"Well, well, you have certainly come up in the world! Monty would have been proud. Used to be the most scapegrace footman," Jamie informed a baffled Fanny. Isabel was well versed on the story. Brett's face was expressionless as he

216

looked on. "Always aiding and abetting my father in any boyish prank he cared to undertake. The bats in the bishop's bedroom makes a most diverting tale. Remind me to tell you of it sometime."

"Everyone here, Griffith?" Brett inquired of the reformed butler.

"Yes, sir. I have installed them, per your instructions, in the library."

"Come, James," said Brett, taking Jamie's arm, "it is time to face your double."

Isabel felt as if her skin had been tightly pinched across her bones as Fanny gaily claimed her arm and they advanced into the house.

The library was exactly as Monty had recalled it from his boyhood days. The room was long, nearly forty feet in length. Three walls were lined from floor to ceiling with books. The fourth wall, opposite her, bore nearly two dozen family portraits. Gazing at them, Isabel was startled at the family features that had been passed from generation to generation. The author of the legacy had chosen well in selecting the library as the site of the Thornwynd succession. Family resemblance would only help the heir, as it would help Jamie.

In the middle of these portraits she suddenly found herself riveted by a familiar gaze. She stared at Montague Shipley, not the silver fox she had known but the dark brown colt he had been as a boy perhaps a little older than what Jamie was now.

"We need all the help you can give us, Monty," she whispered.

"Don't worry, my dear," Fanny said, patting her hand, "Brett will insure that everything goes splendidly. He always does."

Three large crystal chandeliers hung from the paneled ceiling. At the far end of the room was a desk with two leather wing chairs before it. At the opposite end of the library were a sofa, two armchairs, and a chaise longue. There were no other furnishings.

Isabel gazed upon it all with grim satisfaction. There would be enough room.

In the center of the library stood Sir Henry Bevins; Lord Farbel, Jamie's nearest neighbor, a tall, emaciated gentleman of perhaps seventy years; the Reverend Dillingham, a robust cleric of forty-two years who seemed more suited to the hunt than to the church; and Squire Babcock, a compact, dour-looking man in breeches and an out-of-date frock coat.

The bile rose in Isabel's throat. He was an older version of her stepfather! Not as tall, perhaps, but he had the same harsh expression and the same nearly white eyes that gave him an unearthly, almost hellish appearance.

Fortunately he had not yet seen her, and she was able to regain control over her shuddering heart and suddenly inactive lungs. She forced her gaze to the man beside her stepuncle.

Nigel Clark, Jamie's cousin, was perhaps an inch taller than he, though not as broad in the chest or shoulders. His hair was a light brown, as were his eyes. She disliked him on the spot. There was a hardness to his mouth and a hauteur to his air that indicated he thought himself superior to everyone in his acquaintance.

"So, this is the second claimant, eh?" he said, extending his hand to Jamie. "Welcome to Thornwynd, lad."

"Thank you . . . Cousin," Jamie replied, a trifle off kilter, for he had never met a relative before.

Brett then introduced Isabel to the gentlemen before her.

"You are . . . a friend of the family?" the elderly Lord Farbel inquired.

"A close friend," Jamie amended. "She has saved my life times past counting."

"Has she, by gad?" erupted Reverend Dillingham. "Well, there's precedent. There's precedent. The Bible is littered with females defending their cubs from all comers. I salute you, Miss Seton."

"Why, thank you, Reverend," Isabel said.

Jonas Babcock, she knew, had been studying her hard from the moment Brett had introduced her.

218

"By gad, this creature is no Miss Seton!" he suddenly bellowed. "She is a murderess!"

Everyone gasped, even Jamie.

"What are you babbling about, Babcock?" Nigel Clark demanded.

"I tell you, this is no Miss Seton! This is my stepniece, Gleana Isabel Dalton! She murdered my only brother!"

"Hello, Mr. Babcock," Isabel said above the various exclamations from their audience. "How thoroughly unpleasant to see you again."

"Sir Henry!" Babcock shouted. "Arrest this creature at once!"

"Isabel," said Jamie, his young face bloodless as he grasped her arm, "is this true?"

"Yes, child," Isabel said gently.

"Why didn't you tell me?!"

"I did not want you to feel guilty that, in protecting you, I was exposing myself to additional danger. You had enough to worry about on your own account."

"Oh God," Jamie said, agonized. "*This* is the warrant you mentioned that last night in Vienna. You knew Babcock would be here! You knew you were walking into a hangman's noose!"

"I gave my word to Monty to see you safely installed at Thornwynd. Indeed," Isabel continued, breaking into the argument Babcock was waging with Sir Henry, Lord Farbel, and the Reverend Dillingham, "that is why we have gathered, is it not, gentlemen? To install the new heir to Thornwynd? Surely this other matter can wait until we have attended to the more pressing problem at hand."

"I'll see you hanged, Gleana!" Jonas Babcock yelled.

"That is quite enough, all of you," Brett declared in that masterful manner so peculiarly his. The room was instantly hushed. "The succession has always been our first concern. We will deal with Mr. Babcock's charges immediately afterward."

"But she's a murderess, I tell you!" Babcock fumed.

"All in good time, Squire," Brett snapped.

Looking at the earl's hard, impassive face was like looking upon her own death. Everything ended for Isabel in that moment, save one: Jamie.

"Shall we fulfill the legacy?" she inquired.

"Certainly," Jamie replied, studying her for a moment. He seemed to make a decision, for he suddenly adopted a jovial expression and turned to the others. "But where is my uncle? I am longing to meet him."

Isabel smiled inwardly. Monty had taught his son well.

"I had not forgotten Mr. Shipley," Brett said. "Mason!" he called.

Mason stepped into the room, cradling a shotgun.

"What's all this?!" Lord Farbel sputtered, already a good deal put out by the excitement he had been forced to endure thus far.

Mason was followed by a boy of perhaps seventeen, a little shorter than Jamie, certainly more slender, with a shock of brown hair and terrified brown eyes. His clothes were ludicrously ostentatious—white satin with gold silk woven throughout. His neck cloth was so voluminous, Isabel was in fear of seeing him strangled at any moment. Still, he had the Shipley nose, and that was a shock.

The boy, in turn, was followed by a shark. He was a good two inches taller than Jamie and all muscle, not an ounce of fat. His hair was slate gray, like the sky, his eyes a glittering brown, his clothes silver and gray. Isabel had long ago learned what people to avoid at all costs. This was one of the most dangerous men she had ever seen. Her eyes flew to Jamie. His face was impassive, though there was some color in his cheeks as he gazed upon his father's murderer.

Horace Shipley and his pretender were surrounded now by Mason and five others of the Earl of Northbridge's employ who kept their guns trained on the pair.

"Sir Henry!" roared Mr. Shipley, causing at least two witnesses to jump. "I want these men arrested at once!"

"On what charge, Mr. Shipley?" Sir Henry inquired, taking a pinch of snuff.

"Housebreaking!"

The Reverend Dillingham guffawed.

The color rose in Horace Shipley's cheeks as the second Jamie cowered beside him.

"Now, now, Mr. Shipley," said Sir Henry soothingly. "I'm sure that you're exaggerating things."

"Exaggerating?!" Mr. Shipley sputtered. "When armed men burst into my home and lock me in my bedroom, terrorize my poor nephew, and hold me against my will at *gunpoint*, I do not think it is exaggerating to call that housebreaking at the least, even *kidnapping*!"

"What's all this?" said the Reverend Dillingham.

"A misunderstanding, merely," Brett said soothingly.

"*You!*" Horace said venomously, turning upon the earl. "You're behind this outrage. This whole filthy business *reeks* of Northbridge!"

"My brother," Fanny said severely, "is known throughout the country for the propriety of his actions. A Northbridge would never stoop to housebreaking. Housebreaking forsooth!"

"Thank you, Fanny," said the earl with a fond smile. Then he turned back to Mr. Shipley. "I was merely anxious that you attend today's ceremony, Horace. The succession is a momentous event for the Shipleys, after all. I wouldn't want you to miss your nephew's installation."

Isabel considered the earl. He *was* playing this close to the chest. Perhaps she should not have chastised him with such vigor during their adventures, for it seemed his suspicion cut both ways.

"Mason," he said, "you and the others may go now. If you'll wait in the kitchen, I believe Griffith can find you some hot food."

"Very good, my lord," Mason said. He and the others trooped from the library, closing the door behind them.

"Come," Brett said pleasantly to the glowering Mr. Shipley, "I don't believe you've met your other nephew. Jamie, *this* is the despicable blackguard from whom Monty protected you."

Everyone in the room gasped. Horace Shipley's face was vermilion. "I'll call you out for that insult, Northbridge!"

"But I meant no insult," Brett said innocently. "I only repeated what had been quoted to me some days back. Come, Horace, what do you think of the boy?"

Far from mollified, Mr. Shipley looked Jamie up and down with a sneer. "I'll deny to my dying breath that this pasty-faced calfling has any claim to Thornwynd! You think you're so everlastingly clever, Northbridge, but you've been duped! This boy is an impostor!"

"I lay claim to many faults," Brett said coldly, "but being duped is not one of them."

Isabel cringed.

"Let us end this charade once and for all," Brett continued. "It is time to meet the requirements of the legacy."

He sat behind the desk and read from the yellowed parchment before him as the others formed a half circle around him, Squire Babcock still glowering at Isabel. The Thornwynd legacy set out in considerable detail and in the tongue-twisting archaic English of a sadistic Tudor solicitor the requirements attendant on one Baron of Thornwynd succeeding another. First was adequate proof of his identity before several reputable men, as delineated in the legacy. Second was an acknowledgment from the next male heir to the baronetcy that this was the one true heir before them all. Third was an oath that the heir was to take. And last came his signature, below that of his grandfather, on the parchment, witnessed by all the others in the room.

"Therefore," Brett said, setting the legacy back on the desk and rising from his chair, "as executor of the will of Montague Shipley—"

222

"I contest that!" Horace Shipley broke in.

"Oh, do shut up," Brett said wearily. "I believe no one else in this room questions my authority to act in this matter?" He scanned the room. No one demurred.

"We hang upon your lips, sir," Jamie assured him.

A suspicion of a smile quirked the corner of Brett's mouth. "It is my duty," he continued, "to resolve this confusion as to who is the true James Shipley and who the impostor. If the two claimants will stand together?"

Like Mr. Garrick directing *The Comedy of Errors*, the Earl of Northbridge lined Jamie and the pretender up side by side and grouped Mr. Shipley and the witnesses together in front of the desk, opposite the boys.

"As you can see," the earl continued, "we cannot decide who is the real heir by features alone, for they both look like Shipleys. But there are other ways of selecting an heir. Let us demand adequate proof of their identities. You," he said to the pretender, "may go first. State your full name, the names of your parents, and the date and place of your birth."

"I—" The boy cleared his throat and began once again as Horace Shipley glared at him. "I am James Montague Shipley, the son of Montague and Clara Shipley. I was born December fifth, 1787 in . . . in Florence. I have my baptismal record."

He pulled a soiled document from his coat pocket and, hand shaking, gave it to Brett.

"And what of you?" said the earl to Jamie.

"This is a farce!" roared Horace Shipley. "This boy is no more—"

"Do be quiet," Sir Henry complained, nudging him sharply in the ribs. "I want to hear this."

"I am James Montague Shipley," Jamie stated in a clear, proud voice, "first and only child of Montague Wentworth Shipley and Clara Honoria Robinson Shipley. I was born on December fifth in the year of Our Lord 1787 in a rather ornate piazza in the city of Florence. I was, as is natural for a Shipley, a beautiful baby."

223

Brett smiled at this. "And what proof can you offer these gentlemen of your identity?"

"None, save my word and my character," Jamie replied.

"Ha!" Horace Shipley gloated. "Then there's an end to this impostor's claims. *This*," he said, clapping a hand on his claimant's shoulder, "is the *true* James Shipley."

"Not so fast," Brett intervened as he passed the sole baptismal record to each of the required witnesses. Fanny managed to sneak a peek as well. Isabel stood silently in a corner behind the desk, watching everything.

"It seems in order," said Lord Farbel.

"But documents," Brett said, "as I am sure Mr. Shipley will attest, can be falsified. Therefore, we cannot rely merely on this scrap of paper."

"How else are we to tell them apart then?" Reverend Dillingham demanded.

"A stab at common sense would seem to be in order," Brett replied. "The true James Shipley has known many people in his life who can identify him."

"This murderess, I suppose?" Horace sneered, glaring at Isabel.

"There are many who would have met the true James Shipley in company with his father," Brett coldly continued.

"Exactly! *Precisely*," Horace retorted. "I have met my nephew off and on over the years and *this* is he!"

"Piffle," Jamie riposted to all save Isabel's amazement. "Monty took care to keep me from the pollution of your acquaintance, *uncle*. We have never met before this."

"There are other witnesses that I believe we can rely on," Brett intervened. "Dick! Mr. Harvey!"

Dick Rowan and a gentleman almost as small as he, though possessed of a good deal more hair, entered the room.

"I believe Sir Henry Bevins can attest," said Brett, "that the gentleman on the right is Mr. Bartholomew Harvey, Esquire, of Cookson and Sons, solicitors, London."

"Indeed I can," said Sir Henry. "So, Northbridge has lured you into this game as well, has he, Harvey?"

"Yes, Sir Henry," Mr. Harvey replied in carefully rounded tones.

"What the devil for?" demanded Squire Babcock.

"Over three years ago," Mr. Harvey replied, "I was asked to go to the Continent in search of Mr. Montague Shipley to inform him of his father's stroke and to solicit his return to England, if only for a visit. The late Sir Barnaby's solicitor, Mr. Stone, is a cousin of my employers, the Cooksons."

"And did you find Mr. Shipley?" Lord Farbel demanded.

"Indeed I did, my lord. In Brussels it was. Master James and Miss Richards were with him at the time. Hello, Miss Richards."

"Hello, Mr. Harvey," Isabel replied easily. "It is good to see you again."

"I thought her name was Seton," Reverend Dillingham murmured.

"No, no, it is *Dalton*," Fanny whispered.

"Having been in company with both Montague Shipley and his son," Brett continued, "would you feel confident in identifying James Shipley for us?"

"Oh, certainly," Mr. Harvey replied with a pardonable self-importance. "I never forget a face. Part of the job, you know." He walked up to the boys, looked at each, and placed a hand on Jamie's shoulder. "This is James Shipley."

"Thank you, Mr. Harvey," Jamie said with a grin.

"Ah, ah, ah, Horace," Brett said, holding up one hand. "I see you are about to protest this identification. I see the word 'bribery' hovering on your lips. That is why Dick is here. You remember Dick, don't you, Lord Farbel?"

Lord Farbel looked Dick up and down. "Dick Rowan, brother to my man Daniel," he pronounced.

"It is good of you to remember me, my lord," Dick said. "And I am gratified to hear that my brother has come up so well in the world."

"Oh yes, there's no doubt this is Dick Rowan," Lord Farbel informed the others. "You were hired to serve Montague Shipley, were you not?"

"And never left his side till the day he died, my lord," Dick replied.

"Dick should be able to recognize James Shipley, wouldn't you agree, gentlemen?" Brett inquired.

"Indubitably," Reverend Dillingham replied.

"Well, Dick?" said Brett.

"And didn't I raise him from a pup?" Dick demanded. He slapped Jamie on the back. "This is James Shipley and make no mistake."

"This is nothing but flummery and lies!" Horace Shipley sputtered. "One servant may be as easily bribed as another. *My* nephew, the true Jamie, has the family appearance, he can recite the family history verbatim, he knows the Thornwynd password, *and* he has the only documents in the case to prove his identity."

"Now I must challenge that," Brett said mildly. He drew a packet of letters from a coat pocket. "I have here only a dozen of the hundreds of letters my father and I received from Montague Shipley in a correspondence that lasted nearly three decades. Sir Henry and Mr. Harvey have been so good as to authenticate these letters as genuine. Every letter from the day of his son's birth details Monty's pride in Jamie's newest accomplishments. Among those are . . . oh, let's see," Brett said as he began to scan the letters, Isabel watching him with growing amazement, "a fluency in several languages, including French, German, Spanish, and Italian; athletic abilities including fencing, riding, hunting, and dancing; a decided skill with firearms; and an innate acting talent that enabled him to pretend to be everything from a stable boy to a duke's son."

Isabel's mouth fell open. Brett . . . the ever-suspicious *Earl of Northbridge* was proving her Jamie to be the rightful heir!

"While allowing for a father's natural pride in his son's accomplishments," Brett blithely continued, "I believe we can use Montague Shipley's own written testimony to prove without a doubt which boy is the true heir. *I* have been in company with both boys and have had occasion to study them both closely. This one," he said, clapping a hand on Jamie's shoulder, "is by far the superior on horseback, on the dance floor, in use of firearms, and as an actor. Moreover, he frequently uses certain phrases that were particularly Monty's own, and he also has Monty's heart and courage. The same," he said with a chilling glare at the boy trembling at Horace Shipley's side, "cannot be said of our second claimant. But I think language should provide the conclusive test. As we all know, Monty traveled extensively on the Continent, and by his own claim, his son is an adept at several languages. Lord Farbel, would you be so good as to put these boys to the test?"

"Certainly, Northbridge," the elderly Lord Farbel replied with pardonable self-satisfaction. "We'll start with something simple and work our way up, shall we? You there," he said to the ashen boy at Horace Shipley's side, *"comment vous appelez-vous?"*

"Je m'appelle James Shipley, monsieur."

Isabel stared, horrified, at the boy. He spoke French like a native!

Lord Farbel led the boy through a more and more intricate conversation in French. The boy never slipped. But when Lord Farbel switched to Spanish, panic-stricken brown eyes looked helplessly up at Horace. He began to shake as Lord Farbel tried Italian. When Lord Farbel began speaking German, the boy seemed to melt into a little puddle of terror.

"Et vous?" Lord Farbel said to Jamie. *"Comment vous appelez-vous?"*

"Je m'appelle James Montague Shipley, naturellement," Jamie replied fluently, and then led Lord Farbel through a five-minute conversation in fluent French of Thornwynd's history. He switched to Italian to discuss the education he had received on the Continent, then to Spanish to detail a magnificent horse he had received on his fourteenth birthday, and finally to

German to detail the struggles he had had memorizing *Faust*. He began a discussion—in Latin—of Socrates' philosophy, but Lord Farbel held up his hand.

"That is quite enough, thank you. Gentlemen," Lord Farbel said to the others, "I am quite convinced that this is the true heir to Thornwynd."

"And I," said Nigel Clark.

"I've been convinced for some time that this is Montague Shipley's heir," said Sir Henry Bevins.

"Oh, there's no doubt about it," said the Reverend Dillingham. "The boy's Latin is impeccable. And if both Lord Northbridge and Lord Farbel vouchsafe him—"

"A pretty piece of villainy *you've* been enacting," Squire Babcock sneered at Horace Shipley.

They waited for Mr. Shipley's reaction. He stunned them all by turning on the pretender and striking him to the ground. "You cur!" he bellowed. "You lying, deceitful *cheat*! You told me you were my brother's son. You claimed me as your uncle and your protector and all the while you were nothing but a fraud!" He turned to his appalled audience. "It is clear that I have been duped and criminally used by this impostor. I trust, Sir Henry, that you will see him properly charged and jailed."

"No!" the boy shrieked.

"You disappoint me, Shipley," Brett said with a grimace. "You are so wearingly predictable. What about you?" he said to the terrified boy. "Tell us the truth now and things won't go so hard for you."

Sweat poured from the pretender's brow. He was so pale, Isabel thought he must surely faint. "It was *him*!" the boy shrieked, pointing at Mr. Shipley as he scuttled across the floor to escape any further blows. "*He* made me do it! He is my natural father."

"That *would* explain the family resemblance," Reverend Dillingham remarked.

"He said he'd make me rich," the boy sobbed. "I have six

228

brothers and sisters living in Paris to care for. Our mother is dead. How could I say no?"

"Do you stand there and tell me," said Horace Shipley in the greatest disgust, "that you would believe this filthy foreigner and liar over a *Shipley*?!"

"Over *your* word?" Brett said coldly. "Yes. Don't say anything further, Shipley, for I warn you I would like nothing better than to see you entombed in some rotting jail for the rest of your life!"

"Do restrain yourself, Northbridge," Lord Farbel advised. "It won't do for the Baronet of Thornwynd to have an uncle in jail. Very scandalous. Not at all the thing."

"Precisely," said Brett with some bitterness. "Therefore, Horace, you've got a reprieve of sorts. Though you're a murderer and a fraud, you're not going to prison. You're being shipped off to Canada."

"*Canada?!*" Horace Shipley fumed. "What the devil do you expect me to do in *Canada*?"

"Suffer ten times the suffering you have inflicted on Jamie," Brett said.

"You've no right—"

"*Don't push me further, Shipley!*" Brett said in a murderously cold voice Isabel had never heard before. "For now, you will watch the installation of your nephew as Baronet of Thornwynd."

Jamie took his oath. His signature on the legacy followed.

While the gentlemen and Fanny, for she insisted on adding her mite, were gathered around the desk signing the legacy as witnesses, Isabel moved inconspicuously back from the group until she had reached the other side of the room. There she removed her cloak, setting it neatly upon the back of a chair after retrieving the pistols she had secreted in its inner pockets. She wore buckskins and a white shirt, opened at the throat. The pistols were steady in her hands.

"We are all agreed, then," said Brett as Lord Farbel signed

229

the legacy, "that Monty's will is a true document and that I am James Shipley's guardian until he reaches his majority?"

"Oh, certainly, certainly," murmured the others.

"I thank you. Horace Shipley," Brett stated, his blue eyes drilling into Mr. Shipley as the others straightened from their task, "I charge you before these witnesses with the health and safety of James Montague Shipley, Baron of Thornwynd. If any ill fortune strikes the House of Thornwynd, I shall hold you personally accountable and I will hunt you down and kill you like the murderous dog you are."

"You go too far, Northbridge!" Shipley hissed. "Is this how you mean to protect your precious ward? By forcing a duel on me?"

"No, no," Isabel said, walking calmly toward the desk, "that is Jamie's prerogative. Fanny and Brett, if you and the others would be so good as to stand against that wall behind the desk, I would be most obliged."

She had her pistols trained upon the party. Her voice was flat, without any trace of emotion.

"Isabel, what the devil—" Brett began.

"We are attending to a little unfinished business," Jamie said, the pistol he had secreted in his greatcoat now in his hand and aimed at Horace Shipley's head.

"This is an outrage!" Lord Farbel sputtered. "Put down those guns at once!"

"In good time, my lord. In good time," Isabel said soothingly. "For now, you will all cooperate by standing very still and not interfering in an important piece of family business."

"I told you! I told you all!" Jonas Babcock cried. "She's a cold-blooded murderess. Look at her eyes. She's insane! She'll kill us all!"

"Oh, do shut up, Babcock," Isabel said wearily.

"Isabel," Brett said in a low voice, taking a step toward her, "this is insanity. You must know it."

She hid behind the wall in her heart. "You will return to your sister's side, Brett, or I will shoot you."

230

His blue eyes met hers. "You cannot kill me."

"No," Isabel calmly agreed. "But I can hurt you enough to stop your interference."

Their eyes held for a long, suspended minute. Then Brett stepped back to Fanny's side.

"My dear Miss . . . er . . . Dalton," the Reverend Dillingham said with forced geniality, "this is all very melodramatic, of course, but not at all suitable to one of your gentle sex."

"Brett," said Isabel, "be so good as to inform your sister and these gentlemen that I will not hesitate to shoot anyone who makes the slightest move."

"Fanny, gentlemen, Miss Dalton is a woman of her word and an excellent shot," Brett said quietly. "I advise you not to move."

Still keeping the little group under guard, Isabel backed to the nearest library door and shouted, "Dick!"

Dick Rowan, who had slipped unobtrusively from the room, now returned. In his hands were two swords. A pistol was shoved into his belt. He set the swords upon the desk and then, taking the pistol from his belt, aimed it at Horace Shipley's heart. Jamie lowered his gun and began to remove his great-coat. Like Isabel, he, too, was dressed in buckskins and a white shirt.

"You cannot be serious," Mr. Shipley said with a sneer.

Jamie struck him across the face with the back of his hand, the crack reverberating in the room. A little blood trickled from the corner of his uncle's mouth.

"I am deadly serious," Jamie hissed. "You murdered my father. He must and shall be avenged."

"I? Murder your father?" Mr. Shipley said with every aspect of surprise as he dabbed at the corner of his mouth. "Now, how is that possible? I have been in France the whole of this last year, and it is my understanding that my poor brother died in Vienna."

"He died on your orders, *Uncle*. I will not argue the matter with you. I will have my vengeance. Choose your sword."

"Jamie, no!" Fanny cried. "He is a noted swordsman!"

"Jamie, don't throw your life away like this!" Brett said in a low, urgent voice. "You have Thornwynd and your whole life before you. Your shoulder is still weak. Horace Shipley has thirty years more experience and skill than you. He has already killed five men in duels."

"But I was trained by Monty," Jamie calmly replied. "That must balance the scales, don't you think?"

"Isabel, you must stop this madness now," Brett implored. "You gave your pledge to Monty. You are responsible for Jamie's safety. Do not throw him onto his uncle's sword!"

"Last night you and Sir Henry made it abundantly clear that Jamie could find no recourse in the law for his father's murder," Isabel stated, her face expressionless. "Monty's death must be redressed. The onus lies on us both. Pick up your sword, Mr. Shipley."

His eyes on her guns, Horace Shipley removed his coat and then slowly clasped the hilt of his sword.

"This," he said, "is going to be a distinct pleasure."

"Dick, keep our friends under guard," Isabel instructed the little man, handing him one of her guns. "Gentlemen," she said to Jamie and Horace, "follow me." She led them to the center of the room, then turned and laid a hand on Jamie's shoulder. "Remember," she said quietly, "if you fight him with your hate rather than your head, he will kill you."

"Aye," Jamie said softly, his eyes drilling into his uncle, "I'll remember."

"I will call the start," Isabel announced. "Any deviation from the standard rules of fencing will be met by a bullet, Mr. Shipley."

"It will be a pleasure laying this boy's dead body at your feet!" Mr. Shipley growled.

Jamie and he assumed the opening stance, their swords raised, the tips touching between them.

"Gentlemen, *en garde*!" Isabel cried, and then hurriedly stepped back.

The first clash of cold steel rang in the room. Mr. Shipley lunged, his longer thrust driving Jamie back again and yet again. But Jamie parried each thrust and, with a sudden side step, sent Shipley staggering forward. Jamie's sword flashed beneath the crystal chandeliers. A thin line of blood seeped from Shipley's upper sword arm.

Enraged, he began to batter at Jamie with quick furious blows that left the room ringing, for Jamie met every murderous attack with his sword. Back and forth they pushed each other around the library, sweat drenching them both.

Shipley slashed at Jamie's belly.

Jamie danced out of the way and laughed. "You're slowing down, Uncle!"

"And you," Mr. Shipley spat, driving at him, "are just a little too cocksure of yourself!"

"No, no, Uncle," said Jamie, pushing him back, "that is your fault!"

He suddenly spun, the tip of his sword sweeping across Mr. Shipley's chest, leaving a thin line of blood in its wake.

"Twice blooded, thrice dead," he chanted, leaping back from his uncle's enraged counterattack.

Fury drove the older man on, battering at Jamie's defense. Jamie stumbled to his knees. Everyone in the room thought him dead then.

Trembling, Isabel raised her pistol.

But as Mr. Shipley's sword plunged downward, Jamie rolled out of the way and onto his feet, and with Shipley caught off balance, he threw himself against his uncle, knocking him to the ground.

Horace raised his sword to defend himself, rising to his knees. But with one mighty sweep, Jamie tore the sword from his hands and sent it flying across the room.

He stood over his uncle, panting, his sword raised as if he would behead him.

"Jamie, no!" Brett shouted.

It was just the distraction Horace needed. He grabbed a

pocket pistol from his back waistband and leveled it at Jamie's heart.

A gunshot echoed in the library. Mr. Shipley's gun slipped from his fingers as he stared, horror-struck, at the blood flowing freely down his arm.

"Jamie, love—" Isabel cried, starting forward.

Jamie held up his hand with a smile. "I'm well. You always were a superb shot."

"Thank you, love," she said, hugging him.

Jamie pulled away and suddenly raised his sword. Horace Shipley's shriek filled the air, causing more than one witness to shudder, as Jamie's sword slashed across his uncle's face.

"You are marked for what remains of your miserable life, *Uncle*," Jamie spat. "Hear me well: If you ever cross the Atlantic back to England or the Continent, I will kill you. I will kill you as I should have done today."

Jamie threw his sword to the floor and walked back to Isabel. She laid her pistol on a small table and slid her arm around his waist.

"That, ladies and gentlemen," she said calmly, though every vein in her body was vibrating with relief, "is the end of today's performance."

The library remained in stark silence for a moment.

"Help Mr. Shipley to his feet, Dick," Isabel said quietly.

The little man laid his guns on the desk and went over to the shuddering mass that was Horace Shipley. "Here now, be a man," he abjured. "Think you'd never seen your own blood before, the way you're carrying on."

It was at this point that Mason and his five cohorts burst into the library, guns at the ready. "We heard gunshots, my lord!"

"A minor squabble only, Mason," Brett said easily. "Nothing to be alarmed about. You may now take Horace Shipley in tow and escort him to Liverpool as I instructed you earlier. Make sure that he sails on the *Amanda Lee* to Montreal. Swim after him if you have to, but make sure he's on that ship."

"Certainly, sir," Mason replied as, impassively, he grasped

Horace Shipley's good arm and jerked him from the room, the five other guards trailing behind.

"And what shall we do with this one?" Reverend Dillingham inquired.

"You mean the pawn?" Brett inquired, staring at the pretender who was now quite green with terror. "He does present a certain complication. I have no doubt he was browbeaten into this charade."

"I'll not have him punished," Jamie announced. "*I've* no doubt he's been in fear of his life this last month, as have I. He is not accountable for his actions. And he *is* my cousin. I'll not have him harmed."

"Said like a true Thornwynd," Lord Farbel murmured.

"As you wish," Brett said. "But we must do something with the boy." He thought a moment. "Mr. Harvey," Brett called to the solicitor, "could you not find room for a new clerk at Cookson and Sons?"

"I am happy to oblige you, my lord," said Mr. Harvey with a bow.

"I'll arrange to have your family brought to you from Paris," Brett assured the stunned youth. "I daresay work can be found for them all."

"And now will you attend to *my* charges against this heinous woman?" Jonas Babcock demanded.

"Not just yet," Brett said apologetically. "There is still the niggling matter of who has been trying to murder Jamie this last fortnight. Oh, Mr. Clark, if I might just have a word with you?"

Chapter 17

May 17, 1804   Midafternoon

Thornwynd Hall, near Scorton, Lancashire

"CLARK?!" SAID ISABEL and Jamie as one.

"What the devil are you talking about?" Jonas Babcock demanded.

"Yes, what has Mr. Clark to do with anything, Northbridge?" Lord Farbel said.

"A good deal, actually," the earl replied. "Don't you, Nigel?"

"I haven't the vaguest idea what you're talking about, Northbridge," Mr. Clark replied with great unconcern.

"But I think you do," Brett said, sitting on the edge of the library desk and swinging one leg. Isabel and Jamie stared at him in something akin to amazement. "For the last fortnight, someone has spent an extraordinary amount of time, energy, and *money* trying to keep Jamie from reaching Thornwynd. I was puzzled at first. It was probable that Horace Shipley wanted Jamie dead, but I also knew that his pockets were completely to let. How, then, could he pay for the attacks upon Jamie, Isabel, and me on our journey north? The only answer was that he could not. Who, then, I asked myself, would also profit from Jamie's death? The answer was obvious: the next heir to Thornwynd, Nigel Clark."

"This is pure and utter nonsense," Mr. Clark scoffed as

everyone in the room stared at him. "I've money enough of my own. I've no need for the Thornwynd fortune."

"So it would seem," Brett said. "Still, it was your fortune which first made me begin to seriously suspect you. *You* had more than enough money to hire five *dozen* brigands to stop us if you wanted. But what bothered me was that such a show of strength was not at all your style, Nigel. You are not one to use a blunt instrument when a stiletto will do a much neater and quieter job . . . unless you are desperate. And what, I wondered, could make a man of your intelligence and fortune desperate?"

"Good God, the estate!" Sir Henry Bevins burst out. "He had Sir Barnaby's power of attorney. He ran Thornwynd for the last three years of Sir Barnaby's life. *And* he is executor of Sir Barnaby's will!"

Isabel looked at Brett. "Has Mr. Clark been embezzling from Thornwynd, sir?"

"Steadily," Brett replied with an appreciative glance at her.

"That's a damned lie!" Mr. Clark exploded. He took a step toward the earl, hands clenched at his sides.

"It was well hidden, I grant you," Brett continued, unperturbed by this threatening stance. "It took me most of last night going through Wyndham's financial records to pick up your trail. Your own fortune wasn't enough, was it, Clark? Not for a man of your ambition. There was Thornwynd sitting fat and sleek and ready for the plucking. Sir Barnaby's stroke and dependence on you gave you the perfect opportunity to take what you wanted. And you did."

"This is all sheer fabrication," Clark hissed. He turned to the others. "Don't you see what he's doing? With me out of the way, he can plunder Thornwynd with impunity!"

"That won't fadge, Clark, and you know it," Sir Henry retorted.

"My brother," said Fanny haughtily, "is one of the most honest and respected men in England. No one, however, has ever been able to say the same of you, Mr. Clark."

237

"If you were a man—" Clark growled.

"I would take the greatest pleasure in planting you a facer!" Fanny retorted.

Isabel didn't even try to hold back her low chuckle.

"But surely, if Clark *did* embezzle from the estate, he knew that he must be discovered by Sir Barnaby's heir," Reverend Dillingham broke in. "Would not that alone have deterred him from committing so heinous a crime?"

"You have not lived with us long, Mr. Dillingham," Brett replied. "Sir Barnaby was a selfish, grasping, mean-spirited man. I dare say he hinted to Clark that he would leave Thornwynd to *him*. After all, why shouldn't he? Horace had been disinherited, Monty lived a scapegrace life and had visited his father exactly once in thirty years. Nigel, however, had devoted himself to waiting on his grandfather hand and foot for years. The title must go to Monty, but why *shouldn't* Sir Barnaby leave Thornwynd to his daughter's son rather than to a disappointing second son? Unfortunately, Nigel failed to take into account his grandfather's noted cruelty."

"Rather than inheriting what he had robbed, Clark found himself staring discovery and ruin in the face," Isabel said, gazing admiringly at the earl.

"Precisely," said Brett. "His only chance to protect himself was to prevent Monty and Jamie from fulfilling the requirements of the Thornwynd legacy. It must have been a tremendous relief to you, Nigel, to find that Horace had already dispatched Monty. That left only Jamie standing between you and safety. You undoubtedly had your own proof that the pretender was precisely that. All you had to do was keep the real Jamie from reaching Thornwynd in time and you would inherit everything, including proof of the embezzlement. And there was Horace Shipley as your shield. If anything happened to Jamie on the road, Horace would be blamed, not you."

"You're grasping at straws, Northbridge," Clark sneered, resting one hip against the desk. "You can't prove any of this."

"You're only partially right," Brett said, sliding off the desk

238

and advancing on Mr. Clark. "I haven't enough evidence to prove the many ways you tried to harm and even kill us on the road north. But I *can* prove the embezzlement. Unfortunately, that would place an heir to Thornwynd in jail. Not at all the thing, as Lord Farbel would assure us. Therefore," Brett said pleasantly, "I intend to break you. In fact, I've already begun. I recommend emigration within the next twenty-four hours, Clark, if you want to possess more than the clothes on your back. Griffith!" the earl called out.

The bald butler entered the library, shotgun cradled in his arm. It seemed, in his considerable opinion, to be that sort of a day.

"Have a half dozen of my men outside escort Mr. Clark to his home," Brett instructed him.

"I'll see you in Hell first!" Clark roared. He grasped a letter opener on the desk and drove it toward the earl's heart.

"Brett!" Fanny screamed.

But the cry came too late. Before anyone could move, the earl's hand had shot up and caught Mr. Clark's wrist. The letter opener was suspended between them.

"Physical violence isn't really your forte, Nigel," Brett said smoothly. "I have discovered, however, that it *is* mine."

Clark screamed as the letter opener fell to the floor. "My wrist! He's broken my wrist!"

Brett released Clark and took a step back. "Oh, how clumsy of me," he said mildly. "Griffith, take Clark outside to my men. You may summon him a doctor after he has packed his bags."

Clasping his wrist, cursing freely now, Nigel Clark was led from the room, a shotgun barrel pressed into his back.

Isabel stared at Brett, trembling with the horror of what might have been.

"A splendid adventure!" the Reverend Dillingham exulted. "Simply splendid!"

"It was well played, guardian," said Jamie with a grin. "Monty couldn't have done better."

"You overwhelm me, ward," Brett said with a bow.

"You are unharmed, sir?" Isabel inquired in a low voice.

He smiled at her. "I am fine, Isabel."

"Well then," she said, taking a breath, "I consign Jamie to your care until his majority, and I wish you luck of your charge."

"Thank you," Brett said gravely, though there was a glint of amusement in his blue eyes. "I think I will need all the luck I can get."

"I hope," Isabel said, walking up to Fanny and taking her plump little hands into her own, "that you have suffered no ill effects from all this excitement."

"Oh, I'm in fine fettle," Fanny assured her, blue eyes glowing. "I love being in on a good scrap."

"One anticipates with a suitable amount of terror," Brett remarked, "the budding character of her firstborn."

"You must write me all the details," Isabel said, gathering her cloak and pistols, "for I must bid you all adieu. Dick has arranged for my safe passage from this house. I'll send you my forwarding address." Pistols raised once again, she began to back toward the library's far door.

"Somebody stop her!" Jonas Babcock cried. "Sir Henry, I *demand* that you arrest her for the murder of my brother, Hiram Babcock!"

"Neither Miss Dalton's departure nor her arrest are necessary," Brett calmly stated.

"I must disagree with you once again, sir," Isabel said with equal calm, though her wall was crumbling fast. If only he would not look at her so! "I've no liking for a gallows tree." She was nearly to the door.

"Stop her! *Arrest her!*" Squire Babcock screamed.

"I'll do no such thing," said Sir Henry Bevins peevishly. He had never liked Mr. Babcock.

"Then I'll take her to jail myself!" the squire declared, starting forward.

Brett's large hand placed firmly against the squire's heaving chest stopped him in his tracks. "Be not so hasty, Mr. Babcock. You act without right."

Isabel stared at him.

"Right?" spat Jonas Babcock. "I have every right. She murdered my brother!"

"There are some, like me, who would undoubtedly argue—and have—that she shot Hiram Babcock in self-defense. But it is really a moot point after all, for as it happens, the warrant for her arrest has been quashed."

If Isabel had been amazed before, she was now well and truly dumbfounded! She stared across the room at him. "Quashed?" she said faintly.

"Isabel, Isabel, Isabel," the earl said with a sigh, shaking his head as he walked up to her. "I have spent the whole of this last fortnight trying to impress you with the position I hold and the power I wield. Besides, Sir Henry likes you."

"Sir Henry?!" Isabel exclaimed, wholly at sea.

"It's a conspiracy!" Jonas Babcock screamed.

"Balderdash," Sir Henry succinctly retorted. "It's a completely legal dismissal of all charges."

"But how—" Isabel stammered.

The earl's smile was unnervingly gentle. "I've suspected your true identity for some time now, Gleana Isabel Dalton. I have been acquainted with your aunt, Elinore Gunthorpe, for several years. She is, after all, a leader of the *haut* ton in London. She married well, you see. You are very like Mrs. Gunthorpe. Fanny noticed it immediately."

"My aunt? You suspected me because of my aunt?!"

"Only partially. Hiram Babcock's death was well detailed in the newspapers of the time. I was already certain, but once Dawkins had gathered the information I had requested and Fanny assured me that you are the very image of your aunt, I felt free to go to Sir Henry and lay the whole of the matter before him. The Babcocks are a powerful family, it is true, but I believe myself to be somewhat more powerful, and with my protection, Sir Henry felt free to go against them. The warrant for your arrest has been well and truly and for all time quashed, Isabel."

For the first time in her life, Isabel felt close to swooning. She sat down on the nearby sofa with a thump. "This is impossible."

"On the contrary. *Nothing* is impossible for the Earl of Northbridge."

Isabel stared up at Brett as if he had grown two heads.

He laughed down at her. "You are free, Isabel. You may safely stay in England for the rest of your life."

"Aye," Squire Babcock said angrily. "She may stay. But I'll see justice served yet!"

"Raise one finger to harm Miss Dalton," Brett murderously countered, *"and I'll destroy you, Babcock."*

The squire's eyes fell first. With an oath, he stormed from the room.

"And that, ladies and gentlemen," Brett said with a bright smile, "is the end of today's entertainment. Mrs. Worth, Thornwynd's housekeeper, has very kindly provided a sumptuous tea in the dining room for our refreshment. Let us adjourn there that we may drink to the health of the new baron."

His suggestion was happily seconded. Everyone had had enough adventure for one day. Fanny leading the way on Jamie's arm, the company began to troop from the library.

"Just a moment, Miss Dalton," Brett said easily, catching Isabel's wrist in his hand and holding her fast. "I'd like a word with you in private."

"It can wait until after we toast Jamie," Isabel said unsteadily, fear crashing into her once again.

"No, it cannot."

"Let me go!"

"In good time," Brett replied, shooing the last of the legacy's witnesses out of the library and closing the door behind them. He took the precaution of locking the door before releasing her wrist. He then turned to glare down at her, arms

242

akimbo. "I ought to turn you over my knee and spank you, Isabel, for the stunt you pulled today."

"You could try," Isabel retorted, her mouth dry.

Brett chuckled. "Just where were you planning to shoot me if I *had* interfered?"

"In the foot." Why did he seem so happy? He should be furious with her! "No man can seriously interfere in anything when he's hopping around on one leg cursing like a banshee."

"You are a devious female, as I have noted on more than one occasion. But come, why on earth did you let Jamie risk his life like that? He could have easily been killed."

"I had no choice, sir," Isabel said quietly. "Neither Jamie nor I could let Monty go unavenged. It was all I could do to keep Jamie from killing his uncle outright. I could not sway him from vengeance. A duel seemed the only means of avoiding outright murder. Neither would miss with guns. There was a chance of success with swords. It seemed the only option, certainly the only option Jamie would accept. It took an hour's strong argument to get him to agree not to kill Horace if he won."

"And if Shipley had killed the boy?"

Isabel shrugged. "I would have killed him, and that would have been an end to it."

Brett raised his eyes to the heavens in open exasperation. "Except that you would then have been taken and hanged for murder!"

"I hadn't planned to stay around long enough to be arrested," Isabel mildly informed him.

"You both took an unconscionable chance," Brett insisted.

"Shipping Horace off to Canada was no recompense for Monty's death!"

"Of course not. But I have . . . associates in Canada. I have arrangements in place to make the rest of Horace Shipley's life a living hell."

Isabel stared up at Brett as understanding dawned. "I am very glad I am not your enemy."

243

"As am I," Brett said softly with an expression Isabel had not seen before and could not decipher. "And you have been very clever at shifting me from my original point. You should not have risked Jamie's life."

"But Dick had informed me last night that you had sent men to guard Horace. If you had not, I could have attended to the matter myself."

Brett stared down at Isabel, a slow smile creasing his face. "I am very glad you are not *my* enemy. Now then, when are you planning to leave?"

"Leave?" Isabel faltered.

"Don't play innocent with me, miss. I know how your devious mind works. Let me guess: Now that you are an acknowledged murderess, the whole of the ton will learn of it soon enough, and your presence will only damage Jamie's place in society and keep him from an acquaintance that would benefit and advance him as Monty would have wished. Something like that?"

"It's all perfectly true," Isabel said defensively. "Jamie is safe now in your care. He needs the knowledge and skills you can impart to him, not the company of an acknowledged murderess. I . . . I wanted to tell you about Mr. Babcock myself, sir. I owed you that at least. I'm sorry you had to discover it on your own."

"There's still time, you know," the earl replied. "I know only that you were compelled to kill your stepfather. Come," he said gently, somehow making her meet his gaze, "will you not now tell me what happened thirteen years ago?"

Yes, Isabel thought, she could at least give him this moment of truth and trust. She clasped her hands tightly before her, her gaze unwavering. "My father," she began, "died when I was five. My mother was . . . a helpless sort of female. She could not withstand widowhood. When the formal period of mourning ended, she married Mr. Hiram Babcock. He knew the right words to secure a rich widow for his wife, you see. He could be quite . . . charming when he chose.

244

"After the wedding"—Isabel took a breath—"he revealed his true character: He was a drunkard, an adulterer, a monster. He delighted in torturing and killing animals, in abusing our servants, in . . . beating my mother and me any time of the day. The French had nothing on Mr. Babcock's Reign of Terror. There was no escape, you see. My grandparents were dead. My Aunt Elinore had a noted temper and had disowned Mama when she went against her excellent advice and married Mr. Babcock. We were trapped." Isabel's mouth tightened to a grim line. "We were helpless."

She realized that Brett had somehow taken both her icy hands into his. She doubted if she could have continued otherwise. "One day . . . I found Mr. Babcock in a drunken rage . . . strangling my mother. I tried to stop him! But he was so much stronger. . . . My screams brought no help. Our servants were long used to avoiding Mr. Babcock's rages. So, I ran for a gun, but by the time I got back . . . my mother was already dead." She discovered that she was shaking and couldn't seem to stop. "Then Mr. Babcock came at me, blood lust in his eyes, and I . . . shot him. I don't think I meant to kill him, only to stop him. It took a moment for me to comprehend that he was dead. It took a much longer moment to consider the implications. Mr. Babcock, as you know, was the younger son of a very powerful and thoroughly nasty family. They would see me hanged for his murder. I was certain of that.

"I dropped the gun and ran from the library and up to my room. I threw a few things into a valise and left the house no more than five minutes after I had killed Mr. Babcock. I hid for the next few days. Finally I cut my hair, dressed as a boy, and walked into a village to hear the news. There was a newspaper stall. I paid my penny and read that the Babcocks had indeed charged me with murder. There was a warrant out for my arrest."

"Did Monty know?" Brett asked quietly.

"Oh yes," Isabel said with something like a smile. "Monty always knew everything. I lived hand to mouth as a boy for a

245

few months and then was able to get work with a theatrical troupe. I even fooled them into believing I was a boy. But I could not deceive Monty. He was visiting friends in Warwickshire and saw one of our performances, cornered me afterward, and soon got the whole story out of me. There was something about him. . . . I saw the adventure in his eyes, but he was also the safest person I'd ever met in my life. He offered me . . . protection. A family. We left for the Continent the next day. You know the rest."

"Thank you for telling me," Brett said quietly. "I am grateful for your trust."

"And now," Isabel said, taking a deep breath and pulling her hands free from his warm clasp. "it is time to protect Jamie from my past, and to enjoy the future you have so generously given me, by leaving Lancashire."

"Piffle."

"Brett—"

"You cannot leave until after I have asked you to marry me."

If Isabel had been pale before, she became positively ashen now. "M-M-Marry you?"

The earl's fingers gently brushed her cheek. "I'm hopelessly in love with you, sweet Isabel. I must have you as my wife. I need you. My life will be barren without you."

"You're mad!"

Brett sighed heavily. "Isabel, I've already kissed you twice. In some circles, that is tantamount to taking the vows!"

"B-B-But you know what I am, the things I've done, the life I've led! How can you marry me?"

"With a license, a vicar, a ring, and a witness. Fanny has already asked to fill the latter role."

"Will you please talk sense, Brett?" Isabel demanded, unable to stop shaking. "Good God, man, only think of my adventures and disguises and a life spent in gaming houses or on the road or on the run from the local constabulary. I have blood on my hands! You need a wife of noble birth, large fortune, and the grace and assurance of a woman who knows her past spotless, not some mongrel equally at home in buckskins or petticoats! I am no fit bride for the Earl of Northbridge."

"But you are the only wife for Brett Avery," the earl retorted. Then, as Isabel stared up at him—wholly drunk on his words—he pulled her into his arms and kissed her.

Her senses already dazed, Isabel had no defense. She returned his kiss fiercely, her arms wrapping around Brett's neck, her heart singing with the joy of his embrace, her blood flaming her entire body as he kissed her again and again.

"You love me, don't you? *Don't you?*" he demanded.

"Oh, I can't think when you kiss me like that!" she gasped.

"Good," said Brett, and kissed her again. "I want an answer from your heart, not your head. I long to have you stop calling me 'sir' in that odiously proper little voice you use. I long to be your husband, your helpmeet, your friend, your lover, your playmate. I love you, Isabel. Let down your guard far enough to trust me with your happiness for the rest of your life. I love you and will never betray or do you harm. Will you marry me?"

A prompt answer was made difficult by the kisses Brett pressed to her upturned face before returning to her mouth to further persuade her to his cause.

"Oh, please!" Isabel gasped, pulling far enough away to speak, though Brett's strong arms continued to hold her fast. "Do not be so wonderfully distracting when I must answer you clearly."

"*Isabel—*" the earl said in a dangerous voice.

"Oh, I do love you, Brett."

The earl's glower was replaced by an ecstatic smile. It was only through the full use of her strength that Isabel was able to fend him off.

"I have not finished!" she said. "I love you beyond reason, Brett. But only think of your mother having to welcome a murderess as her daughter-in-law!"

"It will add an exotic glow to her reputation that will lure

247

even Lady Jersey to her Viennese breakfasts. Mother will be delirious."

"Fanny—"

"Already regards you as a sister."

"B-B-But what will your *friends* think?! What will your *neighbors* think of me as your wife?!"

"I couldn't care less," Brett retorted.

"But—"

The earl ruthlessly silenced Isabel by kissing her so long and so hard that she ended by finding her cheek resting happily against his broad chest, listening to the thundering of his heart, his fingers slowly sifting through her hair and quite ruining her coiffure. "But you should care," she murmured. "You should be practical. You should remember your position, your respectability, your duty to—"

"*Hang* my duty!" the earl said with the utmost disgust.

Isabel stared up at him in utter amazement.

"I'll have you as my wife and no other," he continued in a very firm tone. "You already have my ring," he said, raising her hand to his lips. "Will you not take the love and the man that go with it?"

"Oh, very well," Isabel said, affecting a petulant sigh. "But *only* because you have obviously become mad as a hatter and *someone* has to look after you."

Brett laughed with a joy she had never heard from him before. She was wholly undone, particularly when he swung her up and into his arms.

"We are going to have the most *famous* rows," he said with a grin, "and a very short engagement."

Isabel brushed her mouth against his. "But if you speak my heart's desire, how will we ever argue?"

Brett's eyes burned into hers. "A *very* short engagement," he said roughly before he crushed her mouth with his own.